ORCHID BLUES

Books by Stuart Woods

FICTION

Cold Paradise*

L.A. Dead*

The Run†

Worst Fears Realized*

Orchid Beach

Swimming to Catalina*

Dead in the Water*

Dirt*

Choke

Imperfect Strangers

Heat

Dead Eyes

L.A. Times

Santa Fe Rules

New York Dead*

Palindrome

Grass Roots†

White Cargo

Under the Lake

Deep Lie†

Run Before the Wind†

Chiefs†

TRAVEL

A Romantic's Guide to the Country Inns
of Britain and Ireland (1978)

MEMOIR

Blue Water, Green Skipper

*A Stone Barrington book

†A Will Lee book

ORCHID

BLUES

Stuart Woods

G. P. PUTNAM'S SONS
NEW YORK

This is a work of fiction. Names, characters, places,
and incidents either are the product of the author's imagination
or are used fictitiously, and any resemblance to actual persons,
living or dead, business establishments, events,
or locales is entirely coincidental.

G. P. Putnam's Sons
Publishers Since 1838
a member of
Penguin Putnam Inc.
375 Hudson Street
New York, NY 10014

Library of Congress Cataloging-in-Publication Data

Woods, Stuart.
Orchid blues / Stuart Woods.
p.   cm.
ISBN 0-399-14777-2
1. Police—Florida—Fiction.   2. Doberman pinscher—Fiction.
3. Women dog owners—Fiction.   4. Policewomen—Fiction.
5. Florida—Fiction.   6. Dogs—Fiction.   I. Title.
PS3573.O642 O74   2001   2001019727
813'.54—dc21

Printed in the United States of America

1   3   5   7   9   10   8   6   4   2

This book is printed on acid-free paper. ∞

Book design by Victoria Kuskowski

This book is for
Phil and Susan Dusenberry.

ORCHID BLUES

He waited until the last of the line had entered the cinema for the eight o'clock movie.

"All right, let's take a tour," he said to the boy at the wheel.

The boy drove slowly around the parking lot.

"Here," he said.

The boy stopped the car.

The man looked at the parked vehicle. It was an older Ford commercial van, well cared for and clean. "Wait a minute," he said. He got out of the car and grabbed his tool bag. "Drive over to the edge of the parking lot and wait. When you see the van's headlights go on, follow me home. I'll be making a lot of turns."

"Yessir," the boy said.

He slipped a pair of rubber gloves on, then walked over to the van and tried the door. Unlocked. It took him less than a minute to punch the steering lock and start the van. He switched on the lights and checked the odometer: 48,000 miles; not bad. He backed out of the parking space and drove out of the lot, onto the highway. In the rearview mirror he watched the boy fall in behind him, well back. He drove for a couple of minutes, constantly making turns, checking the mirror, then he turned down a dirt road, drove a hundred yards and stopped. The boy stopped behind him. He sat in the van and watched the traffic pass on the highway for five minutes, then he made a U-turn and went back to the highway and headed west. He had two hours before the van's owner would come out of the movies and discover his loss, but he needed only half an hour.

Twenty-five minutes later, he drove into the little town, and five minutes after that, he pulled the van into the large steel shed behind his business. Half a dozen men, who had been sitting around a poker table, stood up and walked over.

"Looks good," one of them said.

"It'll do. Only 48K on the clock, and it runs like a sewing machine. Let's do it."

Everybody went to work. First, they donned rubber gloves, then they washed the van thoroughly and cleaned the interior, and fastened two rough wooden benches to the floor. Two men unrolled a large decal and fixed it to the side of the van. Environmental Services, Inc., it read, and in smaller letters, Cleaning up after the world. There was a phone number, too. If anyone rang it, they'd get a pizzeria on U.S. 1. They fixed an identical decal to the opposite side of the van, then changed the license plates, tossing the old ones into the van.

Somebody looked under the hood, fiddled with a couple of things, then closed it. "Good shape," he said. "The man knows how to take care of a vehicle." He checked a sticker on the windshield. "Had it serviced last week; nice of him."

"I hope his insurance is paid up," someone else said.

"All right," their leader said, "let's go over it again." The poker chips and cards were removed from the big round table, and a large floor plan was spread out. "Number two," the leader said, "take us through it."

"We all know it by heart," somebody said.

"You will when I'm finished," the leader said. "Then you can all get a good night's sleep."

When the van was ready they went home and left him alone in the shed. He went to an elongated safe in a corner, tapped the combination into the keypad, and opened it. He removed six Remington riot guns—12-gauge pump shotguns with 18¼-inch barrels, normally used for police work—and took them to the van, laying them on the floor. He went to a locker and removed six blue jumpsuits—all the same size—took them to the van and put one where each man would sit. Back to the locker to find six yellow construction hard hats, six dust masks and six pairs of tinted safety goggles, which he laid neatly on top of the jumpsuits. He then laid a shotgun on each seat, and placed a box of double-aught shells and a pair of latex surgical gloves beside each shotgun. Finally, he went back to the gun safe, removed six 9mm semiautomatic handguns and boxes of ammunition and distributed them inside the van. The weapons had been bought, one at a time, at gun shows or from unlicensed dealers, then stripped, inspected and, if necessary, repaired. Before reassembly, each part of each weapon had been washed clean with denatured alcohol and oiled. There would be no fingerprints or DNA samples on them.

When he was done, he sat down at the table, stripped off his gloves and poured himself a drink from a bottle of bourbon. He looked at the newspaper clipping again. Eleven o'clock at the courthouse. "Happy occasion," he said aloud to himself. "And oh so convenient."

2

Holly Barker opened her eyes and felt for Jackson. His side of the bed was empty, and she could hear the shower running. She moved her hand to the warm place on her stomach and found Daisy's head. She scratched behind an ear and was answered with a small sigh. Daisy was a Doberman pinscher, and she liked to sleep with her head on Holly's belly.

Holly heard the shower turn off and, a moment later, Jackson's bare feet padding across the bedroom carpet. She raised her head, tucked a pillow under it and eyed him—naked, wet hair, in a hurry. She liked him naked.

"So," she said, "where am I going on my honeymoon?"

"Same place as I am," Jackson replied, stepping into his boxer shorts and selecting a white shirt from a drawer.

"I'm relieved to hear it," she said. "And where is that?"

"Someplace you'll probably like," he said.

"*Probably* like? You're not even *sure* I'm going to like it?"

"I *think* you will," he said, "but, in the immortal words of Fats Waller, 'One never knows, do one?'"

"This is how you treat your wife?"

"I don't have a wife."

"You will by high noon, or my daddy will shoot you."

"Ham wouldn't shoot me; he's too nice a guy."

"He would, if he knew you wouldn't tell me where I'm going on my honeymoon."

"*He* knows, and that's enough for Ham."

"Wait a minute," she said. "My *father* knows where I'm going on my honeymoon, and your wife doesn't?"

"I told you, I don't have a wife."

She sat up on one elbow, and the sheet fell away from her breasts. "How will I know what to pack?"

"You packed yesterday," he said, "and I told you what to pack, remember?"

"Men never know what to pack. What if you screw up?"

"I'll just have to take that chance." He pulled on his trousers, found a necktie and started to tie it.

"You're driving me crazy," she said, falling back onto the pillow.

"If you don't pull that sheet over your breasts, you're going to drive me crazy," he replied, looking at her in the mirror.

She kicked the sheet completely off, disturbing Daisy's sleep. "Take that," she said.

"I intend to," he said, "when we arrive in . . . whatchacallit."

"Why are you rushing off?" she asked seductively.

"Don't point that thing at me," Jackson said. "I've got a closing in half an hour, then I have to do some dictating before I leave the office and then, on the way to the courthouse, I have to pick up the tickets at the travel agent's and stop at the bank for some travelers' checks."

"Why didn't you have the tickets sent here?" she asked.

"Because you would have ripped them open to find out where you're going on your honeymoon."

He had her there. She fumed.

He slipped into his suit jacket, adjusted his tie, came to the bed and bent over her.

"Why didn't you dry your hair?"

"I'll put the top down." He kissed her on one nipple, then the other.

She giggled. "Sure the closing can wait a few minutes."

"Would you muss my wedding dress?" he asked. That was how he referred to the white linen suit he had had made for the occasion.

"No, you're too beautiful."

"Tell you what, if you'll call yourself Mrs. Oxenhandler for the rest of your life, I'll tell you where you're going on your honeymoon."

"Jackson, I keep telling you: *nobody* would *choose* to be called Mrs. Oxenhandler. You're stuck, you were born with it. Can you imagine my cops calling me Chief Oxenhandler? They couldn't keep a straight face."

"I think that's a very dignified name for a chief of police," Jackson said, trying to look hurt.

"It's a very dignified name for someone who handles oxen," she said.

"Well," he sighed, "I guess you'll find out where you're going on your honeymoon when you get there."

She pulled the sheet over her head. "You won't even tell me *then!*" she cried. She pulled down the sheet again, and he was standing in the bedroom doorway, looking splendid in his new suit.

"See you at the courthouse," he said.

"In Judge Chandler's courtroom, and you'd better be there early!" she called after him. She fell back on the bed. She would always remember that picture of him, standing in the doorway in his white linen suit and gold tie, with his hair still wet.

Holly got out of bed, brushed her teeth and got into the shower, reaching for the shampoo. She had let her hair grow, and it was nearly down to her shoulders, though she wore it up when she was in uniform, which was most of the time. She was allowing herself two hours for the process—washing, rolling and drying her hair, putting on a little makeup, which she rarely wore, and getting into the short white sheath that would be her wedding dress.

Daisy lay on the bathroom mat, watching her through the clear glass shower door, waiting patiently for her breakfast and to be let out. Holly laughed. Daisy would be her maid of honor; Holly had trained her to carry the bouquet all the way to the front of the courtroom before handing it to her. Daisy could do anything.

Holly felt that she could do anything, too. She was bursting with happiness and expectation and with trying to figure out where Jackson was taking her on her honeymoon.

She got out of the shower and called her office's direct line.

"Chief Barker's office," her secretary and office manager, Helen Tubman, said.

"Hi, it's me. What's happening?"

"Nothing, and if something were happening, I wouldn't tell you," Helen said. "It's your wedding day, so I want you to hang up and do whatever you're supposed to do on your wedding day."

"How many are coming?" Holly asked. She had posted an invitation on the squad room bulletin board.

"Let me put it this way," Helen said, "if there's a murder in the middle of Beach Boulevard this morning, the body will have to lie there until you're married and on your way to the airport."

"Oh, God," Holly said. "That many?"

"That many."

"Tell me their names, and I'll put them to work."

"I'll do no such thing," Helen said. "Now you go get beautiful, and don't bother me again." She hung up.

Holly hung up the phone, laughing, then went to feed Daisy and let her out into the dunes for her morning ablutions. She felt completely, insanely happy.

3

The men assembled after breakfast,
and the leader set up a drawing pad on an easel and ran them through
their individual roles once more.

"Any questions?" he asked.

A hand went up. "Under what circumstances are we authorized to
fire?"

"Danger to your own life or another of us," the leader replied. "The
two guards will already be disarmed, so, unless a civilian is packing,
we're not going to have to deal with being shot at. Of course, there's
always the chance that some cop will wander in to cash a check and
come over all brave, but the sight of our shotguns is going to put the
fear of God into anybody who understands what a shotgun can do."

"Are we authorized to kill, if necessary?" the man asked.

"Only if absolutely necessary," the leader replied. "But if it becomes
necessary, don't hesitate. But remember, the police will work a lot
harder on a murder than a robbery."

The man nodded.

"Anybody else?"

Nobody said anything.

"Just remember: nobody moves until the armored car leaves. The guards will be locked in and safe, and they've got a radio." He looked around. "All right, we drive separately to the shopping center, and each of you waits beside your car. Enter and leave the van one at a time through the front passenger door. Let's go."

The group broke up and went to the four cars parked outside. The leader gave them a ten-minute head start, then he pulled on his gloves, got into his coveralls, hung the dust mask and goggles around his neck and put on his hard hat. He got into the van and drove out of the building, closing the garage door behind him with a remote control. He left the town and drove east, toward Orchid Beach. Half an hour later, he pulled into the parking lot. It was a big shopping center for a small town, anchored by a huge supermarket, with other stores strung out along both sides. The lot was three-quarters full. He drove up and down the lanes, stopping whenever he came to one of his men. Each was wearing a baseball cap, dark glasses and latex gloves. Each entered by the front passenger door, then moved to the rear and took a seat on one of the facing benches. After twenty minutes, all the men were in the van, costumed in their jumpsuits, masks, goggles and hard hats. They began loading their weapons from the ammunition on the bench beside them.

Each had four clips of 9mm ammunition and a box of double-aught shotgun shells. Each loaded four shells into a shotgun, racked one into the chamber, then loaded one more shell. Each put the spare ammo into the side pockets of his jumpsuit.

The leader glanced at his watch. "Right on schedule," he said. Each weapon had had its serial number removed. None would ever be traced, except to the factory where it had been manufactured years before.

As he turned the van into the parking lot, the armored car entered the other end of the lot, exactly on time. He parked the van and switched off the engine. "It's going to get hot in here," he said, "but I don't want anyone to notice a van with the motor running."

He watched as the two guards on the armored car went through their drill; they looked bored. As they unloaded, a civilian, a man, drove up in a convertible, got out and went inside. The guards regarded him closely, then entered. They were inside the building for less than two minutes, then returned to their vehicle and entered it through the rear door, locking it behind them. The driver put the car into gear and drove out of the parking lot.

The leader waited while the armored car stopped for a traffic light, then turned left onto Highway A1A. "Here we go," he said. He started the engine and drove to the spot outside the main entrance that the armored car had just vacated. "Hats, masks and goggles on," he said. He waited ten seconds, then looked at his wristwatch, a chronograph. He pressed a button. "Two minutes," he said, "starting *now.*"

Everybody got out of the van and started for the front door.

4

office for the closing, with ten minutes to spare. His secretary had already set out all the documents on the conference room table, and he checked them once more. He liked for his closings to go smoothly.

His partner, Fred Ames, stuck his head in. "You're working right down to the wire, huh? I like that."

"Gotta bring in some bucks for you to squander while I'm gone," Jackson said. "I'll bet you're off to Vegas tomorrow."

"Tonight," Ames said, grinning. "I've got all your personal stuff ready to sign. It's on your desk."

"After the closing, you and the girls come in; I'll need you all for witnesses."

"Got it."

The receptionist came to the door. "Everybody's here, Jackson."

"Send them in," Jackson said, then stood and shook everyone's hand—both real estate agents, the sellers and their lawyer, and the buyers, who were his own clients.

For the next forty-five minutes, everybody methodically signed documents, stacks of documents. Money, in the form of cashier's checks, changed hands. There was some quibbling about a couple of contingencies in the sales document, and Jackson made small changes, making everybody happy.

Finally, when everything was signed, everybody left, the sellers with a large check and the buyers with the deed to a very fine beach house.

Jackson went into his office, and Fred Ames and two secretaries followed him.

"You know the drill," Fred said, setting the documents on his desk. "Does this document accurately reflect your wishes?"

"It does," Jackson said, and started to sign.

When he was done, and the document had been properly witnessed, Ames set two plastic document wallets on the desk. "The policies came this morning; everything is in order."

"Put them in the safe," he said to his secretary, handing her the wallets. "Everything else, too." They complied, and he shooed them out of his office. He picked up the little recorder, found his notes and began to dictate. He went rapidly, knowing his secretary could follow his rapid speech. An hour and a half later, he stood up, straightened his desk, and left his office. He laid the cassette on his secretary's desk.

Fred stuck his head through the door of his office. "You're really going to do this, huh? After all these years as a bachelor?"

"Looks that way," Jackson said, grinning. "You know, at the closing, nobody said a word about me being in a white suit with a carnation in my lapel?"

"I explained to them," his secretary said.

"Oh. All right, I'm out of here. See you all at the courthouse, and after that, in three weeks."

Everybody waved goodbye.

Jackson drove to the travel agent's office in the shopping center near his office. He had to wait a minute for a parking place outside their door, and as he waited, he noticed a van drive by. "Environmental Services," he muttered aloud to himself, chuckling. "Janitors, I'll bet. The further inflation of the English language. One day, it will explode."

A woman left a parking space and he pulled in. Inside, the receptionist smiled. "You look sensational," she said.

"I know," he replied, giving her a smile.

She handed him a fat envelope. "There you are: tickets, itinerary, reservation confirmations, the works. And a little gift from us: a guide to the best restaurants."

"You're an angel," he said.

"Have a wonderful honeymoon!"

He left the agency and went back to his car. He spent five minutes going through everything in the envelope, making sure that the tickets, reservations and itinerary were perfectly accurate. Satisfied, he started the car and headed up the boulevard. He crossed the south bridge over the Intracoastal Waterway, also known as the Indian River, and in another five minutes reached the bank.

He parked the car and got out. An armored car was unloading at the front door, and the guards gave him a look. He laughed. What bank robber would be wearing a white linen suit?

Only two tellers were open, and there was a line of half a dozen people at each. He got into line behind a blond man of his own height—well over six feet—wearing Bermuda shorts, Top-Siders and a yellow Polo shirt.

The man glanced over his shoulder and grinned. "You look as though you're dressed for a wedding," he said, smiling.

"Guilty," Jackson said, raising his hands.

"Your own?"

"Guilty again. You a local or a foreigner?"

The man laughed. "A foreigner, I guess. I'm down here to buy an airplane from Piper, in Vero Beach."

"Which airplane?"

"The Malibu Mirage."

"Not the turboprop, the Meridian?"

"I'll have to make some more money before I get one of those."

"I fly myself, but I rent. Couple more years, I might spring for something nice. Where you from?"

"New York."

"What do you do up there?"

"I practice law."

"I do the same down here, when I'm not getting married. Have you done your flight training yet?"

"Finished this morning; I'm just picking up a cashier's check, so we can close on the airplane."

The line moved forward, and the man became engaged with the teller.

Something made Jackson look toward the door. Four men were standing there, wearing blue jumpsuits, yellow hard hats, masks and goggles. Each of them was holding a shotgun at port arms. One of the men racked his shotgun, and everybody turned and looked at him.

"Everybody be real calm," the man said from behind his mask, "and we'll be out of your way in just a minute." He turned to the men beside him. "Get started," he said. The three men walked rapidly toward an area of desks, where the bank's officers worked. Immediately behind the desk was a large vault, open.

Jackson noticed the blond man standing beside him. "Looks like we're witnesses to a bank robbery," Jackson said softly, without moving his lips.

"Just do as they say," the man said.

"You bet," Jackson said. He looked to his left to see the men in jumpsuits returning from the vault. Two of them stood guard as the third pushed a hand truck laden with canvas bags. They were going to pass within three feet of him. Jackson concentrated on trying to remember what the men looked like. He could hardly tell Holly he had witnessed a bank robbery and not noticed what they looked like. They ranged from about five-seven to six-feet-four and were identically dressed. What with the masks and the goggles, he could tell nothing about them but their height and weight. The tallest one had some gray hair visible at the nape of his neck. Holly was going to be pissed when he told her about this, and that wouldn't be until they were on the airplane. He wasn't going to have his wedding day ruined by a bank robbery.

As the men approached, one of them backed into Jackson, then whirled around to point the shotgun at him. "Watch it, you stupid sonofabitch!" the man said.

"*You* watch it," Jackson said, fairly pleasantly. "*You* bumped into *me*."

The man made a sort of snarling noise and swung the butt of the shotgun at Jackson's head.

Jackson saw it coming and leaned backward. The shotgun butt brushed against his chin as it passed, and the man, having missed his mark, lost his balance and fell against Jackson.

Jackson pushed him away, hard. "Get off me!" he said.

The man recovered his balance and brought the shotgun to bear on Jackson.

Jackson heard two things, nearly simultaneously. The blond man to his right yelled, *"No!"* and the shotgun must have gone off, because his head filled with the noise and something huge and heavy seemed to strike him in the chest.

As he flew backward he saw only a stretch of ceiling. He didn't feel it when he hit the floor.

5

Holly parked her car at the court-
house, checked herself in the mirror one last time and walked across
the parking lot. Daisy trotted by her side, carrying the bouquet.

Helen, her secretary, and Hurd Wallace, her deputy chief, were
waiting by the side entrance for her.

"Everybody's here," Helen said. "Except the groom, of course."

"Oh, he'll be along, eventually," Holly said. "He had a closing
this morning, and he had to go to the travel agent's and the bank."
They walked through the courthouse doors and started down the
hallway. "He still won't tell me where we're going on our honeymoon."

"Gosh," Helen said, "everybody else knows."

"Even Hurd?"

"Yep," Hurd replied, with a straight face. Hurd spoke only when
necessary, and with an economy of words. Holly had never seen him
laugh, or even smile.

"It's outrageous," Holly said. "Everybody knows but me. If I have the wrong clothes, I'm going to murder Jackson as soon as we get there."

"I'd hate to have to extradite you," Hurd said.

"Aha! It's out of the country!"

"That's why you needed a passport," Helen said. "It's not as though we're giving anything away."

They reached the courtroom and walked through the big double doors. Virtually the whole of the Orchid Beach Police Department was present, most in uniform.

"My God," Holly said, "I hope the criminals are taking the day off, too."

Everybody laughed, a little too heartily.

Her father, Hamilton Barker, a retired army master sergeant wearing an unaccustomed blue suit, stepped forward, took her shoulders and looked her up and down. "You look just like a girl," he said.

"Thanks, Ham," Holly replied, with a touch of sarcasm.

"Well, I can't remember the last time I saw you in a dress. Was it your senior prom?"

"If my father says anything like that again," she said to the assembly, "shoot to kill."

"She doesn't appreciate compliments," Ham said to Helen.

The judge appeared from her chambers, wearing her robes. "All present?" she asked, looking at her watch. She was a sturdily built woman in her fifties, with a mound of snow-white hair.

"Everybody but the groom," Helen told her.

She peered over the bench at Daisy. "I don't usually allow dogs in my courtroom," she said.

"She's not a dog," Holly replied, "she's the maid of honor."

"Oh," the judge said. "In that case, I'll make an exception."

Ham looked at his watch. "Looks like he's going to jilt you," he said, grinning.

"What time is it?" Holly asked. She didn't have a dressy watch, and she wasn't going to wear her steel Rolex with her wedding dress.

"Two minutes to go," Ham said.

Across the courtroom, somebody's portable radio barked something.

Hurd Wallace leveled his gaze at the cop. "Turn that thing off."

But the officer instead began speaking into the microphone clipped to his shirt, then he turned and walked toward an unpopulated corner of the courtroom.

Dammit, Holly thought, I'm not going to have this day ruined by some teenager in a stolen car.

Hurd walked across the room and stood next to the officer, cocking an ear toward the radio. He listened for a moment, then walked back to where Holly stood.

Holly put up her hands, as if to ward him off. "Not today, Hurd," she said.

He leaned close to her. "It's Jackson," he said quietly. "He's been hurt; he's on the way to the hospital."

Holly jerked her head back as if she had been slapped. "How bad?"

"Bad, but he's alive. Come on, I'll drive you."

Holly started for the door, and Hurd turned to the crowd, motioning for Ham Barker to follow him. "Sorry, folks, the wedding is postponed. Everybody back on duty. Jenkins, get your crime-scene team and get over to the Southern Trust Bank on Ocean Boulevard, and be quick about it. I'll join you as soon as I can."

Holly sat rigidly in the front seat of Hurd's unmarked patrol car, willing Hurd to go faster.

"Any details?" Ham asked from the rear seat. Daisy sat quietly in the back, as if she knew something was wrong.

"There was a robbery at Southern Trust," Hurd said. "Apparently, Jackson got in the way."

Holly turned and looked at him. "Gunshot?"

Hurd nodded. "We'll know more in a couple of minutes." He

whipped the car into the emergency entrance of the hospital. Everybody got out and ran inside.

A doctor stood just inside the doorway, wearing a white coat, its right sleeve smeared with blood. "This way, Chief," he said, ushering her toward an examination room. Just outside the door, he stopped her. "I'm sorry to have to tell you this, but he died three or four minutes ago. There was nothing we could do to save him."

Holly turned to face the doctor. "*Nothing* you could do?"

"It was a shotgun blast to the chest; massive damage."

Holly sucked in a big breath and put a hand on the door for balance. "I want to see him," she said.

"All right," the doctor replied. He opened the door.

Holly stepped into the room. An examination table was before her, and the body, draped with a sheet.

The doctor walked to the head of the table and took hold of a corner of the sheet, waiting for Holly.

Holly stepped forward, and her toe caught on something. She looked down to see a yellow knit shirt, covered in blood, at her feet. What? she thought. Jackson wasn't wearing a yellow shirt; it's the wrong man! She rushed to the head of the table.

The doctor pulled back the sheet, revealing only the head.

Holly felt as if someone had struck her in the chest. The tanned face was without color, the mouth slightly open, the eyes closed. It was not the wrong man. She reached out to pull the sheet back farther.

The doctor put his hand on hers. "You don't want to do that," he said kindly.

Holly placed her hand on Jackson's cool cheek and began to sob.

6

Holly got into Hurd's car and slammed the door. Ham got into the back seat. "Take me to the station," she said.

Hurd turned and looked at her, his usually placid visage showing astonishment. "Holly, you ought to go home and rest."

Ham, who was sitting in the rear seat with Daisy, spoke up. "God, you're not thinking of going to work, are you?"

"What else am I supposed to do, Ham? Go home and bounce off the walls? Make keening noises and curse God? Right now, work is all I've got, and there's work to be done."

Hurd recovered himself, started the car and drove off toward the station.

Holly sat mute, collecting her thoughts. She couldn't think about Jackson on a slab in the hospital morgue; plenty of time for that later. She had an investigation to organize, witnesses to question, bank robbers—no, *murderers*—to catch.

First things first. She fished her cell phone out of her purse and dialed a number she knew by heart.

"FBI," a man's voice said.

"Harry Crisp," she replied.

"Mr. Crisp's office," a secretary said.

"This is Chief Holly Barker of the Orchid Beach Police Department," Holly said. "I need him."

"One moment, Chief."

"Holly, how are you?" Harry said cheerfully.

The year before, she had worked a huge case with him on her home turf, and they had become friends.

"What's up?"

"First of all, I have to report to you that the Southern Trust Bank in Orchid Beach was robbed less than an hour ago. Bank robbery is a federal crime, so consider yourself duly notified."

"All right," Harry said. "I'll get people on it right now. Is there something else, Holly? You sound funny."

"A bystander was killed," she said.

"Duly noted; I'll let the crime-scene team know."

"My team will work with them," she said.

"That's not necessary, Holly."

"Yes, it is. The bystander who was murdered was my fiancé."

"Jackson? Oh, my God, Holly, I'm so sorry."

"Be advised right now," she said, "*my* department will work the homicide. I'm happy to have your people's advice, but—"

"Holly, the homicide is ours, too, since it was part of the bank robbery."

"Harry, I'm asking you, don't fight me on this."

He was silent for a moment. "All right, it'll be this way: officially, it's according to the book. Unofficially, and I mean *unofficially*, your people work side by side with mine, on both the robbery and the homicide. All statements to the public come from this office. The U.S. Attorney gets the call on the prosecutions. You'll have to rely on my word and my judgment about the way we handle the evidence. That's the best I can do."

"All right," she said tightly. "But I want your word that no information, no evidence will be withheld from me. I get the reports simultaneously with you."

"I can arrange that. Are you all right, Holly?"

"I'm . . ." She had almost said "fine," but that would be dishonest. "I'm managing," she said.

"I know you will. I'll give my personal attention to the case from this moment forward. If there's anything you need from me, you have only to ask."

"Thank you, Harry," she said. "I'll expect your people."

"They'll be there inside of three hours."

"Bye." She punched off. "Hurd, take me to the back door; I don't want to be seen at the station in this dress."

"Sure."

They drove the rest of the way in silence, then Hurd dropped her off.

Holly walked through the back door of the station, followed by Daisy, and down the rear hallway to her office, closing the door behind her. She locked the door and got out of the dress, then went to a closet for a uniform. Shortly, she was dressed for business in khaki shirt and slacks. "Stay, Daisy," she said to the dog. She took a deep breath and opened the door that led into the squad room.

There was more than the usual hubbub; witnesses were lined up on benches down one wall, and somebody was bringing them coffee and sandwiches. Holly was pleased that her people had been thoughtful.

Then they noticed her, and the room grew quiet. "Carry on," she said to them. "Do it right." She walked over to Hurd's office, rapped on the door and opened it. Hurd was behind his desk. Across from him sat a blond man in his early forties, wearing what Holly recognized as a Hawaiian shirt belonging to Hurd. Both men stood up.

"Please sit down," Holly said.

"Chief," Hurd said, "this is Mr. Barrington. He was in the bank when the robbery took place."

The man held out his hand. "How do you do?"

Holly took his hand. He seemed very quiet and self-possessed for someone who had just witnessed a bank robbery and a murder. Suddenly, she realized why he was wearing Hurd's shirt.

"Mr. Barrington," she said, "you were wearing a yellow knit shirt this morning?"

"Yes."

"Thank you for trying to help him. I'm very grateful to you."

"I'm sorry for your loss," he said.

"I'm going to join you for this one," she said to Hurd, and pulled up a chair.

"Good, we were just getting started," Hurd replied. "Mr. Barrington was just about to tell me what happened."

"Please go ahead," Holly said.

"I went into the bank to pick up a cashier's check. I'm buying an airplane from Piper, over in Vero Beach. Mr. Oxenhandler—that was his name?"

"Yes, Jackson Oxenhandler."

"He came in and was in line behind me; we chatted a little, discovered that we were both lawyers. We talked a little about airplanes; the line was held up by someone depositing a lot of checks and cash."

"Go on."

"Four men came into the bank; they were wearing identical blue coveralls, yellow construction hard hats and masks, the kind you wear when you're sanding floors or dealing with a lot of dust. All four were carrying shotguns."

"Descriptions?" Holly asked. She nodded at Hurd, who got out a notebook.

"Three were around six feet—within an inch or so—one was shorter, around five-nine. The bigger men were middle-age beefy, though the coveralls probably made them look heavier than they were. The shorter one was much thinner. Two of the bigger men had gray hair showing around the edges of the hard hats; one had darker hair, nearly black. The smaller man had sandy hair and eyebrows. He was wearing brown oxford shoes; the other three were wearing sneakers, one pair of New Balance, two of Nike. All four men were wearing wedding bands, and one of the larger men wore what looked like a college ring.

"The shotguns looked like Remingtons, standard police riot guns. I think all four men were wearing shoulder holsters, too, under the coveralls."

"Did any of them speak?"

"One of them, I'm not sure which, told the people to behave, and they wouldn't get hurt. Any other talk was between themselves and quiet. They went immediately to the area where the desks were, and the shorter man indicated that a bank officer was to accompany them to the vault."

"Do you know which officer?"

"One in the second row of desks. I don't know his name, but the robber seemed to know who he wanted."

"Go on."

"Two of the four men guarded us, while one went with the shorter man and the bank officer to the vault. They were in there maybe a minute, and came back with a four-wheeled hand trolley containing a pile of canvas bags, maybe a dozen. As they passed close to where we stood, the taller of the two men bumped into Mr. Oxenhandler, and there was an exchange of words."

"What sort of exchange?"

"Truculent, on the part of the robber. Mr. Oxenhandler replied in a manner that showed no fear. The exchange escalated a little, then, to my astonishment, the taller robber shot Mr. Oxenhandler, who fell backward at my feet. I immediately took off my shirt and applied it to Mr. Oxenhandler's chest, to try to control the bleeding."

"Why were you astonished at what happened?" Holly asked.

"Up to that moment, the whole operation had been quick and professional. The sudden display of anger on the part of the robber seemed out of character with the team, though, of course, the mask may have prevented me from seeing it coming, since I couldn't see any facial expressions."

"After he shot Jackson, what happened?"

"The shorter man came and shoved him toward the door. He said something, but I wasn't able to understand him, because of the mask. The four men left the building, and a moment later, I saw a white van—a Ford, I think—leave the parking lot and drive west, toward the mainland. I shouted toward the desks for someone to call nine-one-one and ask for an ambulance, and I stayed with Mr. Oxenhandler until the EMTs put him into the ambulance."

"Did he have anything to say?"

Barrington looked her in the eye. "He said, 'Holly's going to be very upset about this.' I asked him to relax and be quiet, but he wanted to talk."

"What did he say?"

"He told me he was on the way to his wedding. He didn't seem to be in a lot of pain, but certainly in shock. He said I should tell Holly that he was sorry he ruined everything, but that she should see Fred, that he had everything in hand and under control. Who's Fred?"

"His law partner," Holly replied. "Anything else?"

"No, the EMTs arrived about that time and got him into the ambulance. If it's any consolation, they got there fast and did their work well, did everything they could do. Mr. Oxenhandler didn't want for the proper medical attention."

"Thank you for telling me that, Mr. Barrington. That was an excellent report; tell me, are you a police officer?"

"Used to be. I had fourteen years with the NYPD, finished up as a detective, second grade, at the Nineteenth Precinct, working homicides, mostly."

"You seem young to have retired."

"Medical disability; I took a bullet in a knee."

Holly nodded. "Thank you, Mr. Barrington; you've been a very big help."

"Please call me Stone."

"Stone it is."

"There's something else."

"What?"

"There was something familiar about the robbery."

7

Holly's pulse quickened. "Familiar? How so?"

Stone wrinkled his brow. "It was six or eight years ago, when I was still on the force. My partner at the time, Dino Bacchetti, and I had lunch with an old acquaintance of his who was with the New York State Police. There was a bank in some little town in the Hudson River Valley that had two or three local industries that had the same payday for their workers each week. It was hit by a group who worked with almost military precision, wearing identical outfits and masks. That's about all I remember about it."

Holly turned to Hurd. "You know about this payday thing? Was the bank especially cash-rich today?"

Hurd stood up. "I'll find out." He left the room.

Holly turned back to Stone. "Can you remember anything else about this robbery in New York?"

Stone shook his head. "Not really; it was a long time ago, but when I saw these people this morning, I remembered that much."

"Could you have a word with your state cop friend and see if he has any other details?"

"I don't even remember his name, but Dino will; I'll call him tonight. He's out of the office today."

"I'd appreciate that." She gave him her card and wrote her home number on the back. "You said you were buying an airplane from Piper?"

"That's right, a Malibu Mirage."

"Big single, six places, pressurized, right?"

"That's right."

"Jackson loved that airplane. I think he might have gone for one in a year or two."

"I'm on the step-up program for the new Meridian, which has a single turboprop engine."

"When will you get that?"

"Another year. I'm pretty far down the delivery schedule."

Hurd returned. "I talked to the bank. Three of the big citrus growers had today as payday. The bank ordered extra cash for the workers who come in to cash their checks."

"Inside job," Stone said.

"Sounds that way," Holly agreed. "Hurd, I want you to set up interviews with every single employee of that branch; start with the people on the floor today. Figure out exactly how many of them knew about the big cash order, who's new on the job, and we'll go from there."

Hurd nodded and jotted something in his notebook.

"And I need somebody to run me over to the bank; Jackson's car is still there."

"If you're finished with me here," Stone said, "I'll give you a ride. I've got to get back to Piper and give them a whole lot of money."

"Thanks," she said. "Scratch that, Hurd; I'll go with Stone."

Hurd nodded and left the office.

"I think we're done here, if you're ready," she said.

"My rent-a-car is out back."

Holly went to her office and got Daisy. She introduced her to Stone.

"Beautiful dog," Stone said, scratching her behind the ears.

"She's my best friend," Holly said.

They walked out to the parking lot and got into his car. Stone drove slowly, following her directions.

"You said you practice law?"

"That's right. I have an independent practice, and I'm of counsel to a big firm, Woodman and Weld."

"I've heard of them," she said. "Jackson loved his small practice. He just had one partner, and he liked being in charge of himself."

"I can understand that," Stone said. "I enjoy the independence, too."

"How much longer are you here?"

"Just a couple of days. I take delivery of the airplane this afternoon, then I have to get some dual instruction time in before my insurance company will let me fly it back to New York."

"I can imagine," she said.

They drove along in silence for a couple of minutes. "Holly," Stone said at last, "forgive me for mentioning this, but you seem to be operating pretty well for someone who has just suffered a great personal loss."

"It's something I learned when I was in the army," she said.

"You were in the army?"

"Twenty years. I was an MP; finished up commanding an MP company. I learned to concentrate on the task at hand and forget about everything else. I'm in that mode now, but tonight, I'll probably come apart."

Stone nodded. At the bank, he pulled into the parking lot.

"Let's go inside," Holly said. "I want to see where it happened."

Stone led her inside. "There was a carpet here," he said, pointing. "We were standing right there."

Holly looked around. Everything seemed perfectly normal, except that they had taken the carpet away to have Jackson's blood cleaned from it. She nodded. "Let's get out of here."

Stone walked her out to the parking lot to where Jackson's convertible was parked. "Do you have his keys?"

"I have my own," Holly said, taking the key from her pocket. "Hop in, Daisy."

Daisy cleared the top of the door with room to spare and settled into the passenger seat.

Holly leaned over and took an envelope from the front seat of the car and opened it. Then it hit her. "Oh, God," she said. "Paris." She began to sob. "He was taking me to Paris for our honeymoon."

Stone took her in his arms, and she sagged against him. They stood there for a minute or two, and she gradually got control of herself. He handed her his handkerchief.

"Thank you," she said, blowing her nose and dabbing at her eyes. "And thank God none of my people saw that."

"Don't they know you're human?" Stone asked.

"No, they don't, and they're not going to find out anytime soon, if I can help it."

"Let me drive you home."

"No, it's all right. I'm back in my detached mode again. Sorry about your handkerchief; I'll return it to you."

"No need. It's one of many." He gave her his card. "Here are all my numbers, though, should you need to get in touch with me. I'll be glad to testify, when you've arrested the robbers."

"That's exactly what I'm going to do," Holly said, getting into the car. "I'll see you later, Stone, and thanks."

As she drove away, she saw him standing in the parking lot, looking after her. "What a nice man," she said aloud.

She drove back to the house and put the car into the garage. She managed to get upstairs and undressed before she collapsed on the bed and began crying again.

Daisy hopped onto the bed and laid her head in Holly's lap, making small whimpering noises.

Finally, Holly was able to get up and feed Daisy and take her for her walk on the beach. She passed the evening staring blankly at the TV set, letting the answering machine pick up the phone calls. Finally, exhausted, she struggled upstairs and fell into bed.

In the middle of the night, she rolled over, stretching out a hand for Jackson. Then she sat straight up in bed. She spent the rest of the night staring at the ceiling.

8

Very early, Holly got up, fed Daisy and let her out. She fixed herself some cereal and ate it slowly, watching the sun rise out of the Atlantic. She felt more in control now, but she knew she'd have to be careful with herself, otherwise little things would set her off.

She dressed in her uniform, then went and listened to the messages on the machine. They were all from friends or coworkers and uniformly kind and concerned. She wrote down their names, so that she could return the calls later, then she called the name at the top of the list, her father.

"Hello."

"Morning, Ham."

"How you doing, kiddo?"

"I'm okay, weirdly enough."

"You sound a little dull, not yourself, but I guess that's to be expected."

"Yeah. I'm sorry I didn't get back to you last night, but I just had to sit by myself and let my brain catch up with what's happened."

"Smart move."

"Ham, will you do something for me?"

"Sure."

"Call a funeral home and get Jackson's body collected from the hospital morgue. I want it cremated as quickly and cheaply as possible. Jackson hated funerals and the whole business of being disposed of. He told me he wanted to disappear without fanfare when his time came."

"Okay, I'll get that done. What do you want me to do with the ashes?"

"Just drop them off over here, and I'll take care of them."

"What else can I do?"

"Have dinner with me tonight?"

"You bet. Why don't you come over here, and I'll fix you something."

"I'd like that."

"Whenever you like."

"Great. I'll call you when I get some idea."

"See you."

She hung up, and immediately, the phone rang. She sighed and picked it up; the day had begun. "Hello?"

"Holly, it's Stone Barrington."

"Good morning."

"I got hold of my old partner last night, and he called his friend upstate. What he found out was that the robbery was never solved, and they really only ever had one lead."

"What was the lead?"

"A teller at the bank, a woman, was the only employee who'd been there for less than two years; she'd been there three months."

"And they couldn't get anything out of her?"

"A couple of weeks after the robbery, she vanished, along with a bunch of other people, apparently."

"What do you mean, 'vanished'?"

"She was a member of some religious sect in the Hudson River Valley, twenty-five or thirty people. They simply pulled up stakes and left the state. Apparently, they had spent the weeks before disposing of their property and even their vehicles. A lot of people thought they'd committed mass suicide, and they may very well have, because every effort to track them down failed."

"Very strange."

"Very strange indeed."

"The guy on the New York State Police is doing a follow-up with the FBI office in New York, and he'll get back to me when he knows more."

"Thanks, Stone, I really appreciate this."

"Glad to help. You doing okay?"

"I'm managing."

"Let me know if you'd like to see my new airplane; I'm taking delivery today."

"Okay, I will."

"You can reach me at the Disney hotel in Vero, or on my cell phone; the number's on my card."

"Let me see how things go."

"Take care."

"Bye."

When Holly and Daisy got to the office, the atmosphere had returned to something more normal, since the witnesses had all been interviewed and sent home. She went into Hurd's office. "What's happening?"

"We've got the employee records, and we're going through them now."

"I want to know about the more recent employees." She told him about her conversation with Stone.

"That's real interesting," Hurd said. "I'll rush it." He handed her a sheet of paper. "Here's the tally on what the robbers got."

She took the paper and looked at it. "Holy cow! They had over four million dollars in cash in that one bank?"

"A confluence of four payrolls, not the three we originally thought. They would normally have no more than half a million cash on hand."

She handed the paper back. "I don't suppose there's any indication of the employees' religious affiliation in their records?"

Hurd picked up a file and looked it over. "Nope. That would probably be against some privacy law."

"Hurd, when you interview these people—and I do want them all interviewed again—I want you to tell our people to find out, subtly, if possible, what church these folks go to. If any of them is anything smaller or stranger than Baptist, Methodist, Catholic or some other well-established denomination, I want to know about it."

"Okay, I'll pass the word along." Hurd put down the folder. "Holly, when is the service going to be?"

"Service?"

"The funeral."

"Oh, sorry. There won't be one; Jackson's own wish. He hated everything to do with funerals, and he didn't want to put his friends through that."

"I understand. I'll let our people know."

"Thanks, Hurd." She went back to her office. There was a note on her desk to call Fred Ames, Jackson's partner. His had been one of the messages on her machine. She called him back.

"Hello, Holly. First of all, I want to tell you how sorry I am."

"I know, Fred. It's a big loss to you, too."

"Yes, but still—"

"Don't worry about me; I'm all right."

"Good. Holly, I don't want to rush you on this, but you and I should get together and go over Jackson's estate."

"I guess you're right. Is it important that we do it soon?"

"I think so. There are some unusual aspects, and the sooner we can go over them, the better."

"You don't want to do it on the phone?"

"I'd rather do it face-to-face."

"Late this afternoon be okay?"

"Five is good for me."

"Five it is; I'll see you at your office."

"Bye, Holly."

"Bye." Holly hung up and went back to Hurd's office. "Let me have the personnel files you're finished with, and I'll go over them again. That way, we're less likely to miss something."

Hurd handed her a stack. "I didn't notice anything unusual about any of these, but you're welcome to check them out."

"Are you checking out bank officers, too?"

"Yes, but they're in a separate bunch. You want them?"

"Yes, please."

Hurd got up and went to a table across his office and picked up a stack of a dozen folders. "Here you go."

Holly went back to her office, sat down and opened the first folder.

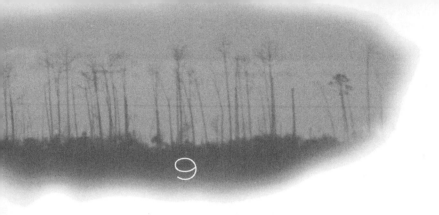

9

Holly arrived at the law offices of Oxenhandler & Ames at five-thirty. The staff had left for the day, and Fred Ames was alone in his office.

He gave her a big hug. "I'm sorry," he said, "and I won't say anything else."

She hugged him back. "Thanks, Fred."

He waved her to a chair. "Have a seat, and I'll make this as quick as possible."

"You make it sound like a trip to the dentist."

"It's not all bad news, but it's not all good, either."

"Shoot."

"Jackson's affairs were in excellent order. He'd seen to that in anticipation of the marriage."

"I'm glad to hear it."

"He left everything to you, except his half of the practice, which he left to me, and a few small bequests. He appointed you and me as his executors; he figured you'd need some help."

"Not only will I need your help, Fred, but I want you to do all the work, at your usual fee. I'm going to be busy."

Fred waved a hand. "Don't talk to me about fees again, all right?"

"All right, I'm sorry."

"The problem with the estate is the law that allows a spouse to leave everything to a spouse with no estate taxes."

"Why is that a problem? It sounds like good news."

"It's a problem, because you weren't Jackson's spouse."

Holly blinked. "Oh."

"You were an hour short of spouse, I guess, and I think it's worth having Jackson's accountant try to make a case to the IRS that you qualify. After all, you'd been living together for a while, and common-law wife might count."

"Common-law wife sounds like a broken-down trailer and a couple of old cars up on blocks in the front yard."

"If it works, don't knock it. Jackson was worth something over three million dollars, including the beach house, his belongings and his investments, so if you have to pay the estate taxes, it's going to bite."

"Listen, Fred, that's so much more money than I ever expected to have in my life that Uncle Sam can have his cut without any bitching from me."

"Still . . ."

"I know, save what you can."

"Right. Now the good news. A couple of weeks ago, Jackson and I took out life insurance policies. We each insured ourselves for a million dollars, and we each had a survivor's policy for another million that would go to the other in the event one of us died. This was to ensure the survival of the practice, since losing a partner means losing a lot of business."

"That's fine with me, but are you saying he left a policy for another million?"

"Yes, and it's payable to you, by name, not to his estate or spouse. What's great about that is that, if you do have to pay the estate taxes, you'll have cash without having to sell assets."

Holly put a hand to her breast. "My God, I had no idea about any of this."

"I don't know if you know this, Holly, but Jackson took that piece of land your house is on in lieu of a fee from a client years ago, then he bought an old Florida farmhouse inland somewhere for a dollar, sawed it in half and had it moved to the lot and reassembled."

"Jackson told me about that."

"So, after a lot of renovations and additions, and in the current real estate market, which is spectacular, that little old farmhouse on the beach is probably worth two million dollars, should you want to sell."

"I don't. Jackson still lives there, as far as I'm concerned."

"As you wish, it's yours to do with as you like. Jackson has a brokerage account and some T-bills, and about forty thousand dollars in cash in the bank. It's going to take a few weeks to get this probated, but you'll have the insurance money in a week or two, so you'd better start thinking about what you're going to do with it. You don't want that kind of money sitting around in a checking account."

"I know Jackson's broker. I'll talk to him."

"Good idea. If you need any immediate funds, I can advance them to you."

"Thanks, Fred, but no."

"That's about it, then. Do you have any questions?"

"No, I don't think so."

They stood up, and he hugged her again. "You call me when you have questions of any kind. Have you made any arrangements for burial?"

"Ham's taking care of that. Jackson wanted to be cremated and scattered without ceremony."

"He told me the same thing."

"Thank you, Fred. I appreciate your help."

She kissed him on the cheek and left.

Holly drove up A1A with Daisy sticking her nose out the window, and across the north bridge, then took a left down a dirt road and arrived on Ham's little island. He had inherited the land and a small house from his old army buddy, who had been Holly's chief until he was murdered.

Ham walked out of the house and gave her a big hug, then held her at arm's length. "You look a little funny," he said, "kind of stunned."

"Stunned is right," she said. She told him about the meeting with Fred Ames.

"Well, I guess you and I are lucky in the people we choose to be close to. I've got my house, and now you've got yours."

"I guess so."

They went into the house and to the kitchen, where Ham had been cleaning fish.

"Fresh out of the Indian River," he said, gutting a sea trout. "The sun is over the yardarm; why don't you pour us a drink?"

Holly went to a kitchen cabinet and found a bottle of bourbon and two glasses. She got ice from the fridge and poured them both a stiff one. They clinked glasses.

Ham raised his glass. "Better times than these."

"I'll drink to that," she replied, sipping the whiskey. This had been their evening ritual since she had been old enough to drink, especially when they were serving on the same post. The bourbon tasted like comfort and friendship.

"You given any thought to what you're going to do?" Ham asked.

"Just what I'm doing," she said. "I'm going to find the people who killed Jackson, and put them in jail and see them tried and convicted, unless they find a way to make it necessary for me to shoot them, which I'd do with pleasure."

"Me, too," Ham said. "As a matter of fact, I was going to offer to do it for you, if you'd look the other way for a minute."

"Tell the truth, I'd rather see them rot in jail."

"I know you don't think much of the death penalty, for a cop, anyway."

She nodded. "That's right. What could be worse than rotting in a Florida prison? Dying would be fun in comparison."

"You got a point, though I favor the penalty, myself, even if I don't get to personally administer it. What about after that's all done? You're a woman of means now; you can do whatever."

"I'm just going to keep on being a cop and keep drinking with you, I guess."

Ham rolled a fillet of fish in flour and dropped it into a pan of hot oil, then he leaned over and kissed her on the forehead.

"You sure know how to make an old man happy."

She kissed him back. "I don't see any old man."

"I'm gettin' there, sugar."

"Not you, Ham, not ever."

Ham blinked rapidly. "Oh, shut up and drink your bourbon."

10

back to work on the bank's personnel files.

Hurd Wallace came and leaned on her doorjamb. "Why do you think we'd be more interested in somebody who's new at the bank than somebody who'd been there for a long time?"

"Standard operating procedure," she said. "New employees are more likely to be involved in crimes against their employers than long-time ones. Didn't they cover that when you went to the academy?"

"Yes, they did," Hurd said, "but there's all kinds of reasons for an old employee to get involved: somebody has debts, maybe gambling or drugs; somebody has an affair and wants to run away with the new girlfriend and ditch the wife, needs funds."

"I agree," Holly said. "All I'm saying is let's start with the classically most likely employees and work our way down the list."

"There're two on your desk, there," Hurd said.

Holly picked up a folder. "Emily Harston?"

"Yep, and the other one is Franklin Morris. He's a new manager at the bank, been there four months."

Holly dug out the file. "Came from their home office in Miami; twenty-seven years old, married with a young child, senior loan officer. Would a loan officer know how much money was in the vault on any given day?"

"Probably not, unless he made it his business to know."

Holly turned to the other file. "Emily Harston has been there seven and a half months, a teller. Married, no kids, home address, P.O. Box 1990, Vero Beach."

"Kind of funny to have a post-office box as a home address," Hurd said.

"Good point." Holly turned to the next page. "Here we go: twelve Birch Street, Lake Winachobee. Where's Lake Winachobee?"

Hurd looked blank. "You got me, but there're a lot of lakes in Florida."

Holly got a Florida road atlas from a bookcase and spread it on her desk. Hurd came and looked over her shoulder.

"Well, we've got Lake Okeechobee, to the southwest," she said, pointing at it.

"Florida's largest lake." He pointed at a patch of water to the west. "What's this?"

Holly took a magnifying glass from her desk. "That's it; Lake Winachobee; about a tenth the size of Okeechobee." She looked more closely. "But there's no town by that name, and only one road going to the lake."

"Maybe she lives down that road somewhere."

"Could be. Who talked to her?"

"I'll find out." Hurd went into the squad room.

Holly continued looking at the area of the lake through her glass. Little lines indicated that it was a swampy area.

Hurd came back with Vicky Berg, one of her policewomen. "Here's your interrogator."

"Morning, Vicky. You talked to Emily, ah, what's her name?"

"Harston. Yes, I questioned her."

"What were your impressions?"

"She's late thirties, pretty in a plump sort of way, very quiet. And pregnant, I think, unless her weight just made her look pregnant."

"Anything else?"

"She answered my questions as best she could, gave me a good account of the robbery, but she didn't volunteer anything."

"She was reticent?"

"Yes, much more than the others. All the others I questioned couldn't stop talking about the robbery."

"Did you read anything into that?"

"Not really. I just thought she was probably shy or not a talkative person. She did strike me as being very bright, though; something in her eyes said that to me."

Holly looked back at Emily Harston's personnel file and read from a few lines at the bottom. "Mrs. Harston appears to be an intelligent person, and she has experience as a teller, having worked at a credit bureau at her former home in Idaho. Her former supervisor there gave her a very good recommendation, said she was honest, good at math and very competent." Holly peered at the signature at the bottom of the page. "Looks like it's signed J. Williams."

"His signature is on most of the forms. He must be a personnel officer."

"Has anyone interviewed Mr. Willams?"

"Not yet."

Holly stood up. "I think I'll go see him."

At the bank, Holly asked for Mr. J. Williams.

"That's Mrs. Joy Williams," the receptionist said. She made a quick call. "She's in. Just go up the stairs there; she's in room three-oh-eight."

Holly climbed the stairs, walked down a hallway and found the office. A fiftyish woman in a dark suit rose to greet her.

"Mrs. Williams?"

"Call me Joy, Chief. Have a seat."

Holly sat down.

"I expect you're investigating our robbery."

"I am."

"Well, that's about the most excitement we've ever had around here. I've been here fifteen years, and . . ." Her face fell. "Oh, my goodness, I'm so sorry. You lost—"

"Yes, but . . ."

"I shouldn't have said that."

"Please don't worry about it, Mrs. Williams."

"Joy, please."

"Joy, have you been in personnel for the whole time you've been at the bank?"

"Just for the past eight years."

"So you know most of the people who work here?"

"I know all of them."

"What about the newer people, Franklin Morris and Emily Harston?"

"Frank came to us from Miami, and he's fitted right in around here. He's made friends in the bank, and he and his wife go to my church."

"Which church is that?"

"First Baptist."

"What about Emily Harston? She's pretty new."

"Yes, but she's a real good worker. I've had very good reports from her supervisor."

"Do you know where she goes to church?"

"No, I don't. Emily doesn't live in Orchid Beach, and I don't think she's mixed with folks the way a lot of others do."

"Her personnel file says she lives in Lake Winachobee. Where is that?"

"You know, I'm not real sure. I remember when I hired her, she said it was half an hour, forty-five minutes away, depending on traffic."

"Do you know her husband?"

"No, I haven't met him. We had a company picnic last month—it's an annual event—and she didn't come. She said the next day that she hadn't been feeling well. I think she's probably four or five months along. Pregnant, I mean."

"Do you know if she's particularly friendly with any of the other employees?"

"Well, I see her in the bank's kitchen at lunchtime, and she usually sits alone, unless one of the other tellers joins her. We've just got a microwave and a refrigerator and a few tables; most people bring their own lunch."

"Is there anyone else at the bank who's new?"

"Those are the only two," Williams said. "We don't have a lot of employee turnover; this is a good place to work."

"Joy, can you think of anyone at the bank who may have been having financial difficulties? I mean, a lot of debt, late paying bills, checks bouncing, that sort of thing?"

"No, I can't think of anyone. The bank expects its employees to be financially responsible. If an employee had his wages garnished or bounced checks, he'd be in trouble. We're a bank, after all."

Holly stood up. "Well, thank you, Joy. I wonder if you'd do me a small favor."

"Sure, if I can."

"Would you come downstairs with me and point out Frank Morris and Emily Harston?"

"Sure, be glad to."

Holly followed her down the stairs and stopped at the bottom.

"Now, look over there at the platform—that's what we call it—that's where the bank's officers sit."

"Right."

"Frank is at the third desk on the right."

Holly found him, a slender, rather handsome man with dark hair and a mustache.

"And Emily is in the fourth teller's cage over there."

Holly saw the woman, and she was as Vicky had described her: plump and pretty. "Was she at that cage during the robbery?"

"I believe so; that's her regular position."

"Thank you, Joy. You've been a big help."

"Do you think that either one of them was somehow involved in the robbery?"

"Oh, no, Joy, nothing like that. We just always look at the newer employees in a case like this. I'm sure they're both fine people."

"I'm relieved to hear that," Williams said.

Holly thanked her for her help and left the bank. Outside, she sat in her car and waited. The bank closed in a few minutes, and she wanted to see where Emily Harston went when she left work.

11

Emily Harston left the bank five minutes after closing time and went to her car, an older, but presentable, pale blue Ford Escort. She got in, fastened her seat belt, backed out of her space and drove away. Holly, parked on the street nearby, followed her.

Holly stayed four or five cars back, even though she was driving her usual unmarked car. If Emily Harston was connected in some way to the bank robbery, this was no time to spook her.

Emily drove to a strip shopping center on the west side of Orchid Beach, parked her car and went into the supermarket. Twenty-five minutes later, Holly watched through a window as she paid for her groceries in cash. She emerged from the store pushing a heavily laden cart and went back to her car. She loaded the groceries, returned the cart to the place provided and drove out of the parking lot, turning west again.

Holly followed at an even more discreet distance as Emily proceeded across the South Bridge and headed west toward the interior of the state. Twenty minutes later, she signaled left, made the turn and disappeared from sight. Holly slowed as she approached the turnoff and was surprised to see that there were no street signs or signposts at the turn, just a dirt road headed straight south. Holly could see down it about a quarter of a mile, and the blue Escort was no longer visible.

Holly turned into the road and drove slowly down it. After a quarter of a mile, the road turned southwest, and there followed another straight stretch. Half a mile later, the road turned south again, and this time, Holly stopped her car, got out, walked to the turn and peered down the road. Another straight stretch lay ahead.

She got back into her car and drove until she came to another turn in the road, then she got out and looked again. This time she found herself looking down what appeared to be the main street of an old Florida town, no more than two hundred yards away. The street continued past a number of storefronts on both sides until it seemed to disappear into the lake. She went back to her car and got out a large-scale Florida atlas and found the correct page. The lake was there, but the town was not. She looked at the publication date of the atlas and found that it was less than a year old.

Holly sat and thought about this for a moment. She had found what appeared to be a town that did not appear on a recent map, which was very unusual. New towns did not pop up all that suddenly in Florida or anywhere else. She was reluctant to proceed into the little town until she knew more, so she turned her car around and drove back toward the highway. She passed no other cars, and she noted that there were no other roads turning off this one.

Daisy, who had been sleeping soundly in the rear seat, woke up and put her muzzle on Holly's shoulder. "You have a nice nap, girl?" Holly asked, scratching her under the chin, a favorite place. Daisy sighed sleepily. Holly punched the speed-dial button on her cell phone for Ham's number.

"It's Ham here," he said.

"Hey, good dinner last night."

"Glad you liked it."

"You want to go fishing tomorrow?"

"Sure, what time you want to come over?"

"Not there. I want to make a little expedition."

"To where?"

"If you'll get out a map and look very closely, you'll find a lake called Winachobee, about twenty-five or thirty miles west of Orchid Beach." She heard a rustling of papers.

"That little old thing?" Ham asked. "It's probably just a mud hole."

"It's not all that little. You must be using a small-scale map."

"Well, yeah, I guess so."

"I got a glimpse of it a few minutes ago, and it looked fairly substantial. There's a little town on the shore."

"I don't see the town."

"I don't think it appears on any map; that's what intrigues me. Why don't you put your boat on the pickup and collect me early tomorrow morning. I'll explain on the way."

"Okay, you're on."

"See you then." She hung up. "You want to go fishing tomorrow, Daisy?"

Daisy made a compliant grunting noise. Holly swore sometimes that the dog could talk.

Her cell phone rang.

"Hello?"

"Hi, it's Stone. Are you on the road somewhere?"

"Yeah, I'm a few miles west, heading back toward Orchid."

"You want to see my airplane?"

"Sure, when?"

"How about right now?"

"Where are you?"

"I'm on the Piper ramp at the Vero Beach airport."

"I can be there in twenty minutes."

"The tail number is November one, two, three, tango foxtrot."

"I'll find you." She punched off and took a right on Highway 1.

Stone Barrington was standing next to his new airplane, talking to another man as she pulled up. "Stay, Daisy," she said, and got out of the car.

Stone introduced the man as his instructor, then the man left. "Climb in," he said.

She walked up the airstair door and into a leather-upholstered cabin. Four seats in club style made up the rear portion, and she climbed forward into the copilot's seat.

Stone followed her and sat in the left seat. "What do you think?"

"It's beautiful; it even smells beautiful. Awful lot of gauges and instruments, though. I'm used to simpler airplanes, like Cessna 172s."

"It's a much more complicated aircraft," Stone said.

"When do you fly her home?"

"Probably the day after tomorrow. My first flight went well."

"Let me run something by you."

"Okay."

She told him about following Emily Harston and about the little town she discovered.

"Seems strange, doesn't it?" Stone said.

"Yes, it does. Have you ever run across anything like that?"

"Can't say that I have."

"Could you call the guy in New York and see if you can find out anything more about the place these people lived, the ones who disappeared?"

"Sure, glad to."

"I'd appreciate it if you'd call me at home tonight and tell me what you find out. Ham and I are going out there tomorrow."

"Ham?"

"My father. He's a retired army master sergeant and a fisherman. We're going to poke our noses into that place, on the pretext of looking for some fishing, and see what we can see."

"This is all very interesting. I'd want to come, if I wasn't flying again tomorrow."

"Maybe next time," she said. She looked at her watch. "Well, I'd better get back to the station."

They both got out of the airplane.

"She's a lovely color, too." The airplane was a rich cream on top and a deep red on the bottom.

"Thanks. Holly, I think you ought to be very careful tomorrow. Don't press your luck in this place."

"Don't worry."

"Good idea, I'll do that."

They shook hands.

"I'll call you tonight after I've called New York," he said.

"Thanks, Stone." Holly got back into her car and, with Daisy, drove back toward Orchid Beach.

12

Holly reached home as the sun was setting over the island. Preoccupied with thinking about the little town she had found, she entered the house expecting Jackson to be watching the evening news with a drink in his hand, and the cold darkness shocked her.

She found a light, fed Daisy and let her outside, then went and sat in Jackson's chair, feeling bitterly lonely. She flicked on the news, just to have some noise in the house, but the screen was a blur in her mind, and so was the sound.

Then Daisy scratched on the door, and Holly went to let her in. She stood, looking out at the sea reflecting the dying light in the sky, and she thought it made the water look as if it were lit from underneath. She loved this time of day. Sometimes she'd lure Jackson away from the TV, and they'd sit on a dune with a drink and watch the light die.

She was surprised by a hunger pang and went to the fridge to see what she could have for dinner. She settled for a frozen meal, since

Jackson had pretty much cleaned out the fridge in anticipation of their honeymoon absence. She sat in front of the TV while a rerun of *Law & Order* played. She'd seen it already, and even though she had, she wasn't able to follow the plot anyway, in her present state of mind. She seemed unable to organize coherent thoughts about anything, and her mind wandered. Fragments of days with Jackson played around in her brain, and sex entered into the mental pictures. She would never make love again, she was sure. After Jackson, what would be the point?

The phone rang, and she picked it up.

"Hello?"

"Hi, it's Stone."

"Oh, hello." She had forgotten she had asked him to call.

"I talked with the ex-trooper personally this time, but he wasn't able to help much. This group, this religious sect that disappeared, apparently did so in an orderly fashion. I think I mentioned before that they had sold their property and their vehicles. In the months after the bank robbery, the trooper ran a check to see if any of their driver's licenses had been transferred to another state, but nothing turned up."

"Did they actually look for these people?

"Yes, but not very hard. After all, they had no hard evidence against the woman who had been a teller, and she had resigned from her job and had given two weeks' notice, so there was no question of her running from the law. These people left the state the same way thousands of others move, except they didn't leave a forwarding address. The only mail they received after their departure was junk mail, so they had apparently closed out all their accounts—phone, electric, etcetera—and paid whatever was due. No bill collector or lawyer turned up looking for them. The trooper was unable to find out what means of transportation they had used to leave town. One day they were there, the next they were gone."

"What sort of area did they live in?"

"A county of small towns and farms. The group owned a sizable farm, but they sold it. They left it in perfect order for the new owner, complete with a tractor and other essential equipment, so apparently they didn't plan to take up farming again in another location."

"It's just a total blank, isn't it?" she said.

"Seems that way, and it's a little late in the game to start tracking these people. If they left no trace then, there would certainly be no trace now."

"I suppose you're right."

They were both silent for a moment.

"How are you doing?" he asked quietly, and in such a way that she knew it wasn't simply a polite question.

"I'm just sitting here letting my mind wander, and all I seem to be able to think about is Jackson. Have you ever lost anybody?"

"My parents, but not in the same way. They had long and productive lives and, when they finally became ill, died quickly."

"Have you ever lost a friend by violence?"

"I've known cops who were killed in the line of duty. I've never personally known an innocent bystander like Jackson who died in a crime."

"You know, it's said that when people have limbs amputated, the nerve endings in the stump make them think they can still feel the leg or arm."

"I've heard that."

"That's how it feels, as if some important part of me had suddenly been amputated, but I can still feel it. It's still real."

"It won't always be that way."

"I'm afraid to hope for that. I might feel better not losing that part of me completely."

"After my father died—he followed my mother by a couple of years—I would find myself dialing his number, expecting to talk to him. It took a couple of weeks to get past that. I'd want his advice, and I'd just pick up the phone, then feel like an idiot."

"I'm not the first to feel this way, I know," she said, "but it's the first time for me, and I don't like it."

"I wish there were something I could say to make it better."

"Thanks. I guess I'll just have to find a way to deal with it. It's okay when I'm working—I told you how I can switch it off. But when I got home tonight . . ." Her voice trailed off.

"Have you had dinner yet?" he asked.

"Yes, I just ate something, but thanks for asking." She was sorry she had eaten; she would have enjoyed his company. "Jackson would have liked you," she said.

"I liked him, for the brief time we knew each other."

There was an awkward silence.

"Listen," he said, "I've got a nervous feeling about this little town you found. When you go out there tomorrow, let your office know about it and arrange a check-in schedule."

"I really don't think it's dangerous," she said.

"Don't take a chance. If these are the people who robbed the bank, *they* don't take chances, and they don't mind killing. It would make me feel better if you kept in touch with your office."

"Oh, all right, if it'll make you feel better."

He gave her his cell phone number. "And you can call me, if you need to."

"Don't worry, I'll be with Ham, my dad. Nothing bad could happen to me in his company."

"I hope you're right," Stone said. "Good night."

"Good night." She hung up and tried to watch Sam Waterston win his difficult case.

She woke up in the middle of the night, still in Jackson's chair.

13

Ham turned up at eight o'clock—
late, for him—and demanded coffee before they left for their trip.

"I guess we're fishing in more ways than one, huh?"

"Yep," Holly said.

"What are we fishing for?"

"Bank robbers, but I don't suppose they'll be wearing ID tags. Apart from that, I just want to get a close-up look at the place, get the feel of it."

"Okay, you're the boss," he replied, downing the last of his coffee.

"Daisy, sit," Holly said to the dog. "No dogs today, you're staying home."

Daisy looked hurt.

"Don't try the guilt thing," Holly said sternly. "Stay. Let's go, Ham."

Ham had loaded a light aluminum skiff, a couple of rods and a tackle box into the bed of his pickup truck. "Camouflage," he said, nodding at the dingy. They got into the truck and started toward the mainland.

"I hope you aren't packing," she said.

"Funny you should mention it," he replied.

"Give it to me," she said.

He handed her his Beretta 9mm, and she stuffed it into the glove box.

"Lock it when we get there," she said.

"What about you?" he asked.

"I'm light. I don't want anybody thinking we're the law."

"I'm a retired military guy," he said. "*You're* the law."

"I'm retired military, too, and don't forget it today. Forget about the law part. Oh, I almost forgot." She took out her cell phone, dialed the station and asked for Hurd Wallace.

"Deputy Chief Wallace," he drawled.

"Hurd, it's Holly. Ham and I are going out to Lake Winachobee to take a look at a little town on its northern bank."

"Okay," Hurd replied.

"I want to be cautious about this, so I'm going to call in every hour at fifteen minutes past, give or take. If you don't hear from me for two hours in a row, call the sheriff and come find me, and bring some backup, too."

"What are you getting into, Holly?"

"I don't know, and that's why I'm being cautious. Don't do anything rash, but if I miss two calls, come get me."

"All right, but you watch yourself. Ham, too."

"Thanks, I'll talk to you later." She punched out.

"You really think that's necessary?" Ham asked.

"I sure hope not."

As they approached the turnoff to Lake Winachobee, they ran into a line of stopped traffic, and two minutes passed before they were able to turn left. A sheriff's deputy, probably an off-duty hiree, was directing traffic, and they followed a dozen other cars down the dirt road.

"We must be in the next county," Holly said, checking the map. "That's not an Indian River County deputy. Yes, here it is—Deep Lake County. I've never even heard of it."

"Doesn't seem to be much to it," Ham said, glancing at the map.

"Except all this traffic."

"Maybe they're having a fishing tournament," Ham said.

"You see any fishing gear on these cars and trucks?" Holly asked.

"Now that you mention it, no, but I see a lot of rifle racks."

"Who are these folks? What do you think?"

"They look pretty ordinary," Ham said. "There's one truck just like mine, the rest are American cars or SUVs. I don't see any Japanese or German stuff."

"So they're patriots."

"Automotive patriots, anyway," Ham said.

"I guess we're dressed the part," Holly said. They were both wearing old camouflage fatigue tops over jeans, their usual fishing outfits. There was a faded spot on Ham's sleeves where his stripes used to be.

The traffic moved swiftly down the dirt road, kicking up dust. Ham rolled up the windows and turned on the air conditioning.

Holly could see the row of Main Street buildings ahead, but before they reached them, another deputy directed them to turn right, along with all the other traffic.

"I hope this isn't some kind of Klan meeting," Ham said. "I might have to shoot somebody."

They were directed into a large clearing in the pines, and ahead stood a tent that would house a small circus. They parked the truck, and Holly insisted that Ham lock the glove box. Everybody was filing toward the tent, and they fell in with the group.

They were an ordinary, blue-collar-looking group, Holly thought, though some of them looked more prosperous than that. There were families with small children and teenagers, all neatly dressed—no long hair or tattered jeans.

"Must be a revival meeting," Ham said. "These look like church folk."

Holly looked around for posters or flyers advertising the event, but saw nothing. Just outside the tent they joined a line that had formed, and a couple of minutes later they were approaching a ticket desk, except no tickets were being sold. Instead, people were laying twenty-dollar bills on the counter, and they were being put into a box.

"Thank you," a woman behind the table would say, as the people laid down their money.

Ham came up with two twenties, put them on the table and got thanked, but no tickets were offered, no hands stamped. They pushed past a canvas flap and stepped inside the big tent.

Holly stopped and blinked. At least three hundred people were milling about among exhibits, and there was a loud murmur of constant conversation. The tent, to her surprise, was air conditioned, and it seemed to be filled with displays of guns—everything from pistols to assault weapons. There were booths with World War II Nazi memorabilia and displays of Confederate swords and uniforms. Everybody was busily doing business, buying and selling.

Holly and Ham exchanged a glance.

"I wasn't expecting this," Ham said.

"Neither was I," she replied, "but if we're going to blend in, we'd better start shopping—window-shopping, at least."

They moved off to their right, toward a large display of black powder handguns.

Ham picked up an old Colt Buntline revolver and handed it to Holly. "Can you imagine wearing that thing on your hip?"

"Nope," Holly said. "Not without developing a list."

They moved slowly on, taking it all in, then Holly stopped and stared. "What the hell is *that?*" Holly gasped.

Before them lay a weapon a good five feet long, made of black steel, with a stock of some sort of plastic and a very large scope.

"That, my dear, is a Barrett's fifty-caliber rifle," Ham said.

"What is it for?"

"Just about anything you want it to be, I guess. I saw one used during Desert Storm. A sergeant I knew put two phosphorus-tipped shells through an Iraqi armored personnel carrier and blew it to hell. The other carriers in the column stopped, and troops started pouring out of them; they couldn't surrender fast enough." Ham reached into the display, picked up a cartridge and handed it to her. "This is what it fires."

Holly was astonished. The cartridge was six inches long and seemed to weigh half a pound.

"They developed that ammunition for the Browning machine gun in World War One, but it didn't really get used much until World War Two. You can put one of those babies right through an inch and a half of rolled steel armorplate."

Holly set the cartridge back where it came from. "That's downright spooky," she said.

14

Holly turned to find a fit-looking man in his mid- to late forties standing behind her. His graying hair was cut short, and he was wearing a military-style jumpsuit.

"That thing is hell on wheels," he said. "I've never seen one fired in anger, but I once saw somebody put a round through a six-hundred-pound safe, and I mean all the way through." He turned to Ham. "You say you saw it fired in Iraq?"

"I sure did," Ham said.

"What was it like?"

"Awful, for the men in the carrier. I was a mile away, with the shooter. He said he could hit a playing card with it from that distance."

"A good shooter can hit a playing card from *twice* that distance, in no wind, if he has time to bracket," the man said.

"From *two miles?*" Holly asked.

"I kid you not, little lady."

Holly thought he had a lot of balls calling her that, since he wasn't quite as tall as she.

The man turned to Ham and stuck out his hand. "I'm Peck Rawlings," he said.

Ham shook his hand. "Ham Barker. This is my daughter, Holly."

Rawlings nodded at where Ham's stripes used to be. "You ex-military?"

"We both are," Ham said. "I put in thirty-eight years, and Holly did a double sawbuck."

"What kind of service?"

"I was in Special Forces for a long time, then I trained a lot of folks, and then they started pushing a lot of paper at me."

"Yeah, they'll do that," he said.

"What about you?"

"Oh, nothing exotic. I was just a grunt noncom. What about you, little lady?"

"I commanded an MP battalion," she said, "and if you keep calling me that, you're going to get even shorter."

The man gave her a shocked look, then burst out laughing.

"Holly doesn't take any shit from anybody," Ham said.

Rawlings bowed from the waist. "I apologize, ma'am," he said. "Just a figure of speech."

Holly nodded, and as she did, they were joined by two other men.

"Oh," Rawlings said, "these are my neighbors, Jim Cross and James Farrow."

Hands were shaken all around.

"What brings you folks to our little event?" Rawlings asked narrowly, and it was clear he wanted an answer.

"We didn't come to your event," Ham said. "We were just looking for some bass fishing, and we saw the lake on the map and just wandered down this way. Haven't seen the lake, yet. What's the fishing like?"

"Not bad, but nothing to write home about," Rawlings said. "That's a nice pickup you're driving."

"Ford'll sell you one," Ham said, "but not cheap."

"Where do you folks hail from?"

"Over at Orchid Beach, in Indian River County."

"Oh, yeah, that's pretty ritzy over there, isn't it?"

"Some parts are," Ham said.

"What do you do over there?"

"Every day, I explore the meaning of the word 'retired,'" Ham said.

"So do I," Holly chipped in.

"What sort of little town you got here?" Ham asked.

"A homogeneous one." Rawlings chuckled.

"I didn't see it on the map."

"That's the way we like it. You know, I can't remember anybody ever turning up here who didn't have an invitation."

Ham turned to Holly. "Well, I guess we're intruding here, babe; let's take a hike."

Rawlings threw up his hands in a placating manner. "Hold on, now, Sarge; I didn't mean any offense. It's just that this is a private affair, here, and we're unaccustomed to visitors."

"Sorry, I never heard of a private gun show," Ham said.

"Well, it is, but we're glad to have you. Just go on and wander around and pick up some hardware for yourself, if you're in the market. When you get ready to leave, though, I'd appreciate it if you'd check with me, so I can clear you out."

Ham looked at Holly. "You want to stay?"

Holly shrugged.

"All right, we'll have a look around," Ham said. "Thanks."

"And we're going to have a little firepower demonstration a little later," Rawlings said, "if you're interested."

"I'll let you know. C'mon, Holly." They walked slowly on around the big tent. "Well," Ham said, "I guess we're getting the feel of the place."

"Not a very good feeling, is it?" Holly asked.

"You notice anything unusual about this crowd?" Ham asked.

"You mean the lack of anybody any color darker than pink?"

"That, and the absence of any girls in cutoffs with bare bellies or guys with nose rings. I mean, this is still Florida, right?"

"It reminds me of the crowd at a PX," Holly said, "absent the people of color."

"I guess I've gotten so used to what you might call a more diverse population of former hippies and current rappers that I find it strange to be in this crowd. And it's not exactly comforting, either."

"I know what you mean."

They looked at weapon after weapon, at ammunition-loading kits, at holsters, at collections of knives and at more than one collection of Nazi memorabilia.

"I don't think I've ever seen this many Lugers in one place," Holly said.

"Me neither." Ham looked to his right. "What's going on?"

The crowd had thinned, and now people were streaming out the back entrance of the tent. There had been no announcement, no signal.

"Let's find out," Holly said. She and Ham went with the flow, and soon they were back in the humid Florida outdoors, walking down a broad path through pines. Shortly they emerged into a large clearing and stopped in their tracks.

"Good God!" Holly said under her breath.

15

Before them was a slanting pit, bulldozed out of the sandy Florida earth. It was shallow at the end near them and deepened as it went back another two hundred or so feet. At the far end it was maybe ten feet deep, and earth was piled up behind it for another twenty feet. At the deep end of the pit was the ruin of a school bus, two dead pickup trucks and a collection of other junk vehicles. Immediately before them, as the crowd strung out across the width of the pit, was an assortment of weapons, most of them automatic, on tripods, in shooting stands of various kinds and some in the hands of shooters of both genders.

Ham went to a picnic table, picked something out of a box and returned to Holly. "I reckon we'd better use these," he said, offering her a set of foam earplugs.

Holly rolled the plugs into narrow strips, then inserted them into her ears, where they expanded quickly to fill the ear canals.

"There's the Barrett's rifle," Ham said, nodding toward the firing line.

"I can't hear you," Holly said. "I've got plugs in my ears."

"What?"

"What?"

Ham pointed, and Holly followed his finger toward the evil-looking weapon, mounted on the roof of a Humvee, which was parked on the firing line.

"Oh," Holly said.

"What?"

"Oh, shut up, Ham!" she half shouted.

Ham started to reply, but, at some unnoticed signal, all hell broke loose.

A cacophony of gunfire erupted, and Holly saw holes appearing in the rusted bodies of the vehicles, but not the school bus. Glass shattered and danced in the light.

The earplugs were not enough, and simultaneously, Ham and Holly clapped their hands over their ears. The firing continued for a full five minutes, then, apparently at another signal, abruptly stopped. The shooters all lowered their weapons, and all turned to look at the Humvee. A man climbed up onto the vehicle's roof and shoved a large clip into his weapon, then sat down cross-legged and sighted on the school bus. The crowd grew quiet.

The shooter took his time, then squeezed off a round. Holly was amazed at how much noise the gun made. Then the projectile hit the front of the school bus and two things happened almost at once. First, the bus's hood flew into the air, then it was followed by the engine, which popped up out of its bay a good three feet high.

Then the shooter sighted again and put three rounds into the bus, along its length. Abruptly, the bus exploded into a huge ball of flame.

Ham reached over and pulled one of Holly's earplugs out. "That's your phosphorus-tipped round."

"But why the big explosion?" Holly asked.

"I guess they must have put a few gas cans in the bus."

The crowd erupted in cheering, and the man on the Humvee roof stood up and took several bows.

"Well," Holly said, "I don't think I've ever seen anything quite like that."

"I have," Ham said.

With the show over, the crowd began to drift away from the pit, back toward the tent, revealing picnic tables spread along the grass on the lakeward side of the tent. Holly had not noticed until now that they were on a rise, and that the lake could be seen a couple of hundred yards away.

"I don't think I feel like staying for lunch," Holly said.

"Let's take a hike, then," Ham replied. "But we're supposed to check with that Peck Rawlings guy first."

"There he is," Holly said, pointing.

Ham led the way, and they approached the man who was, apparently, their host. "Mr. Rawlings?" Ham said.

Rawlings turned. "Call me Peck," he said.

"Well, Peck, we're going to be on our way. You said to check with you first."

"What did you think of our little demonstration?" the man asked.

Holly tried to muster some enthusiasm. "That was really something," she said.

"Yeah, boy," Ham echoed. "I haven't seen that much firepower all at once since Desert Storm."

"We do that at every show," Rawlings said.

"How often do you have them?" Ham asked.

"Oh, every now and then."

"Why don't you put us on your mailing list?" Holly asked.

"We don't have a mailing list," Rawlings said.

"Well, whatever," Holly replied.

"Ham, you want to give me your number?"

"I'm in the book," Ham said. "C'mon, Holly, let's hit the road."

"Right," Holly said.

Rawlings pulled a small walkie-talkie from his shirt pocket. "Hey, Charlie," he said.

"Yeah, Peck?"

"Our guests are departing in a Ford pickup with a boat in the back."

"Got it."

Rawlings put the radio away and stuck out his hand. "We'll see you again sometime, Ham."

"Maybe so," Ham said.

"You never know." He offered his hand to Holly. "See you, little . . . uh, excuse me, Miss Barker."

"It's Holly," she said, shaking the man's hand.

"Bye-bye." Rawlings turned and walked toward the picnic tables.

Back in the truck, Holly called Hurd again and checked in.

"What's going on out there?" Hurd asked.

"I'll fill you in later," she said, and punched off.

"What'd you think of our morning?" Ham asked.

"Funny what Americans do for recreation, isn't it?"

16

Ham drove back to Holly's house,
and, once Daisy had been properly greeted and apologized to for her
lonely morning, they had some lunch.

"I like a ham sandwich," Ham said, munching away.

"I believe I knew that about you," Holly said. "Hence, the ham in
the fridge."

"I knew a woman once who said she liked a Ham sandwich, with a
big H."

"You don't have to spell it out for me, Ham. It's more than I want
to know about your life."

"You mean, a father shouldn't have a sex life?"

"No, just not one that his daughter knows about."

"Oh. I didn't know you were so sensitive."

"Funny, you never asked any questions about *my* sex life," she said. "I mean, when I had one. See what I mean?"

"Point taken," Ham said.

"And anyway, how did this woman make a Ham sandwich, without another woman to help?"

"I wasn't going to bring that up," Ham said, washing his sandwich down with a beer.

"Ham, are you telling me you had a threesome?"

Ham took another swig of the beer. "You said that, I didn't."

"That is appalling," she said.

"What's appalling about it?"

"Not the idea of a threesome; just the idea of you in one."

"You don't find the idea of a threesome appalling?"

"Not if I got to pick the guys."

"Now you're telling me more than I want to know."

"Truce on sex lives?"

"Truce," Ham said, raising both hands as if to ward off ideas of his daughter in a threesome.

"Okay, then." Holly turned her attention to her own sandwich.

"So," Ham said, "were you ever in a threesome?"

"*Ham!* I thought we had a truce!"

"I was just curious."

"Well, put away your curiosity."

"I just never thought you were the type, that's all."

"The type? What type?"

"The type to be in a threesome."

"I don't know whether to take that as praise or criticism."

"Suit yourself."

"You really want to know about my sex life, Ham?"

"Not really. I mean, not unless you want to tell me."

"What kind of father-daughter conversation is this?"

"One we should have had a long time ago."

"Well, we did have it, as I recall, when I was about nineteen."

"You call that a conversation? You wouldn't say a word. I figured you were working on becoming the world's oldest virgin."

"At nineteen?"

"But then that young lieutenant came along and fixed that."

"Which young lieutenant was that?"

"Wasn't but one," Ham said smugly.

"Oh, yeah? There might have been a platoon of young lieutenants, for all you know."

"You thought you could hide that stuff from your old man?"

"I *did* hide it from my old man."

"Then how come I knew about the young lieutenant?"

"Okay, how'd you know about him?"

"It was easy."

"How?"

"Well, you know when you came back from that weekend in the mountains when you lost your virtue?"

Holly turned pink. "You thought that, did you?"

"I didn't think; I knew."

"How, Ham?"

"I just walked up to him in the orderly room on Monday morning and stood about six inches from his nose; I looked him in the eye and said, 'Good morning, Lieutenant. Have a nice weekend?' And he turned purple."

Holly put a hand to her brow. "Oh, God."

"The same color you are right now."

"I am *not* purple."

"Close."

"Not anywhere near close. A little red, maybe. Who wouldn't be?"

"You didn't see *me* turn purple when we were talking about *my* threesome," Ham said.

"My God, Ham, the lieutenant and I didn't have a threesome."

"Who said you did?"

"You implied it, just now."

"You inferred it, maybe."

"You are impossible. We're not talking about sex lives anymore, is that clear?"

"Not even about my sex life?"

"Yours is the most off-limits—right after mine."

"Well, if you want to hide stuff from your old man."

"I'm not hiding anything."

"You're not talking about it."

"That's not the same thing as hiding it."

"Sure, it is. If you're not talking, you're hiding."

"Ham, what exactly is it you want to know?"

"Me? I don't want to know anything. We're only talking about this because you brought it up."

"I didn't bring it up; you did."

"Whatever you say," Ham said smugly.

"You did! I didn't!"

"I'm not going to argue with you about this, Holly."

Holly turned to where Daisy lay. "Daisy, bite Ham."

Daisy got up, went over to where Ham sat at the table and took his ankle in her mouth.

"Harder," Holly said.

"Ow!" Ham yelled.

"Now, Daisy, tear off his leg and hit him over the head with it."

"No, no, Daisy!" Ham cried, prying her jaws from his ankle. "Don't hurt your grandfather!"

"Is that how you think of yourself? As Daisy's grandfather?"

"Well, she's the closet thing to a grandchild I've had so far."

"Daisy," Holly said, "if he starts asking about your sex life, kill him."

Somewhere in the house a small chime rang.

"What's that?" Ham asked.

"It's a car coming down the road," Holly said. She looked at the umbrella stand by the door and confirmed that the barrel of Jackson's shotgun still protruded from it.

"You worried?" Ham asked.

"I guess what we saw this morning spooked me a little," she said. She got up. "I'll see who it is."

She walked toward the front door with some trepidation.

17

Holly checked the peephole first, but all she could see was the rear end of a black car parked outside. She couldn't see anybody at the door. She hooked the beefy chain on and cracked the door.

"Expecting enemies?" a man's voice asked.

"Harry?"

"One and the same."

Holly opened the door and flung her arms around the man. "Come on in the house. Ham's here."

She led Harry into the living room. "Ham, it's Harry Crisp, remember?"

Ham stood up. "Sure, you're the Fed who worked with Holly on that Palmetto Gardens thing."

"One and the same," Harry replied, shaking Ham's hand.

"Harry has risen in the world since then," Holly said. "He's now the agent in charge of the Miami FBI office."

"Mostly thanks to you and Holly, Ham," Harry said, dragging up a chair.

"Can I get you something to drink?"

"How about a pitcher of martinis? Just kidding. A Diet Coke will do, if you've got it."

Holly turned to Daisy. "Daisy, bring Harry a Diet Coke."

Daisy trotted to the refrigerator and, taking in her teeth a towel that had been tied to the handle, opened the door and gingerly fished out a Diet Coke, swung a hip against the door to close it, then trotted back to the living room and handed the Coke to an astonished Harry.

"You're a very handy dog, Daisy," Harry said, scratching her ears.

"She gets handier," Ham said. "She'll bring a beer, if you ask her politely."

Harry popped the can top and took a swig.

"What brings you up here?" Holly asked.

"I came up to make sure my people were doing a good job on your bank robbery."

"That's awfully nice of you, Harry. You didn't have to come yourself."

"I felt I should, owing you, and all."

"That's very kind."

"I also liked Jackson a lot."

"Me, too. Anything to report?"

"My people have done a first-rate job, just what I expect of them, except for one thing."

"What's that?"

"We don't have a thing to go on. I've never seen a cleaner crime—not a print, not a fiber, not a smidgen of DNA."

"Which crime are we talking about, the robbery or the murder?"

"Both. I don't think I've ever seen a case so completely free of anything to go on."

"I may have something," Holly said.

Harry looked at her blankly. "And you didn't tell my people?"

"I only got it this morning, Ham and I."

"Tell me."

"The robbers got unlucky just once, maybe."

"How?"

"There was an ex-cop from New York named Stone Barrington in the bank at the time of the robbery, standing next to Jackson, talking to him."

Harry screwed up his face. "Barrington? That's a familiar name, somehow. I can't remember, but it'll come to me."

"Anyway, when Jackson was shot, Stone tried to help him, and, later, when he came to the station to be questioned about the robbery, he mentioned something."

"He recognize one of the robbers, I hope?"

"Nothing as good as that. He remembered something from his time on the New York force, a bank robbery in some little town up the Hudson somewhere."

"Wait a minute, I've got it. Barrington was a homicide detective in the Nineteenth Precinct—this was, I don't know, seven or eight years ago. You remember the Sasha Nijinsky case?"

"The TV anchorlady who took a dive off a tall building?"

"That's the one. Stone Barrington and his partner—some Italian name, I can't remember it—"

"Dino Bacchetti."

"Yeah, that's it. They were the lead detectives on the case, and there was some question for a while whether Nijinsky had survived the fall and had been kidnapped, which is what Barrington thought. In the end, he got bounced off the force because he wouldn't go along with the official position on the case. I'm sorry, I'm getting you off track. Tell me about this robbery."

"A small bank was hit in much the same way as this one—very clean and professional—but nobody got killed. They suspected a woman who worked in the bank, but after she was questioned, she disappeared, along with everybody in a little religious community of some sort that was based on a farm near the town."

"How many people we talking about?"

"I don't know, a dozen or two, maybe."

"And they left town?"

"Not just left town, vanished into thin air. Nobody ever heard of them again."

"I don't know about this one, but I can check it out," Harry said. "The Bureau would have been involved; I'll put somebody on it."

"I'd appreciate that."

"Is that it?"

"No, there's more."

"Tell me."

"As a result of what Stone told me, and because it looked as though it might be an inside job—"

"That's our view, too."

"Did you question a woman named Harston?"

"Pregnant lady?"

"Yes."

"Yeah, but my man thought she was clean."

"She's one of only two employees hired in the last year; the other was transferred from another branch and seemed clean to me."

"That would be the loan officer?"

"Yes."

"We thought he was clean, too. What makes you think the Harston woman might not be?"

"She lives in a strange little town called Lake Winachobee, half an hour west of here. It doesn't appear on any map. This morning, Ham and I went out there, on the pretense of looking for some fishing in the lake of the same name, and we stumbled into a huge gun show."

"Gun show?"

"A really big one, set up in a circus tent."

"Well, there are lots of those all over the country."

"Yes, but apparently, this one is by invitation only."

"Invitation by whom?"

"I don't know, but Ham and I were spotted immediately as not being on the party list, and three men came over and checked us out."

"Give you a hard time?"

"In a polite way. When they heard that we, especially Ham, were ex-military, they relaxed a little. Ham dropped a few names—Vietnam, Desert Storm—and they seemed to like that."

"You get their names?"

"One was named Peck Rawlings."

Harry took out a notebook and wrote down the name.

"The other two we talked to were named Jim Cross and James Farrow."

Harry wrote them down. "I'll run them through the system and see if the computer likes them."

"I'd appreciate that. They had one hell of a firepower demonstration, too." Holly told him about the pit and the old cars.

"I've heard of that sort of thing. It's how they get their jollies, I guess."

"I guess."

"And they had this weapon called a Barrett's rifle."

"That, I know about," Harry said. "It was one of the reasons for the raid on that Branch Davidian place, out in Waco."

"How so?"

"Our people got a report that they had one or more Barrett's rifles; that's why all that armor was brought in. There were rumors that a round from that thing would penetrate a Bradley fighting vehicle. Nobody knew for sure, and that made everybody very nervous."

"I can see how it might," Ham said. He told Harry about his experience with the Barrett's rifle in Iraq.

"Very scary weapon," Harry said, nodding.

"I find this little town scary," Holly said. "It has really given me the willies. Can you check it out?"

Harry looked serious. "Well, if this is a tight little group, like the Branch Davidians, it takes a lot of time to penetrate one of those. I don't think it would be good for me to just send a carload of agents out there and start questioning people. Better they don't know we're looking at them."

"I think Ham might hear from them again," Holly said. "They seemed real interested in him."

Harry turned to Ham. "You think they might contact you?"

Ham shrugged. "Who knows?"

"If they do, will you play along a little?"

Ham shrugged again. "Let's see how it goes. I don't have much time for people like that."

"Don't mention that to them," Harry said.

18

Holly arrived at her office on Monday morning to find a message to call Joy Williams at Southern Trust; it was marked "urgent." Holly picked up the phone.

"Joy Williams."

"Hi, Joy, it's Holly Barker, from the Orchid Beach Police Department."

"Oh, Chief," Williams said. "Thanks for calling me back so quickly."

"What can I do for you?"

"Well, I feel kind of embarrassed about this."

"About what?"

"About my assessment of a certain person at our meeting the other day."

"Which person is that?"

"Franklin Morris."

"The loan officer?"

"That's the one."

"What about him?"

"Well, he didn't show up at church on Sunday, which is unusual. I can't ever remember his missing a service."

"Do you think something may be wrong with him? Ill, maybe?"

"Ill, no; wrong, yes."

"Tell me."

"Well, he didn't show up for work this morning, either, and he's usually here by eight. I called his home, and there was no answer."

"Did you send someone to his house?"

"I went myself."

"And what did you find?"

"I didn't find anything."

"I'm sorry, I don't understand, Joy."

"I mean, there wasn't anything to find. Nobody answered the door, and when I looked through a window, the house was empty."

"You mean there was nobody home?"

"There was nothing there—no people, no furniture, no nothing."

"You mean, he has decamped?"

"I think that's the perfect word, 'decamped.' I checked with his immediate supervisor and the other people on the platform, and none of them had heard a word from him."

"As I recall, you said he had come from your Miami branch?"

"No, I said he had come from Miami. We don't have a branch in Miami."

"I must have misunderstood," Holly said. "Did he come from another bank?"

"Yes, he had previously been at South Beach Bank. When he applied here, he said he wanted to get his family away from the big city and into a smaller, friendlier town."

"Did you check his employment there?"

"Yes, I faxed them and asked about him. I got a faxed reply the same day from the president of the bank. He said he understood

Franklin's reasons for wanting to leave Miami, and he gave him the highest recommendation."

"Have you spoken to the Miami bank president about this?"

"Not yet. I thought maybe you should speak to him."

"I'll be over there shortly," Holly said, "and we'll get to the bottom of this."

"Thank you, Chief."

Holly went to Hurd Wallace's office. "Remember the young loan officer who was the other recent hire at Southern Trust?"

"Yep."

"Sounds like he's taken a very big powder. I'm going over there now to find out what I can."

"Need any help?"

"Not yet. I'll call you if I do."

Holly collected Daisy and drove over to the bank. When she entered Joy Williams's office, the woman looked flustered.

"What's wrong, Joy?"

"I called South Beach Bank, and the number had been disconnected. So had the fax number."

"You said the president of the bank faxed you a recommendation?"

Williams handed over a letter. Holly took it, sat down and read the letter.

"It looks genuine enough," Holly said.

"Yes, it has all the right elements for a bank letterhead," Joy agreed.

"Did you try information, to see if the bank had moved?"

"I did. There was no listing for a South Beach Bank anywhere in Dade County. Also, I looked them up in a directory of banks, and they simply don't exist."

"May I use your phone, Joy?"

"Of course."

"And I wonder if you'd do me a favor while I'm calling."

"Anything."

"Would you please go down to the platform and ask Mr. Morris's coworkers not to touch his desk or anything on it?"

"Of course." Joy got up and left the office.

Holly dialed the station and got Hurd. "Will you send our tech over here? I want to go over Morris's desk and see if we can pick up some prints we can run. I want anyone who might have touched his desk printed, too."

"Sure thing. They're on their way."

Holly walked down to the platform, where Joy Williams had gathered the bank's officers together.

"Oh, here's Chief Barker, now," she said.

"Good morning, folks. I guess Joy has asked you not to touch Mr. Morris's desk?"

Everybody nodded.

"I've got a fingerprint technician on the way here now to see if we can lift Mr. Morris's fingerprints from his desk. It's important for me to know if any of you have touched the desk."

A young woman's hand went up.

"Your name?"

"Sally Duff," the young woman said. "I'm Mr. Morris's secretary. I mean, I work for all the people on the platform. I think I've touched it."

"We'll want to get your fingerprints, too," Holly said.

"But I haven't done anything wrong," she protested.

"I know that. We just have to be able to distinguish your fingerprints from Mr. Morris's."

"Oh, I see."

Joy Williams spoke up. "I have a record of Franklin's fingerprints," she said. "We take everyone's prints for their personnel files. It's a security precaution."

"Did you have anyone run the prints through the state or federal computers?" Holly asked.

"No, I'm afraid not," Williams replied, sheepishly.

So much for security, Holly thought.

An hour later, Sally Duff had been fingerprinted, and the technician had gone over the desk.

"What's the story?" Holly asked.

"There's more than one set of prints here, but there are lots and lots belonging to one subject. I suspect that would be Franklin Morris."

"Did you compare them to the prints in his personnel file?"

"Yes, and they're different."

Holly turned to Joy Williams. "How were Franklin Morris's prints taken?"

"By our security department. I sent him down there, and he came back with a fingerprint card."

Holly looked at the file. "This card?" It was a standard form available from security supply businesses.

"Yes, that one."

She removed the card from the file and handed it to the technician.

"Take this back to the station and run both sets of prints. Tell Hurd I've gone to Morris's residence."

"Yes, ma'am."

Holly looked at the address on Morris's employment application. "Is this the correct address?" she asked.

"That's it," Joy replied.

"Thanks for your help, Joy. I'll let you know what we come up with."

Holly left the bank and started toward Franklin Morris's house.

19

The house was a neatly kept 1950s ranch house in an older section of town, near a golf course. It was made of pink stucco with a concrete tile roof, like more than half the houses in Orchid Beach. Most of those that hadn't been built of these materials had been remodeled in them. She parked in the driveway, walked up the front flagstone path and rang the doorbell.

She hadn't expected an answer. She tried looking through the front window, but the venetian blinds had been closed. Through a crack at the end, she could see a corner of what appeared to be an empty living room. She walked around to the back of the house and flipped open her cell phone and called Hurd.

"Hurd Wallace."

"I'm at the Franklin Morris residence, and I want you to go over to the courthouse and get a search warrant." She gave him the address.

"What's my probable cause?"

"A bank officer has left town abruptly a few days after the bank was robbed. I think that ought to do it. When you get the warrant, bring it over here and bring the tech with you."

"Will do." Hurd hung up.

Holly tried looking in through the rear windows, but each was covered either by venetian blinds or a shade. There was a small pool in the backyard, and she noted that it was clean and that the grass around it had been recently mowed. In fact, the whole place seemed to be very well kept. She sat down in a poolside lounge chair and closed her eyes for a minute.

"Sorry to wake you," somebody said.

Holly opened her eyes to find Hurd and the tech standing there. "Oh, I thought I'd close my eyes for a minute, and I guess I must have dozed off."

"We've tried all the doors. They're locked."

"Okay, then, let's break in."

"Can I do it?" the tech asked. "I love this part."

"Try not to knock the house down," Holly said. His name was Tommy Ross, and he was a sweet, if naive, kid.

Tommy approached the back door of the house, which had glass panes over a wooden bottom. He made ready to kick it in.

"Tommy," Hurd said, "just break a pane and reach inside."

Tommy looked disappointed, but he found a brick bordering a flower bed and broke the pane. A moment later, they were in the kitchen.

"Nice kitchen," Hurd said. "The owner must have replaced it when he remodeled the house." He went to a cork bulletin board in the kitchen and looked closely at the notes posted. "A grocery list, and a list of chores around the house." He took a thumbtack from the board and pinned the search warrant to the cork.

Holly pulled on some latex gloves and motioned for Hurd and Tommy to do the same. Then she began opening drawers and cabinet doors. "Well, they took the dishes, but not the cleaning stuff under the sink," she said.

Tommy stood at one end of the kitchen counter and sighted down it from a low angle. "This looks clean as a whistle," he said. "It's been wiped down, probably with some sort of cleaner."

"One of the ones under the sink," Holly said. "Go find the master bathroom and check that."

Tommy left the room, and Holly and Hurd walked into the living room. The place was broom clean and, except for some abandoned things—an ashtray, some bad art on the walls—was empty.

Tommy returned. "No luck; been wiped down."

"Try the front doorknob," Hurd suggested. "That would have been the last thing they touched."

Tommy checked and came back, shaking his head. "Clean."

"Dust some surfaces," Holly said. "Try the doorknobs and the mantel."

"This looks like our inside guy," Hurd said.

"It does," Holly agreed. "I wonder if he's in cahoots with the Harston woman, or if we were just barking up the wrong tree."

"I don't suppose there was some legitimate reason for them to move in a hurry?" Hurd said.

"Let me fill you in," Holly replied. "Morris, if that's his name, was hired on the strength of a recommendation from the president of a nonexistent bank in Miami. He moved up here, bringing a wife and a small child with him, and he stayed until the bank was robbed, then he disappeared without a word to anybody sometime between Friday afternoon, when he left work, and this morning. Probably on Saturday night, since he didn't show up for church. I wonder how much furniture they had."

"That's a thought," Hurd said. "I'll check the truck rental places in town." His cell phone rang. "Hurd Wallace," he said, then he listened. "Thanks." He hung up.

"What?"

"The fingerprints on the card in Morris's personnel file belonged to a security guard at the bank."

Holly laughed ruefully. "Morris is smart. He must have gotten the guard to give him a demonstration of fingerprinting, then filched the card. Anything on the desk prints?"

"The secretary and Morris's boss. Apparently both left this morning."

"So Morris cleaned up after himself there, too."

"Looks that way."

Tommy came back again, looking frustrated. "Zip," he said. "Absolutely zero."

"Try the lawn furniture in the backyard," Holly said. "Oops, my prints will be on the one I sat in, but only on the armrests."

Tommy disappeared again.

Hurd called the station and ordered the detectives to start phoning truck rental places. "He had to move his stuff somehow," he said.

"Let's go talk to the neighbors," Holly said. They walked out the front door. "You go left, I'll go right."

Holly rang the first bell and got a young mother with a baby on her hip. "Good morning," she said. "I wonder if you saw the folks next door over the weekend?"

"No, we were at my parents' house in Orlando this weekend. Is everything all right over there?"

"Apparently, they've left town," Holly said.

"Really? I played bridge with her on Thursday afternoon, and she didn't say a word."

"Do you know what kind of car they drove?"

"He had one of those convertibles—Chrysler, I think—and she had a van. I'm afraid all vans look alike to me. I hate them."

"Colors?"

"The convertible was white, and the van was a kind of wine color."

"Have you been inside the Morrises' house?" Holly asked.

"A couple of times. They didn't have a lot of furniture yet, so she didn't really have people over."

"How much furniture did she have?"

"They had a sofa and a recliner in the living room, and a pretty big TV, and I guess they had a bed. She said they were saving up to buy more; that the bank frowned on its people carrying too much credit card debt."

"Thanks," Holly said, handing her a card. "If you should hear from them, would you give us a call?"

"Sure."

Holly walked on, talking to the neighbors. Finally, at the house directly across the street, she got lucky. The owner, a man in his late seventies or early eighties, remembered something.

"I fell asleep in front of the TV on Saturday night," he said, "and I woke up in the middle of the night. I do that a lot, since my wife died. I got up to turn off the lights, and I happened to look out the window, and I saw two cars and a trailer pull away from the Morris house."

"What kind of cars?"

"Their cars, a convertible and a van."

"And the trailer?"

"It didn't have any markings, like those U Haul things. Looked like a horse trailer to me. Wooden sides."

She thanked the man, then returned and reported to Hurd.

"You got more than I did," he said.

"When you get back, put out a report on the two cars and the trailer. I guess the van would have been pulling the trailer."

"If they left Saturday night, they could be well out of the state by now."

"Yes, they could. Alert the state patrol in Georgia, Alabama and the Carolinas."

"You know," Hurd said, "I don't think I've ever run into one like this."

"That's what Harry Crisp said," Holly replied.

20

Holly went back to the station and found another message from Joy Williams at Southern Trust. She returned the call.

"It's Holly Barker, Joy."

"Oh, thank you for calling me back. Something else came up that I thought you ought to know about."

"What's that?"

"Late Friday afternoon, just before closing, Franklin Morris cashed a check for $3,000 at a teller's cage. His whole balance was $4,248.22. Management here has started an investigation of all of Franklin's transactions at the bank, too, but we don't really expect to find anything much. Franklin's approval limit for a loan was only $25,000, without an approval from a senior bank officer."

Holly thought for a moment. "Did he have to have somebody's signature to cash a $3,000 check?"

"Not really, since he was a bank employee. The teller would have checked the computer for his balance, of course, but if he had the money in the account, she would have given it to him without question."

"I see. Which teller did he go to?"

"He went to Mrs. Harston's window."

"I see."

"But hers was the only window open at that hour. All the others would have been checking out for the day, and her window was kept open for last-minute customers. The tellers take turns being the last to close, because it means the last teller will have to stay another fifteen minutes or so."

"Thank you, Joy. Is there anything else?"

"Did you go out to the house?"

"Yes, and you were right. They've left the place."

"Are you going to arrest Franklin?"

"We've put out a bulletin to various state police organizations, because we'd like to question Franklin. Even if he didn't have anything to do with the robbery, we'd want him for fraudulently obtaining employment with your bank."

"You're going to arrest him, then?"

"I haven't requested a warrant yet, but I will."

"Thank you, Chief."

Holly hung up and called Harry Crisp.

"Hey, there, I was just about to call you."

"What's up?" she asked.

"I checked out the three names from Lake Winachobee, and came up with nothing—no arrest records, no outstanding warrants."

"That's what you'd get if they were assumed names, isn't it?"

"Exactly. What I'd like is some fingerprints."

"I'm not sure how we'd get those," Holly said.

"I wouldn't try right now. Just keep it in mind. Now, why were you calling me?"

"Remember Franklin Morris?"

"The loan officer? Sure."

"He bailed over the weekend."

"Quit his job?"

"Quit the town. He and his wife are gone, their house is empty, and he took most of the money out of his bank account on Friday afternoon. A neighbor says he and the wife pulled out in a van, a convertible and a horse trailer in the wee hours of Sunday morning."

"Uh-oh."

"Also, we've learned that he got his job with a fraudulent recommendation from a nonexistent Miami bank."

"I'll get a warrant. This is a federal matter."

"Okay. I've already put out an APB in five states for the cars, but we have no plate numbers."

"I'll check the car registrations and get the numbers."

"Thanks, Harry."

"So he fooled us both in the interviews, huh?"

"Looks that way. On the other hand, he might not have had anything to do with the robbery; maybe he just thought that the investigation might bring too much attention to bear on him."

"That's a possibility, I guess, but I'm inclined to discount it, for the moment."

"Me, too."

"Okay, Holly, let's keep in touch about this."

"Bye, Harry."

The phone on her desk rang as soon as she put it down.

"Holly Barker."

"Chief, my name is Warren Huff."

"What can I do for you, Mr. Huff?"

"I was just over at a house I own that I rent out, and I found it empty and a search warrant in the kitchen."

"That would be the Franklin Morris house."

"Yes, ma'am. It was a real shock finding it empty."

"I can imagine. Did Morris owe you a lot of rent?"

"No, he didn't. I got a check in the mail this morning for a month's rent, mailed on Friday, and I still have a month's rent as a security deposit. There was a note attached that said I could keep the deposit."

"I see. Then you have no complaint against Mr. Morris."

"Well, he had a lease that he ran out on, but I guess I'm not out any money."

"Mr. Huff, I'd like to send somebody over to have a look at the check and the envelope it came in. Would you put it aside without touching it again?"

"Sure, if you say so." He gave her the address of his office.

"Thanks, Mr. Huff." She hung up and called Tommy Ross and asked him to go and dust the check and envelope for prints.

The phone rang again. "Holly Barker."

"Hey, it's Ham."

"Hey, Ham. What's up?"

"You know that Peck Rawlings guy?"

"Yep."

"I had a phone call from him just now."

21

Lunch at Ham's was always fish, freshly caught. He rolled a couple of plump sea trout in flour and dropped them in hot oil.

Holly didn't rush him. It was best not to rush Ham, he'd get around to it.

Halfway through lunch, Ham got around to it. "So, ol' Peck called me this morning."

"What'd he have to say?"

"I think Peck thinks I'm his kind of folks."

"Good."

"Good? I found it kind of insulting."

"Did you tell him that?"

"Nope."

"Good."

"Said he wants to bring me something to read."

"Bring? He's coming over here?"

"Around six, he said."

"You think he wants to recruit you?"

"Maybe."

"How do you feel about that?"

"How do you want me to feel?"

"I don't want you to get in over your head, Ham."

Ham snorted. "Over my head? I've spent more time in over my head than anyplace else."

"I guess you have. What I meant was, if these people are who I think they are, it could get dangerous."

Ham shot her a withering look. "More dangerous than 'Nam? I don't think so."

"All right, I had to say it."

"Sort of a disclaimer, huh?"

"Sort of. I just want you to go into this with your eyes wide open."

"What do you want me to get out of this guy?"

"Nothing, at first. Don't ask too many questions. Let him tell you."

"You want me to be sneaky, huh?"

Holly laughed. "Real sneaky."

"That's one of the things I do best."

"Okay, I want to know how many of them there are, where they came from, how they support themselves, and anything else you can find out."

"I guess I can find out most of that just by going out there again."

"I guess so."

"But if I start asking him where he's from, he'll get suspicious."

"Right."

"Something else he's going to be suspicious about, kiddo."

"What's that?"

"You."

"Me?"

"He's got to read the papers and watch TV. Pretty soon, he's going to figure out who you are and that the man they shot in the bank meant something to you."

"How are you going to handle that?"

"Well, I've got to tell him something. You want him to think you're a closet Nazi or something?"

"You might let him think that I'm not totally averse to his views."

"I guess I could do that. You think he'll buy it?"

"When he finds out I'm the chief of police, he's going to be cautious."

"I guess he might be."

"Maybe you better bring it up, so he won't find out from somebody else."

"Okay." Ham took a bite of fish. "I think it might be best if I let him know, somewhere along the line, that I didn't approve of Jackson much and that that was a sore spot with you."

"Good idea. I don't think he liked me too much when we met."

Ham chuckled. "Well, when you offered to make him shorter, that probably didn't go down all that well."

"He'll have me pegged as somebody he can never trust."

"I guess he will."

"So you've got to make out, one way or another, that you and I aren't as close as we could be."

"I guess I can do that."

"I wish there were some other way to do this, but I think Harry Crisp is right: it would take too long to put an FBI agent in there."

"Probably."

"Ham?"

"Yep?"

"See if you can find out if this outfit has a name. That could be a big help."

"You mean, if they call themselves the United White Brothers of the Klan, that could tell you something?"

Holly laughed. "No, I mean if they have a name, we can use it to find out more about them. There are people who track extreme organizations, keep files on them."

"Okay, I'll see what I can do."

Holly looked at her watch. "I've got to get back to work. Call me when he leaves, will you?"

"I will."

She gave him a big kiss on his forehead. "Don't piss him off, Ham; I wouldn't want to lose you."

22

Ham selected a weapon, field-stripped it and spread the parts out on a towel draped over a table on his back porch. Then he waited.

At six o'clock sharp, there was a loud knock on the front door, and a male voice yelled, "Ham?"

"Yo!" Ham yelled back, then went to the door, wiping his hands on a paper towel.

Peck Rawlings stood on the front porch, a thick envelope tucked under one arm. "Hey, there."

"Hey, Peck, come on in," Ham said, opening the door. "Come on out on the back porch. Can I get you a drink?"

"Well, I guess the sun is over the yardarm," Rawlings replied. "Sure, if you've got some Scotch."

"Go on outside and grab yourself a chair, while I pour." Ham went to the kitchen, poured himself a bourbon and Rawlings a Scotch, then joined him.

Rawlings was bent over the table, examining the pistol. "What the hell is *that?*" he asked.

Ham handed him his drink, set his own down, quickly reassembled the pistol, screwed on the silencer, and handed it to Rawlings. "There you go."

Rawlings examined the evil-looking .22 automatic. "Jesus, Ham, that's an assassin's weapon. Where'd you get it?"

"Oh, when I was in 'Nam I ran a few errands for the Company, and they issued me the thing. Somehow, it got lost, and they never got it back. Pretty pissed off, they were."

"I can imagine."

"They were manufactured in small numbers—handmade, really—specifically for the Company. They were used in wet work all over the world, I believe." He took the pistol back from Rawlings, shoved in a clip, and worked the action. He took aim from the porch at a stand of cattails and fired, making only a tiny *pfft* sound, and cutting the head neatly off a cattail. "That was a .22 Magnum round, believe it or not." He handed the pistol back to Rawlings. "Try it."

Rawlings took aim at a cattail, fired a round, and missed. He handed the pistol back. "That's really something," he said.

"A little different from your Barrett's rifle, but it gets the job done. And nowhere on it is there a serial number or any mark that would identify who made it."

"I don't suppose you'd like to sell it?"

"You'd have to pry it from my cold dead hand," Ham said.

"I don't blame you."

"Sit down and drink your drink, Peck."

The two men settled themselves and sipped their whiskey.

Ham said nothing, just looked out at the Indian River. He'd wait for Rawlings to get around to it.

"Pretty place you got here," Rawlings said, finally.

"Yep, I sure love it."

"How'd you ever come by it?"

"The easy way. Fellow I was in the army with died and left it to me."

"You're a lucky guy."

"I sure am."

Rawlings was quiet for another moment, then he shoved the thick envelope across the table to Ham. "I brought you something to read."

Ham opened the envelope and shook out a book. "Ah, *The Turner Diaries*," he said. "I read it twice, years ago." He shoved it back across the table.

"No, keep it. That's an autographed copy," Rawlings said.

"Well, thank you, Peck. I'll treasure it."

"What did you think of the book?"

Ham had read it when he'd found a buck sergeant who served under him reading it. He thought it was the most outrageous collection of lies, bigotry and downright trash he'd ever come across. "Prescient," he said. "The naked truth, well told."

Rawlings grinned. "It sure is, ain't it?"

"It is."

"Ham, I think you're my kind of guy."

You do, do you? Ham thought. You go right on thinking that. "What kind of guy are you, Peck?" he asked.

"Me and my friends are what you might call patriots," Rawlings said. "In our fashion."

"And what fashion is that?"

"You might say we're working toward the goals expressed in that book," Rawlings said.

"And just how do you go about doing that?" Ham asked, looking curious. "Without getting sent to prison, I mean."

"Slowly, carefully, and above all, quietly."

"I should think so," Ham said, nodding. "I've often wondered if there was anybody actually doing anything."

"More than you might imagine," Rawlings said.

"That's interesting to hear."

"Just how interesting, Ham?"

"*Very* interesting. Tell me more."

Rawlings shook his head. "Not right now," he said. "You and I will have to get to know each other better before I can do that. You'll recall I said that we work carefully."

"Sure, I understand. You go right on doing that."

"With that in mind, I'd like to know a little more about your daughter."

"Holly?"

"Right, Holly. She seemed to me to be a little—"

"Annoying?" Ham ventured.

"If you'll forgive me saying so, yes, annoying."

"Well, Holly's not the smartest girl who ever came along. I mean, she's my daughter and all, but we've never seen eye to eye about a lot of things, so we don't see all that much of each other."

"Looks like you go fishing together."

"That's about all we have in common," Ham said. "If we can get through a couple of hours of fishing without getting into an argument, we're doing well."

"What do you argue about?"

"Well, politics, and, until recently, her boyfriend."

"What about him?"

"He always looked like a Jew to me, although he denied it."

"So she finally dumped him?"

"No, somebody dumped him for her. He got blown away in a bank robbery, just as they were about to get married."

Rawlings's eyebrows went up. "A bank robbery?"

"Yep. He apparently shot off his mouth—he had a real smart mouth—to somebody who was holding a shotgun, and the shotgun just happened to go off. Good riddance, if you ask me."

"You know, I think I saw something about that in the papers. Is your daughter a cop?"

"She's the fucking chief of police!" Ham spat out. "Can you believe it? She was an MP in the army, and not all that good at it, and an old buddy of mine got her this job. Just between you and me, she's not all that good at this one, either."

"Well, ain't life funny?" Rawlings said. He looked at his watch. "Well, I've gotta be somewhere." He stood up. "Thanks for the drink, Ham. I'll see you around."

Ham shook his hand and showed him to the door, then watched him drive away. He went back into the house and called Holly.

"How'd it go?" she asked.

"Not so hot," Ham replied. "We got to talking about you, and I broke the news to him about your being a cop. He didn't take it too well; a minute later, he was out of here."

Holly sighed.

"Yeah," Ham said. "You better think of something else."

Holly called the Miami bureau of the FBI and asked for Harry Crisp. He came on the line immediately.

"Hey there, Holly."

"Hey, Harry. I've got bad news."

"What?"

"The Lake Winachobee people didn't bite on Ham."

"Not even a nibble?"

"When Ham mentioned I was chief of police, the guy went cold and got out."

"Out of where?"

"He came to Ham's house."

"Why did Ham mention that you were a cop?"

"We figured they'd find out anyway—read the papers or something. Ham told him we don't get along, and that he didn't like Jackson, thought he was a Jew."

"Why the Jewish reference?"

"Rawlings brought along an autographed copy of *The Turner Diaries*."

"Oh."

"I'm really disappointed. I thought Ham could take this guy."

"You know, when we were involved in that Palmetto Gardens thing, I had a look at Ham's service record."

"You can do that?"

"Let's just say I did it. After what I saw in there, I would have thought that Ham could handle just about anything, anytime."

"That's pretty much the truth. Except for me."

"How's that?"

"He could never handle me, but I always let him think he could."

"Oh."

"What are we going to do now, Harry? Can you put somebody into that group?"

"It would take months, Holly, maybe longer. Did Ham get a name for the group?"

"No."

"If we had a name, if we knew who we were targeting, then that might help. I might be able to find an undercover guy who had some up-front credentials with right-wing groups who could go in there fully recommended. I mean, if they're associated with other groups. But if we don't know who they are, then we don't know which buttons to push."

"Well, so far we know they're weapons nuts, that they're anti-Semitic and antisocial, and of course, that they rob banks and kill people."

"Let's not get ahead of ourselves. We don't know that last part."

"You're right, I'm jumping ahead."

"We've got to do this one step at a time."

"Have you heard anything on Franklin Morris and his wife?"

"Not a peep. It's like they drove off the edge of the earth."

"I'll bet you anything they're out at Lake Winachobee right this minute."

"If we had probable cause to think so, we could go in there with an arrest warrant."

"Yeah, but it wouldn't be worth it. We might pick up Morris, but the current charges against him are minor, and the group would know we were onto them."

"I suppose we could take a look at them from the gun show angle, but once again, we'd tip our hand that we were interested in them."

"This is depressing."

"The only thing we can do right now is to just wait for something to happen."

"What, for them to rob another bank? Kill somebody else? They're flush with ill-gotten cash right now, and they've got no reason to do another bank."

Hurd Wallace stuck his head through her doorway. "Holly, Joy Williams from Southern Trust is on the line. She says it's important."

"Harry, can you hold on for just a minute?" Holly asked.

"Sure."

She punched the hold button, then answered the call. "Hi, Joy."

"Chief, I've got some news, and it's bad."

"What's the problem?"

"The bank has completed its audit of Franklin Morris's loan portfolio, and it looks like he's taken us for about $175,000."

"How?"

"By making loans to fictitious small businesses with bogus documentation, all of them under his $25,000 limit for loan approvals."

"Joy, I've got the FBI on the other line; I'll have them get in touch with you."

"All right, thanks, Chief."

Holly pressed another button. "Harry, you there?"

"I'm here."

"Southern Trust just called. They've audited Franklin Morris's records and he's embezzled $175,000 from the bank by making bogus loans. I told them I'd get you on it."

"That's weird," Harry said.

"What's weird about it? Isn't that sort of what we suspected?"

"Yeah, but if he's in cahoots with the Winachobee folks, who may have just stolen millions from the bank, why is he doing nickel-and-dime loan embezzlement that would have gotten him caught before he could steal very much? It doesn't make any sense."

"You have a point."

"And if the Harston woman is the group's inside person for the bank robbery, why would they need Morris in there? Certainly not for the money, and Harston could have told them all they needed to know about when the bank had a lot of cash on hand. They wouldn't have needed Morris for that."

"So?"

"So, maybe Morris is an independent, or working with another group with less ambition than the Winachobee folks. Maybe the bank was just unlucky enough to have two employees independently planning to steal them blind at the same time."

"That's a mighty big coincidence, isn't it? Didn't you once say to me that you didn't believe in coincidences?"

"I must have been drunk," Harry said. "Coincidences happen all the time. I know of one case where two pairs of guys showed up to rob the same bank at exactly the same moment. They ended up shooting it out with each other, two killed, two wounded."

"That's a pretty big coincidence, I guess."

"You bet your ass it is, but coincidences happen."

"I guess they do."

"Well, I'd better get another investigation going into the Morris embezzlement. I'll talk to you later."

"Okay, Harry, take care." Holly hung up, depressed.

24

Holly was getting ready for bed when the phone rang. "Hello?

"Hey."

"Hey, Ham. What's up?"

"I just got a dinner invitation."

"Do we have to talk about your sex life again?"

"Sex wasn't mentioned, but I'm keeping an open mind about it."

"Ham, I'm tired. What are you talking about?"

"I've been invited to the Peck Rawlings home for a fried chicken dinner."

Holly's heart leapt. "That's great! When?"

"Tomorrow night."

"God, what a relief! I've been feeling lousy for most of the day because I thought we were at a dead end."

"Not yet, apparently."

"What, exactly, did Rawlings say?"

"He said, 'Ham, why don't you come out here tomorrow night for a fried chicken dinner?'"

"What else?"

"Then I said, 'Peck, I think I'd enjoy that.'"

"I mean, what else did Rawlings say?"

"He said, 'Come out here about six. You turn right just as you enter Main Street, and we're the first house on the left.' Then he hung up."

"I've got to call Harry right now. I'll get back to you."

"Okay."

She hung up and dug out Harry Crisp's home number.

"Hello?"

"Harry, it's Holly. We're back in business."

"How?"

"Rawlings has invited Ham to dinner."

"That's great. It means they're still interested in him, in spite of his daughter being in law enforcement."

"Isn't it great?"

"Maybe. Let's not get ahead of ourselves."

"Well, they're not inviting him out there to shoot him."

Harry said nothing.

"Are they?"

"I shouldn't think so. But listen, Holly, it's important that he not do anything to arouse their suspicions on this visit. I mean, don't hang a wire on him or anything."

"I'll admit, I had been thinking about doing that."

"Just tell him to play it loose."

"That's what Ham does best."

"Thanks for letting me know about this right away," Harry said. "Now, let's both get some sleep. Call me back when Ham reports in."

"Okay, Harry, good night." Holly hung up and called Ham back.

"Hey."

"Harry's excited, too."

"What do you want me to do out there?"

"Eat fried chicken and listen a lot, nothing more."

"You don't want me to burn down the place or anything?"

"Nope. Just be Ham, or a reasonable facsimile who's also a bigot and a crypto-Nazi."

"I guess I can handle that, as long as they don't give me a lie detector test."

"They're still feeling you out, Ham. I don't think these people recruit all that readily; they're very careful."

"That's what ol' Peck told me at our first meeting: careful and quiet."

"Ham, how do you feel about doing this?"

"Funny, but I'm kind of looking forward to it. I mean, you can do only so much fishing and play so much golf before you start getting a little fuzzy around the edges. You want me to take along a tape recorder or something like that?"

"Harry says no, and he's right. Just go as you are, and play it very cool. These are suspicious people—paranoid, even—and we don't want to do anything to worry them."

"I get the picture."

"Don't swear any blood oaths just yet, either. Play a little hard to get; make them work to get you."

"Hard to get, huh? Are we back to my sex life?"

"Come on, Ham, you were never hard to get in your life. This'll be a new experience for you."

Ham laughed. "It sure will be that, and I have to tell you, I'm starting to look forward to it. I've always loved fried chicken."

"Okay, Ham, if you think of anything else, call me tomorrow at the station. Otherwise, just call me as soon as you're safely out of there. I want to hear all about it."

"Oh, you'll be the first to know everything," Ham said.

"Ham, just a thought: Take along a gun."

"You want me to go armed?"

"Not exactly. Just put your nine-millimeter in the glove compartment and don't lock it. If they get curious, it would be nice for them to find it."

"Whatever you say, darlin'. You sleep well, now."

"Believe me, I'm going to."

25

Ham dressed in khakis, a polo shirt, and a light sweater, the way he might if going to dinner at anybody's house. He checked himself in the mirror, the way he had sometimes done before combat missions, to see if he looked the proper warrior. This was the first time he had been a warrior in a polo shirt.

Feeling a little buzz of anticipation—not quite nervousness—he stuffed his 9mm semiautomatic into the glove compartment of his truck and drove west toward Lake Winachobee. He followed the dirt road the way he had on his last visit, but this time he wasn't diverted, so he drove right to the beginning of Main Street and stopped. Clapboard buildings lined each side of the street, and they might have been something out of the early twentieth century, or maybe Disneyland. There was a general store and half a dozen small-town businesses. He turned right, and drove down the dirt road. The sun was just setting, and the lights had come on in the first house on the left. It was a one-story house, but new-looking, neat, with a trimmed lawn and flower beds hugging the house. There was a three-car garage and, off in the woods, some sort of metal utility building. He turned into the driveway, switched off the engine, and got out of the truck.

The front door of the house was opened immediately by Peck Rawlings, who came out to greet him. "Hey there, Ham," he said, pumping his hand. "Glad you could make it."

Ham shook his hand. "Thanks for asking me, Peck."

"Come on in the house and meet some folks." He led the way inside.

Three couples were sitting in the living room, and the men all stood up. Ham had met two of them before.

"You remember Jim and James, I guess, from the gun show."

"Sure," Ham said, shaking their hands.

"And this is Mack Harston," Rawlings said, indicating a bulked-up man in a tight shirt.

"Mack, how you doing?" Ham said, shaking his hand.

Harston nodded.

"That's his wife, Emily," Rawlings said, pointing at a pregnant woman by the fireplace. "This is my wife, Betty, Jim's wife, Edie, and James's wife, Laurel," he said, pointing out the other women.

"Are you married, Ham?" Emily Harston asked.

"My wife died many years ago," Ham replied. "I never remarried."

"I'm so sorry," she said.

"Thank you."

"Ham, can we get you a drink?" Rawlings asked.

He noticed that the other men had drinks, but not the women. "Sure, Peck. Bourbon on the rocks, if you've got it. Anything else, if you haven't."

Rawlings nodded to his wife; she went to the kitchen and returned with the drink. When she opened the door, the smell of good cooking filled the room.

Ham accepted the drink. "Better times than these," he said, raising his glass.

"Hear, hear," Rawlings said.

"Are you right on the lake?" Ham asked. "I couldn't see from the front of the house."

"Yep, it's right out back."

"Pretty spot," Ham said. "Pretty little town, too. Looks like you've got just about everything you need out here."

"We go to town to the supermarket and the drugstore, but that's about it for outside shopping, except once in a while we go over to the outlet mall in Vero Beach and load up on stuff."

"I do some shopping out there myself," Ham said. "Everything's cheap."

Rawlings nodded, then there was an awkward silence, which Ham decided not to fill.

He sat back and waited for someone to say something.

"I hear you're ex-army," Harston said, finally.

"That's right," Ham said. "I retired a couple of years ago."

"How'd you happen to choose Orchid Beach?"

"I had an old service buddy who had already retired there, and he talked me into it."

"That the same one who died and left you the house?" Peck asked.

"That's right."

"Lucky break," Harston said.

"If you don't mind losing a friend," Ham said. "I'd rather have had the friend."

"Death comes to us all," Jim said.

There was a murmur of agreement.

"And taxes," Ham echoed.

Nobody said anything.

"What church do you go to over at Orchid?" James asked.

"I don't go," Ham said. "My wife was a Baptist, and I used to go sometimes with her. Me and my Maker seem to get along all right without any meetings on Sunday mornings."

Everyone got quiet again. Ham waited them out.

"You do much shooting?"

"I do some bird hunting from time to time," Ham said.

"Peck says you're quite a shot with a pistol."

"The army trained me. It's like roller skating; you never forget how."

"I never knew anybody who could cut a cattail," Harston said. "Peck told us about your shot."

"I was in an outfit in 'Nam had half a dozen guys who could do that. It helps your accuracy if you're shooting to stay alive."

"I guess it might," Harston said.

It helps if you practice every day, too, Ham thought.

Mrs. Rawlings went into the kitchen again for a few minutes, while the men chatted and the women remained strangely silent, then she came back. "Dinner is served," she said.

Ham followed the group into a large kitchen, with a dining area at one end. A large table had been set there, and it practically groaned with food. Ham took the seat offered him and waited to see if someone would ask a blessing. No one did, so he dug in with the others. "This is very fine cooking, Betty," he said, biting into a fried chicken breast.

"Betty's the finest cook I know," Peck said, biting into his own chicken.

The food was Southern—corn, collard greens, black-eyed peas, cornbread and biscuits, and of course the chicken. Ham ate well, but saved a little room.

"How about some dessert?" Betty asked, as she and the other women cleared away the dishes. "We've got some pecan pie."

"I'd love that, Betty," Ham said.

"Be right back."

"The women'll leave us after dessert," Rawlings said, "then we can talk."

Ham nodded as if he understood. Nothing about this evening so far was any different from a hundred other evenings he'd spent at the home of fellow soldiers, except there had been less drinking. He hadn't been offered a refill after his first bourbon, and iced tea had been served with dinner.

Betty returned with the pie, and when that was gone, coffee. "I've put a pot in your den," she said to her husband.

"Gentlemen, why don't we go in there and have our coffee?" Rawlings said. He led the way across the living room and into another room that had been paneled in pine and furnished with leather easy chairs.

Ham looked around him and saw the largest private collection of weapons he had ever seen outside a military arsenal. There were hunting rifles and shotguns, but the bulk of the weapons were military—assault rifles, pistols, machine guns. The Barrett's rifle occupied a place of honor over the fireplace.

Ham gave a low whistle. "Hey, Peck, looks like you've been shopping at your own gun show."

Peck gave a little smile and indicated where Ham should sit. "I like to be well armed," he said.

Ham laughed. "That's an understatement."

Peck poured everybody a drink from a decanter. "On the day," he said, "it'll all get used."

The other men raised their glasses. "On the day," they said in unison.

Ham didn't have the slightest idea what they were talking about, but he raised his glass, too. Then everybody sat down.

26

Peck Rawlings got the ball rolling. "Well, Ham, tell me something: what do you think of our current president of the United States, William Henry Lee?"

Ham said nothing, but held his nose.

Everybody smiled a little.

"I guess you've got some support around here for that opinion," Rawlings said.

"I believe somebody took a shot at him during the campaign," Ham said. "Pity he wasn't a better shot."

"You think his opponent was the better man, then?"

"Yes, but not much better."

"Who would you have preferred?"

"George Wallace, maybe, but he wasn't running, and anyway, he was a little too far to the left for my taste."

Rawlings seemed pleased with that assessment.

"And what do you think of our present form of government?"

"I think it was a great idea that got royally screwed up along the way, especially in the twentieth century."

"I can't say I disagree with you," Rawlings replied.

Ham sipped his brandy.

Mack Harston leaned forward in his chair. "Would you change things, if you could?"

"Sure, but what could *I* do?"

"Maybe more than you think."

"I'd be interested in hearing about that," Ham said.

"It's better to light a candle than to curse the darkness," Jim said.

"So I've heard, but I'd prefer a flashlight."

"Your proficiency with various weapons might represent a flashlight," Rawlings said, getting up and taking a manila folder from his desk. He sat down again and opened it. "Your service record says you fired Expert with everything the army gave you."

"My service record?" Ham said, genuinely surprised. "You've got my service record?"

"I have," Rawlings said.

"How in the hell did you do that?"

"Let's just say that we've got friends in useful places. I get the impression from reading it that you don't have much compunction about killing."

"I've never had any compunction about killing somebody who needed it, but I don't intend to spend the rest of my life on death row. They say the death penalty isn't a deterrent, but it sure is for me."

"That's a smart way to think," Rawlings said.

The phone on the desk rang, but it was picked up somewhere else in the house. A moment later, Emily Harston came to the door. "It's okay," she said to her husband, then she closed the door.

Ham sipped his brandy. "You planning on killing somebody, Peck?"

Rawlings smiled. "Oh, I'm just speaking hypothetically."

"Okay."

Suddenly Rawlings stood up, placed the file on his desk and turned to Ham. "Well, Ham, it's been a real pleasure having you out here." The others stood up, too.

Ham figured he'd been dismissed, so he stood up, too. "I've enjoyed it. Please tell Betty for me that it was a real fine dinner, and I appreciate the trouble she went to."

"That's what women are for, isn't it?" Rawlings said, leading the group out of the den and toward the front door. On the front steps, he paused and offered Ham his hand.

Ham took it.

"Thanks again for coming," he said.

"Good night," Ham replied and walked out to his truck. He got in, started it, backed out of the driveway and drove away. When he was back on the main road, he opened the glove compartment. His pistol was still there. He drove on slowly toward Orchid Beach.

Then, as he reached the outskirts of town, he saw a vehicle a couple of hundred yards behind him, lit by a streetlight but showing no headlights. "Why, I believe I'm being followed," he said aloud. The vehicle followed him all the way to the turnoff to his little island.

When he reached the house, he went inside, and instantly, he had the feeling that someone had been there. He switched on some lights and walked slowly around the place. The chair where he watched TV in the evenings had been moved. He knew, because there were indentations in the rug where the chair legs had formerly rested. A phone was on the table next to the chair. First, he switched on the TV and found a noisy cop show, then he picked up the telephone receiver and, while holding down the flasher, unscrewed the mouthpiece, then removed the disk that rested there. Behind it was a small electronic something-or-other that had been soldered into place. His phone had been bugged. He gently replaced the disk and screwed the receiver together again.

He went into his little office, opened a desk drawer and found his portable cell phone. He unscrewed the cover and examined the insides. Apparently, they had missed it. He went back to the living room, then through the kitchen, and closing the door softly behind him, out to the little dock behind the house. He sat down on a post and called Holly.

"Hello?"

"It's me. You been home all evening?"

"Yep."

"Didn't leave the house?"

"Only for a few minutes, to walk Daisy. How was your evening?"

"Let's talk about it tomorrow," he said. "Lunch?"

"Sure. Your place?"

"No, not here. Your place, at noon. When I get there, don't say anything until I've looked around."

There was a brief, puzzled silence. "Okay," she said finally.

"See you then."

"Good night."

Ham punched off, then returned to the house, turned off the TV and went to bed. When he had been asked to leave so soon after dinner, he had thought he'd somehow screwed up, but if they had tapped his phone, he was still in the game. He slept well.

27

Ham arrived at Holly's house shortly after noon, and there was a car outside he didn't recognize. He let himself in through the front door and found Holly and Harry Crisp waiting for him. Holding a finger to his lips, he indicated that they could come outside through the beach door.

When they were outside Harry shook Ham's hand. "What's up?"

"I guess Holly told you I went to this little dinner party last night."

"Yes, that's why I'm here. What did you find out?"

"I found out they kept me there just long enough to tap my phone."

"No kidding?" Holly asked.

"I kid you not, kiddo."

"What kind of tap?" Harry asked.

"They soldered something inside the talking end of the receiver."

Harry nodded. "Was that the only one?"

"I have no idea. They didn't seem to mess with my cell phone, though. Would a tap on the phone let them hear anything in the house?"

"I don't know, but I'm going to get somebody out there to go over your place, so we'll know exactly what we're dealing with."

"Tell us about your evening," Holly said.

"We had a drink and chitchatted, then we had a good dinner. After that, the other men and I went into Rawlings's den and had a brandy and talked."

"What did you talk about?" Harry asked.

"They were looking into my politics; I pretty much told them I'm to the right of George Wallace, and they seemed to like that."

"What else?"

"They were interested in my weapons experience. Rawlings had a copy of my service record, can you believe that?"

"I can," Harry said.

"Harry should know," Holly said. "He has your service record, too."

Ham laughed. "Everybody's all over me. Does that mean they've got somebody in records at the Pentagon?"

"Nah," Harry said. "All it means is they've got somebody who can hack his way into a Pentagon computer and print out your record. Mind you, it would take a pretty smart hacker."

"There was a computer in Rawlings's den," Ham said.

"What else did you talk about?"

"There was some talk of how my weapons experience might do some good for their cause, whatever that is, then it got cut short. The phone rang, it was answered in another room, then one of the wives came in and said everything was okay. Next thing I knew, I was being politely shown the door."

"The call was from whoever bugged your phone," Harry said, "reporting that the coast was clear. Why do you think they might have bugged Holly's place?"

"I don't know that, I was just being careful."

"I'll have somebody here before the day is out to go over both places."

"Oh, they followed me all the way home, too. There was a car behind me with no headlights."

"I guess they wanted to know if you were reporting to somebody when you left," Harry said. "Did anybody follow you over here today?"

"I didn't spot anybody, and believe me, I looked. These folks have a way of making me paranoid."

"Just play it straight ahead; lead your life the way you usually do, and ignore them. Sounds to me like they're interested enough in you that they'll be in touch."

"Tell me about the town and the house," Holly said.

"Looks like something that Walt Disney might have designed. A general store and a couple of other little businesses on Main Street. The house is ordinary-looking, fairly new, middle-of-the-road furniture. Rawlings has the biggest collection of guns I've ever seen off a military base, and believe me, I've seen some collections."

"What kind of guns?"

"Everything from antiques to handguns to military automatic stuff."

"Where does he keep it?"

"In plain sight, on the walls of his den."

"Be interesting to plow through it and see how much of it is illegal."

"Is it legal to own a Barrett's rifle?"

"What's a Barrett's rifle?"

"It's a fifty-caliber sniper's piece that can take out an armored personnel carrier."

"I've never heard of it, but I'll check it out."

"We saw it fired the first time we were out there," Holly said. "It was scary."

"Anything else they talked about?" Harry asked.

"They sort of implied that somebody with my shooting skills could make a difference in the world."

"You think they want you to shoot somebody?"

"The first thing they asked me was what I thought of the president."

"And you said?"

"I just held my nose and expressed my preference for George Wallace. I thought Adolf Hitler might be going a little too far."

"Ham, did you come away thinking that they wanted you to shoot the president?"

"It's hard to say, Harry. Asking about the president might just have been their way of asking about my politics. Still, they were awful interested in how well I shoot."

"And how well is that?"

Holly spoke up. "As well as it can be done," she said. "And with anything."

"I don't like the reference to the president," Harry said.

"Harry," Holly said, "do you think we ought to bring the Secret Service into this?"

"Not yet," Harry said quickly. "They'd be all over it, going in there with a search warrant, and we'd lose any hope of penetrating this group."

"That sounds a little like interservice rivalry to me," Ham said.

"Well, I guess it is, but it's my call on when to bring them in. Don't worry, I'm not going to let the president be put in jeopardy."

"Or Ham, either," Holly said.

"Of course not," Harry said quickly. "I wouldn't be using Ham at all, if I didn't think it was the only way into this group."

"Actually," Ham said, "I'm kind of enjoying this. I've taken a real dislike to these people, and it would tickle me to blow them out of the water, whatever they're doing."

"Any other impressions of last evening?"

"Well, I got the idea that they weren't hurting for money."

"Of course not," Holly said, "they just robbed a bank."

"I guess they could be making good money from this gun show of theirs," Harry said.

"You'd have to move a lot of weapons," Ham replied. "But I bet they could move a lot of weapons, if they felt the need. I bet if you wanted a couple hundred assault rifles or fifty Uzis, they could find them for you in a hurry."

"Anything else about last night?"

Ham thought for a minute. "Something they said," he replied.

"What?"

"It was when the brandy was poured, kind of a toast."

"What was the toast?"

"They all said, 'On the day.'"

28

Holly was on the way to work when her cell phone rang. "Holly Barker," she said into the instrument.

"It's Hurd," he said. "Franklin Morris's car has been found."

"Where?"

"At the Pirate's Cove Marina, in Sebastian."

Sebastian was the next town north of Orchid Beach, on the Indian River. "He didn't go far, did he?"

"Nope."

"Grab the tech and meet me there."

"You know the place?"

"I know it. It's near that seafood restaurant, Captain Hiram's, isn't it?"

"That's the place."

"I'll be there in twenty minutes," she said, then punched off.

The Pirate's Cove Marina had fallen on hard times and had been closed for the better part of a year, not having found a buyer who would rescue it from bankruptcy. Holly remembered it from when she had first arrived in town, and, she thought, it had gone downhill fast. There was a chain at the entrance, with a sign saying, Strictly No Admittance. Trespassers Will Be Shot. The chain was lying in the dirt road.

Holly parked and got out of the car. A small group of people were standing down at the water, next to a boat ramp. A Sebastian police car was there, too, and a wrecker. Holly walked down to the ramp.

"Good morning, Sergeant," she said to the Sebastian cop. "I'm Chief Holly Barker from Orchid Beach."

"How you doin'?" he asked, looking her up and down.

Holly was used to that and ignored it. "I hear you found a car we've been looking for."

"There it comes," the cop said, nodding toward the water. The wrecker's cable stretched down the ramp and into the water, and the machinery was making terrible groaning sounds. A foot at a time, the Chrysler convertible backed up the ramp, leaking water. "That's too nice a car for somebody to do it that way," the cop said.

A man wearing a wet suit walked over, a set of fins in his hand. "That ain't all that's down there, Sergeant," he said. "There's a van and a trailer, too." He pointed. "Right about yonder."

"Well, that's the damndest thing I ever heard of," the cop said.

"We've been looking for all three," Holly said. She looked down at the rear end of the convertible. "Sergeant, would you do me a favor?"

"If I can," the sergeant replied.

"Will you run the plate on that convertible for me?"

"Sure," the cop said and went to his patrol car.

Holly watched the car continue its progress up the ramp. Finally, it was high and dry enough for the wrecker to tow it to one side. The man in the wet suit unhooked the cable from the convertible's rear bumper and began pulling the hook toward the ramp. "One down, two to go," he said, half to himself. A moment later, he pulled down his mask, put on his flippers and walked down the ramp until he disappeared underwater.

Hurd pulled up in his unmarked car, with the tech beside him in the front seat. He got out and walked over to where Holly stood, glancing at the convertible. "It got wet, huh?"

"Yep," Holly said, "and the van and the trailer are still out there." She turned to the tech. "See what you can find in the convertible," she said. "Sergeant, you mind if my tech goes over the car?"

"Well, if you'll share information, that'll be all right. Save our man a trip down here."

The horse trailer was backing up the ramp now, spilling water from between its slats. "Fully loaded with furniture," Holly said. "Now, I wonder where Mr. and Mrs. Franklin Morris could be?"

"Afoot, I reckon," Hurd said.

The sergeant came back from his patrol car. "The plate on the convertible belongs to a Buick in Fort Lauderdale," he said. "Reported stolen eight months ago—the plate, not the car."

"Thanks, Sergeant." She turned to Hurd. "Morris took a pretty big chance driving around with that plate on his car. If he'd been stopped for speeding or a broken taillight, he'd have been in trouble. Tell our man to get the VIN off the convertible, and let's run that. I'm sure the convertible must have been stolen, too."

The diver was going back into the water with the hook again.

"I don't get it," Hurd said. "If they were going to ditch the vehicles, why didn't they just walk away from the house and leave everything there. Why go to the trouble to pack everything up, then dump it all in the river?"

"Doesn't make any sense, does it," Holly said, half to herself. She was starting to get a bad feeling about this.

The van started up the ramp now, water pouring from an open driver's-side door.

"Come on, Hurd," she said, then started down the ramp. She approached the vehicle, taking care not to touch it. "Raymond!" she yelled, "get over here."

The tech trotted toward them, carrying his bag.

Holly stuck her head inside the van. The front seat was empty, but a woman's foot, wearing a sock, but shoeless, rested on the back of the passenger-side seat. Holly looked into the rear seat. "Mr. and Mrs. Morris, I presume."

An hour later, the tech had finished. "They each took two in the head," he said, "small caliber, probably a twenty-two, maybe a twenty-five caliber. No exit wounds, so the ME will recover the lead. A lot of trauma about the head and shoulders, too—both of them."

"How long have they been in the water?" Holly asked.

"The ME will give us a final answer, but my best guess is, since the night they disappeared. They're pretty soggy but well preserved. The water is cool, down by the bottom, I reckon."

"I guess that tells us that Franklin Morris wasn't working independently," Holly said. "Whoever he was working with must have thought he was too much of a liability after the robbery."

"And who do you think that would be?" Hurd asked. "The folks out at Lake Winachobee?"

"This doesn't add up at all," Holly said.

29

Holly, in a phone conversation with the Sebastian chief of police, arranged for her department to take possession of the two bodies and three vehicles, then she had the bodies removed to the Orchid Beach medical examiner's offices and the vehicles taken to the police garage, with orders that no one was to touch them until she arrived. Then she went to her own office and called Harry Crisp.

"We've found Franklin Morris and his wife," she said.

"Locally?"

"Next town up. Both cars and the trailer had been rolled down a boat-launching ramp at a defunct marina. Both bodies were in the car."

"Cause of death?"

"My tech says two each in the head, but the ME hasn't done his report yet. You want to send somebody up here?"

Crisp thought for a moment. "How long have the bodies and the vehicles been in the water?"

"My tech says since the couple disappeared."

"Have you been over the vehicles yet?"

"No, I wanted to talk to you first."

"If they've been in the water for that long, we're unlikely to find anything useful. Why don't you have your man go over the vehicles, then send me his report, along with the ME's."

"Glad to do it," Holly said, relieved, as she didn't want to wait for Harry's people before starting on the vehicles.

"Get back to me," Harry said.

As she hung up, it occurred to Holly that the FBI wasn't much interested in the Morrises; they were small potatoes.

Holly went to see the medical examiner. The two bodies lay side-by-side on stainless-steel tables in the lab, with a sheet over each. On a smaller table nearby, two piles of clothing and possessions lay.

The ME took a deep breath and started. "Cause of death is easy: two gunshot wounds to the head of each."

"How long have they been dead?"

"Probably since soon after they left their rental house," he replied. "Before they were shot, their hands were secured behind them with duct tape, and they were pretty badly beaten up; you might say, tortured. Both show evidence of lots of blunt trauma, probably from fists and boots."

"Anything else you can tell me?"

"Not much else to tell," he said. "You might look through their effects over there." He nodded toward the small table.

Holly slipped on some latex gloves and went through the clothing first. The couple had been dressed nearly identically, in jeans, knit shirts and sneakers. One of the woman's shoes was missing and so was her purse. The man's wallet was on the table, and Holly emptied it. There was more than a thousand dollars in cash, credit cards in several names, and three driver's licenses, all with different names, but each bearing the photograph of the man the bank employees had known as Franklin Morris. There was also a Rolex wristwatch and a signet pinky ring, both of which were engraved with the initials S.C.L., which did not match the names on any of the credit cards or licenses. Holly dropped all the effects into a plastic bag and gave the ME a receipt for them.

"Thanks, Doctor," she said. "Will you fingerprint them and take DNA samples?"

"Sure, that's standard. What then?"

"Eventually, we'll get a burial order, but first I want to try to identify them. Just keep them on ice for the time being."

"As you wish."

Holly left the ME's office and drove back to the station. She collected Hurd Wallace, the tech and four other officers, and together they walked over to the garage, across the parking lot.

The three vehicles were lined up in separate service bays. Holly called the group together. "Here's what we've got," she said. "These two people were tortured, then shot to death. Unless somebody tortured them for the fun of it, which I doubt, the torturers wanted something from this couple, and they may not have gotten it. I want two people on each vehicle. I want everything removed and examined, then I want you to take the vehicles apart."

"What are we looking for?" the tech asked.

"I don't know, but I think I'll know it when I see it. Let's get started, everybody."

The group began work, and as they began removing things from the vehicles, Holly walked back and forth from one to the other, watching their progress. The couple's belongings were unloaded from the trailer and set aside, and Holly examined them. There were suitcases and boxes of clothes; there were small pieces of furniture and kitchen equipment; there were a couple of soggy file boxes. And there was a computer. Holly slipped on some gloves and started to go through the contents of the file boxes.

She found multiple birth certificates in different names for both people and blank letterheads from various financial institutions, none of which Holly had ever heard of and which she suspected were non-existent. Some of the papers had melded together while wet and would probably not be salvageable, she thought, but everything she saw in the file boxes had something to do with obtaining false identities or stealing identities from other people.

Hurd came over, and she showed him the materials. "Looks like these folks were hardworking con artists," he said.

"Did you finish with the convertible?"

"Pretty much. We've taken everything off it we can unbolt and looked in every cavity without finding anything. Harvey is taking off the tires now, to have a look inside them."

Holly walked around the convertible, which now looked as if it were at the beginning, rather than the end, of an assembly line. She looked in the trunk, which had been stripped of its spare tire, tools and lining. "Did the VIN get run yet?"

"Yes," Hurd said. "The convertible was stolen in Fort Lauderdale on the same day that the plates were stolen from the Buick. The van was stolen a couple of weeks later. I'm not quite sure how you trace a horse van. It doesn't seem to have a VIN, and it didn't have any plates, either. I guess we can run a check to see if any horse trailers were reported stolen in the past few months, but even if we find out where it came from, I don't know what that's going to tell us."

"It might tell us where they went after they left Lauderdale," Holly said. "Call the station and send somebody over to the ME's office to pick up the fingerprints of the corpses and their DNA samples. Run the prints first, on both the state and federal computers, and see if we get a hit."

Hurd pulled out his cell phone and made the call, while Holly walked around the van, which was nearly as disassembled as the convertible. "Anything?" she asked the officers working on the van. Both shook their heads. She walked over to the horse trailer, which looked more whole than the other two vehicles.

"There's not all that much to pull off it," a young officer said.

"Let's get in on a hoist and look underneath," Holly said. The two officers maneuvered the trailer over the hoist, and soon it was six feet off the ground. Holly walked around under it, dodging drips of Indian River mud. "Pretty dirty," she said. "Use the pressure washer."

She stood back as the underside of the trailer was cleaned, then she looked again.

"What's this?" an officer asked.

Holly joined him at the rear of the trailer, where a metal box had been fixed to the chassis. "That doesn't look like it belongs on a trailer," she said. "Get it out of there."

The officer went to get a radial saw and returned. "Looks like it's been welded there," he said. "This blade ought to do the job." He put on goggles, switched on the saw and began working on the welded seams. After a few minutes of noise, the box dropped onto the garage floor.

Holly walked over and inspected it more closely. "Looks like some sort of strongbox," she said. "There's a keyhole. Anybody a good lock picker?"

"I'll give it a shot," Hurd said. He found some small tools and began working on the lock. Ten minutes later, it snapped open, and Hurd lifted the lid. "Well, I'll be," he said.

The box, which was about twelve by eighteen inches and four inches deep, contained bundles of money that had been shrink-wrapped. Hurd cut one open and found the bundles to be made up of fifty- and hundred-dollar bills.

"I think we've found out what these people were tortured for," Holly said. "Let's get it back to the office and count it."

Half an hour with a calculator later, Hurd looked up from his tally. "I make it $161,000, even."

"I guess a lot of people would torture and kill for that," Holly said.

"I guess they would," Hurd said.

"It's got to be what they embezzled from the bank," Holly replied. "They must have spent the rest."

"But who killed them?" Hurd asked.

"So far, I've got only one suspect, or rather, one group of suspects."

"How are we going to tie these murders to them?"

"I don't know," Holly said, honestly.

30

Shortly after Holly's telephone conversation with Harry Crisp, he called back.

"Never mind sending all that stuff to me," Harry said. "I'm coming up there. I want to talk to you and Ham."

"Sure."

"Can I take you to dinner?"

"Maybe we should just cook a steak at my house. I don't know if
it's a good idea for the three of us to be seen together in a restaurant."

"Okay, can you meet me at the Vero Beach airport?"

"You're flying up here?" Holly asked, surprised.

"Yeah, we've got a light airplane attached to the Bureau. It's better
than a three-hour drive."

"You want me to put you up for the night?"

"We'll see when I get there."

Holly called Ham on his cell phone. "Where are you?" she asked.

"Fishing," Ham said.

"I don't guess your boat is bugged."

"It isn't. I checked."

"We're having dinner with Harry at my place, seven o'clock."

"Okay."

"Let yourself in if I'm not there."

"Right."

Holly watched the Piper Saratoga set down and taxi up to Sun Jet Aviation. Harry got out and walked over to her car, carrying a briefcase and a small bag, then the airplane taxied away.

"I guess you're staying overnight," she said, as he got into the car.

"I guess I am. Thanks for the offer."

"Anytime. What's up?"

"Did you bring the material from the Morris investigation?"

"It's at the house, and Ham's waiting for us."

"I'll bring you up to date when we get there. No need to do it twice."

They drove the rest of the way chatting desultorily, or mostly, in silence. When they got to the house, Holly pointed at the living room coffee table. "Everything is there, except the corpses," she said.

"I'll go over it later," Harry replied.

Holly got them all a drink, and they sat down.

"Okay, first of all, Ham's phone is bugged, and only his phone, not the rest of the house. However, Ham, they can listen to what's going on there, even when the phone is not off the hook. I wouldn't say anything in the living room or on the phone that you don't want these people to hear."

"Okay," Ham said.

"I guess I'm not bugged," Holly said, "if we're talking about this."

"That's right. Your place is clean, but be on the alert for signs that anybody has been here. They might decide to add you to their surveillance list." He pulled a small box from his pocket. "See the needle there?" he asked, pointing to a meter.

"Yep."

"You can wave this at a phone, and if it's bugged, the needle will move. You might just check it out now and then, and if you get a reading, let me know, and we'll go over the whole house again."

"Thanks, Harry."

"Now, let's go over the Morris stuff," he said.

Holly fed him the ME's report and her tech's report, then showed him the money. "I guess you'll return that to the bank."

"To their insurance company," Harry said. "They've probably already been paid for their loss." He looked carefully at the fake IDs and birth certificates. "These are pretty good," he said, "but a lot of people could do them with a computer and a laminating machine."

"I'm sorry to hear it," Holly said. She nodded at a cardboard box. "Morris's computer is in there. We don't really have anybody who can go over it, but I'm sure you do."

"Right, I'll take it back with me," Harry said. "It could be important."

Holly got up and started dinner, while Harry and Ham talked. He still hadn't told them why he was there.

When they had finished their steaks and were having coffee, she asked. "Harry, you haven't told us why you wanted to come all the way up here."

"We've come up with something," Harry said, "and it isn't good."

"What?"

"I mean, it's good for the investigation, but it's not good for Ham."

"Tell us," she said.

"Ham, you remember you said that when you were out at Rawlings's house, they drank a toast?"

"Yep. 'On the day.'"

"That's right. We ran it through one of our databases in Washington, and we came up with something."

"You came up with something from three words?" Holly asked, surprised.

"Yes, the Bureau has come across it before."

"Where and when?"

"Several years ago, in an investigation in Atlanta. There was a right-wing militia group called The Elect, based in Atlanta, but with, apparently, other outposts. Ham, did anybody ever mention The Elect?"

"Nope. I think I'd remember that."

"Well, don't ever mention it to Rawlings and his people, but if they mention it to you, I want to hear about it."

"Okay."

"Anyway, 'On the day' was a kind of motto with these people. They killed a Republican candidate for the U.S. Senate, and they made an attempt on Will Lee's life, when he was running for Senate the first time."

"Did they have anything to do with the attempt on his life when he was running for president?"

"It's possible, but we're not sure. There was a little nest of these people in Idaho, and they may have had a connection to the Atlanta outfit. We never had any firm evidence to that effect, because when we went after this guy, the others bolted, and we've never found them. They had been robbing armored cars and, generally, getting up to mischief. One of them actually made two attempts on Lee's life."

"How many of them?"

"Three families."

"And you've never found a trace of them?"

"They were apparently well prepared, had escape routes and identities all worked out ahead of time. It was all very slick."

"But you got the man who tried to kill President Lee?"

"The man's son shot him. We questioned the boy and his family, but we never got anything out of them connecting him with The Elect."

"Spooky," Ham said.

"Yes, it is, and Ham, if you get any indication of these people at Lake Winachobee being part of The Elect, I want to know about it instantly."

"Okay," Ham said.

"Ham, I'd love it if we could take down the group, but if these people are part of it, then they're very, very dangerous. You keep that in mind."

"Okay," Ham said.

"God, I'd love to bust them," Harry said.

Ham raised his coffee cup. "On the day," he said.

31

A month passed. Holly noticed that the emotional detachment she felt from the experience of Jackson's death when she was working had begun to lap over into the hours when she was not.

She still had moments when she couldn't stop the tears, moments when she was alone in the dunes with Daisy, or sometimes when she woke up in the middle of the night and reached for Jackson, but they seemed to come less often and with less intensity. If she wanted to really feel sorry for herself, to feel what she had felt when Jackson had died, she could, but it took more and more effort. She wondered if time really healed all wounds, or if she was just becoming a harder person. She didn't want to become a harder person, but how else could she protect herself from the pain?

She found work less and less interesting, particularly since she had not been able to connect the Morris murders to the Winachobee group, or anybody else, for that matter. And as for the Winachobee group, they had gone very quiet. Ham had not heard from them, and they had not come to her attention again, except through an occasional call from Harry Crisp, and those were coming less and less frequently.

The Morrises themselves remained an enigma. Their fingerprints were not known to any law enforcement computer, nor were their photographs. The name Franklin Morris, with its corresponding birth date, did not appear on any legitimate birth certificate known to any county database in Florida or in any other state. The young couple were a blank, and none of the names they had used on various identity papers rang any bells with anybody, either. It was Holly's slowly developed opinion that they were not connected with the Winachobee group; rather, that they were a couple of freelance hustlers who were either new to the game or who had never been caught. Still, they were working with *someone,* she believed, or else why would anyone have had a motive to kill them? They had failed to share their ill-gotten gains with whomever they had promised to share it with and had been killed for it. Also, they must have learned what criminal skills they had—car theft, fake identities, loan embezzlement—from somebody, but who? Holly had no idea.

The phone rang. "Holly Barker."

"It's me," Ham said.

"Hey, Ham." She had not seen as much of him as usual, because it seemed better not to, if they were under scrutiny from the Winachobees.

"I'm on a pay phone. I got a call at home from Peck Rawlings," Ham said.

Holly's heart skipped a couple of beats. "Tell me," she said.

"They're having another one of their gun shows tomorrow, and they invited me to come out there. You, too."

"Great," she said.

"I said I'd ask you, but I think it's better if you don't come."

"Why?"

"Because I've told them we don't get along all that well, remember? I think I ought to tell them you weren't interested."

"Well, maybe you're right."

"I think you ought to check with Harry Crisp on this, though."

"Okay, I'll call him right now. Hang on, I'll make it a conference call." She put Ham on hold, got Harry on the phone, then pressed the conference button. "Everybody there?"

"I'm here," Ham said.

"Me too," Harry replied.

"Harry, they've invited Ham out to another gun show, and me, too, but Ham doesn't think I ought to go."

Ham explained himself.

"I think Ham's right," Harry said. "They need to get used to him without you—after all, you're the law."

"Yeah, I guess," Holly said.

"I know you'd rather be out there amongst 'em," Harry said, "but I think Ham's got to carry the water on this one."

"I guess you're right, Harry."

"What about me?" Ham asked.

"Oh, all right, you're right, too."

"I don't hear *that* very often," Ham said, and Harry laughed. "Harry, you got any special instructions?"

"Nope, just go out there and do what you do. I don't want you carrying any recorders or cameras, either."

"I've got to win their trust, huh?"

"No, not that," Harry said quickly. "If they see you trying, they'll wonder. Let them come to you. Don't make any moves."

"He's right, Ham," Holly said. "Did they say anything except come to the gun show?"

"They mentioned lunch by the lake," Ham said.

"Nothing more sinister?"

"Not unless you consider barbecue sinister."

Harry laughed. "Be patient, Holly, this is going to take a while."

"You're right, Harry," she said. "Ham, take your cell phone this time, just in case you need help."

"No, don't," Harry jumped in. "You need to go naked into the jungle."

"Won't be the first time," Ham said.

"Bye," Harry said, and hung up.

"Listen, I'll call you back on my bugged phone and invite you, okay? Then you can turn me down."

"Okay." Holly hung up.

A couple of minutes later, Ham called again.

"Holly Barker."

"It's your old man, Holly."

"How are you?" she asked, as if she didn't care.

"I'm okay. You and I got an invitation from those folks out at the lake to go to their gun show this weekend and have some lunch with them. You want to go?"

"I'll pass, Ham. Those people are boring."

"Suit yourself, Holly."

"I mean, you don't really like them, do you?"

"I had dinner out there last month. They seem like nice folks, and they have some interesting ideas."

"Yeah, sure. Listen, thanks for the invitation. I gotta run. Take care of yourself."

"Well, somebody has to," Ham said petulantly, then hung up.

Holly hung up, too. "Let's see what they make of that conversation," she said aloud.

32

This time, Ham wore a freshly starched set of camouflage fatigues. He figured he'd fit right in with the mindset of these people, and he was right.

When Peck Rawlings saw him, he beamed from ear to ear. "Well, Ham, you're looking sharp today," he said, shaking hands.

"I'm okay," Ham said. He unzipped the canvas bag he was carrying and showed Peck the silenced CIA-issue pistol. "I thought some of your folks might be interested in seeing this," he said.

"Damn right they will," Peck replied. "Come on, let's find some of the boys right now."

Peck collected a dozen men, only a couple of whom Ham had met, and escorted them out to the firing range. "Gentlemen," he said, "Ham Barker has brought along something I think you'll find very interesting. Ham?"

Ham took the pistol from its holster, removed the clip, checked that the breech was empty and passed it around, watching as each of the men inspected it.

"Never seen anything like it," one of them said.

"It's not likely you will," Ham said. "I'm told they were made in very small numbers for a government agency that appreciates these kinds of toys." He took the pistol back, loaded it and screwed the silencer into the barrel.

"Pick out a target," Peck said, waving an arm at the range.

Ham lifted the pistol, took brief aim at a whiskey bottle sitting on top of a burned-out car halfway down the range and fired. The shattering of the bottle made more noise than the pistol had.

There was a murmur of approval from the crowd.

"That was a hell of a shot from a hundred yards," Peck said. "I'm a pretty good shot, and I don't know if I could hit anything with a handgun from that distance."

Ham shrugged. "Some of you fellas want to try it out?" He watched as the men, one by one, fired the weapon. One or two of them came close to their targets, but none hit them.

Jim, whom Ham remembered from before, stepped forward with another military-looking weapon—a long-barreled rifle with a large scope affixed. "Show us what you can do with this, Ham," he said.

Ham took the weapon and inspected it. "I believe I've seen one of these before," he said, "when I was in Special Forces." He looked around him. "What can I safely take a shot at that's a little farther away?" he asked.

Peck looked back toward the town and pointed to the water tower, half a mile away. A bunch of welcoming balloons was tied to the top of it. "See if you can hit the top balloon," he said. "The round will end up in the lake."

Ham sighted the rifle. The balloons stood straight up in the calm air. "Good day for it," he said, and popped the top balloon with a single round.

"You think you could do that with the Barrett's rifle?" Peck asked.

"Given an opportunity to sight it in, probably," Ham said. "I fired it a few times in Iraq and did pretty good."

"Maybe we'll try that on another occasion," Peck said. "Come on, everybody, let's eat some barbecue."

Ham unloaded and stowed his pistol, and the group walked to the lakeside, where a group of women had set up a chow line beside a dozen picnic tables. Everybody grabbed a plate, and shortly, they were seated at a table, eating barbecue. Ham noticed that Peck and Jim stuck with him, and another man, one he hadn't seen before, joined them.

"Ham," Peck said, "this is John."

The man, who was tall and slim like Ham, and who wore round, steel-rimmed glasses, offered his hand. "How do you do, Ham?"

"Good to meet you," Ham said. "Just John?"

"That's what they call me," the man replied, biting into some cornbread.

"That's all that's necessary," another man said, and the group nodded as one man.

Ham sensed, from the deference shown to John, that he was somebody special to these people. "John, it is," he said, and dug into his barbecue.

"I had a look at your military record," John said after a moment. "You had an interesting career."

"I guess I did," Ham replied.

"Must be a little boring, being retired."

"A little," Ham agreed. "There's just so much fishing a fellow can do."

John nodded in agreement. "That's how I felt when I retired."

"What service?" Ham asked.

"I wasn't in the military," the man said. "You might say I served another master."

Ham started to ask what master but thought better of it. He nodded and continued with his lunch.

"I wonder," John said, "if you'd like to give some of our people a little instruction in the finer points of shooting?"

"Sure," Ham replied. "What sort of shooting?"

"The kind you were doing a few minutes ago," he said. "We've got some good shots in our outfit, but none as good as you."

"If they've got talent, I can train them," Ham said. "They'll have to work at it, though."

"Oh, they'll work at it," John said, "or answer to me. After lunch, we'll take a little trip down to another range we've got out in the pines, and you can watch our people shoot."

"Be glad to," Ham said. "This is damn fine barbecue, Peck. You folks sure do eat well."

"We do that," Peck replied. "John always enjoys our ladies' cooking, too, don't you, John?"

"I do," John replied. "Your women are the best cooks in the group, and that's a fact."

And just what group is that? Ham wanted to ask, but didn't. He sat, ate his barbecue, which really was sensational, and listened to John talk to the men, apparently about nothing. The others were reverentially quiet.

33

Holly had just come home from work when Ham let himself in through the beach door.

"Hey," she said, giving him a kiss.

"How you doing?"

"I'm okay. I got your message."

"Then where is Harry?"

"Come with me," she said, leading him out the door to the beach. Daisy padded along behind, running through the dunes, sniffing out dune mice. Holly led him down the beach a hundred yards, then turned down a path through the dunes to the house next door.

"Whose place is this?" Ham asked.

"Just follow me, Ham." She rapped sharply at the door of the house and let herself in. Harry and two other men were sitting in the living room, drinking beer.

"Hi there, Ham," Harry said.

"You're living next door now?" Ham asked, shaking his hand.

"What you've found out so far about the people out at the lake has made me commit to a full investigation. We rented the place. It's convenient, and it keeps the heat off Holly."

"Good idea," Ham said.

"Ham this is Doug, one of our agents, and this is our ace techie, Eddie. Eddie the Hacker we like to call him."

Ham shook their hands, then he noticed that the dining-room table was filled with computers, printers and some equipment he didn't recognize.

"You want a beer?" Harry asked.

"You betcha," Ham said, accepting a cold Heineken.

"I want to hear about this John character," Harry said, "and Eddie is going to do up a computer-generated face for us."

"Okay," Ham said, and allowed himself to be sat down beside Eddie at the dining-room table.

"Let's start with height and weight," Eddie said.

"Six-three, a hundred and eighty pounds, about like me," Ham said.

Eddie made some entries into the computer, and a male figure, faceless, appeared on the large, flat-screen monitor before him. "Okay, hair color?"

"Gray."

"Short? Long?"

"Fairly short and very curly."

Eddie typed away. "Like this?"

"No, even curlier, almost like a sheep."

"Like this?"

"That's it."

"Face thin, medium or fat?"

"Thinnish, strong jaw."

"Like so?"

"Stronger."

"Better?"

"Very good."

"Nose: fat or thin, straight or curved?"

"Thin, straight and short."

"Lips?"

"Thin."

"Color of eyes?"

"I'm not sure; maybe blue or green."

"We'll start with blue." Eddie typed some more, then a face appeared on the screen, very complete, almost like a photograph. "How's that?"

"Good, but he had pretty thick eyebrows, and they were black."

Eddie made the adjustment.

"Higher cheekbones," Ham said.

Eddie typed some more.

"And his ears were fairly small and lay flat against his head," Ham said.

Eddie made the changes.

"Jesus, that's good," Ham said, impressed.

Eddie hit some more keys, and the face turned to its left a quarter turn. "Does it still look good?"

"Yep."

Eddie turned the face to profile. "How about now?"

"The nose isn't turned up like that, it's straight, but the length is right. He looks older than your picture, too."

Eddie typed some more. "What age?"

"Fifty, maybe, or a young fifty-five. No, that's too old. He's fairly youthful-looking, no sagging chin or bags under his eyes."

"We'll make him fifty and well preserved," Eddie said.

Ham watched the changes in the image. "Try forty-five."

Eddie adjusted the picture.

"Eddie, that's the guy. Dead ringer. I swear, I didn't know it could be done that well."

"Okay, now let's compare him to the database," Eddie said.

"Just a minute, I forgot the glasses. They were round, steel-rimmed, on the small side."

"Like this?"

"Rounder. That's it. Now try your database."

Eddie typed for another thirty seconds, and the screen went blank. "This'll take a few minutes," he said. "It goes faster if you don't watch it happen." He stood up, walked back to the living-room sofa and retrieved his beer.

"Anything else you can tell us about this guy?" Harry asked.

"I'd say he was a natural-born leader, considering the respect he got from everybody. They seemed a little in awe of him. He was the first one to actually ask me to do something for the group."

"What did he ask you to do?"

"To train some of his people in shooting."

"Shooting of what?"

"He didn't say; just shooting. I gave them a little demonstration, and somebody asked me if I could shoot like that with the Barrett's rifle."

"What did you tell them?"

"I told them I could, if I had an opportunity to sight it in."

Eddie got up and went back to the computer.

"How's it going?" Harry asked.

"Coming along. It's a big database, remember, and a lot of John's features are common to a lot of other people. Give it a few more minutes."

"Does John live out at the lake with the group?" Harry asked.

"My impression—and nobody actually told me this—was that he didn't, that he was visiting. It was the first time I'd seen him there, but it's possible that he lives there, but had been away and had just returned."

Eddie spoke up. "We've got some faces," he said. "Come take a look."

Everybody gathered around the computer screen. Faces were materializing, some clear, others still filling in. Most of them were front and profile shots of people holding numbers under their chins.

"Same general types," Eddie said.

Ham pointed at a photograph. "Isn't that a woman?" he asked.

"Yes, but she answers the description," Eddie replied, "and she turned up, even though I specified male."

More pictures became clear, and Eddie slowly scrolled through them, more than two hundred. Then he stopped at the last frame.

"What does that mean?" Ham asked. The frame was empty and had the word "restricted" stamped across it.

"That means it's a face somebody doesn't want us to see," Eddie replied. "Could be someone in the witness protection program."

"John said he was retired, like me, and I asked him if it was from the military. He said not exactly. Could the restriction be because the guy worked for one of the civilian intelligence agencies?"

"Maybe. If so, his records would be in another database, one we don't have ready access to. The people in this one are people who have been arrested, done time or, at least, are suspected of a crime."

Eddie turned to Harry. "There's a file number here, Harry. You know somebody who might give us access?"

Harry was staring at the blank rectangle and rubbing his chin. "All I can do is try," he replied.

34

Holly played hostess and cleared the dishes away from the coffee table, and the empty cartons that had once held Chinese food. Doug put on a pot of coffee, and they waited for Harry, who was on the phone in the den. Finally, he came back.

"Here," he said, handing the computer-generated picture of John to Eddie. "E-mail this to the address at the bottom of the page."

Eddie did as he was asked, then came back. "What now?"

"We wait," Harry said.

"Are we going to get access to the file?" Holly asked.

"Not exactly," Harry said.

"What does that mean?" Ham asked.

"It means we're not going to be able to penetrate the restriction on this photograph and download this guy's file. I'm not sure that even a court order would produce it."

"Then what are we waiting to hear?" Holly asked.

"I know a guy who agreed to look at the picture," Harry said. "He can probably get a look at the file, and if he's had enough to drink, he might tell us some of what's in it. I got him at home, and he'd already had at least one Scotch."

"And who is this guy?" Ham asked.

Harry wagged a finger. "Don't ask."

"Oh."

"Yeah."

"Harry," Holly said, "I'm beginning to get the impression that nobody in the federal law enforcement community talks to anybody else outside his own agency."

"This guy's not in the law enforcement community; you might say he's quietly in the law-*breaking* community, in his way. But you're right: the level of interagency cooperation only tends to rise when somebody can recognize some self-interest in a situation. If this guy helps us, then I'll have to help him sometime, ignore a regulation or two, and I probably won't like doing it."

They fell silent for a while, watching the flames from the driftwood fire. Nobody seemed to want to add another log.

"What's your best guess on this John guy, Harry?" Holly asked.

Harry shook his head. "No point guessing; he could be anybody. And if my buddy won't help, and if the guy has never been arrested, then we're going to have one hell of a time figuring out who or what he is."

"I could maybe get his fingerprints," Ham said. "You know, steal a glass he's used, or something like that."

"It might come to that," Harry said, "but I don't want you to take the risk, unless it's the only way. Anyway, if his photograph is restricted, it's very likely his prints will be, too."

The phone rang, and everybody sat up. Harry went into the den to answer it, and he didn't come back for twenty minutes. When he did, the group was all ears.

"Well, I don't know how much help this is going to be," Harry said, when he had settled into his chair once more. "My guy was able to access some records, records that even he was not supposed to have access to, so this one is going to cost me."

"Come on, Harry," Holly said, "spit it out."

"All right, he worked for one or more government agencies as an independent contractor—always paid in cash, no social security number involved, no paper trail, except in those inaccessible files."

"You mean he was, like, a government assassin?" Holly asked.

"No, not that. I'm not even sure those sorts of operators exist anymore, if they ever did."

"They did," Ham said quietly. "I knew some."

"Anyway, the name on the file—and this doesn't mean it's his real name—was Alton Charlesworth."

"Has to be his real name," Ham said. "Who'd pick a name like that?"

"You have a point," Harry said. "But Charlesworth was involved in technical and financial stuff, breaking into bank records, tracing the movement of money from bank to bank and country to country. It was wet work, involving burglary at the very least, and maybe much worse."

"Any specific examples?" Holly asked.

"My guy wouldn't give me any. He did say that if you wanted to hide some assets or launder some money, Charlesworth would be your man. He hinted at darker deeds, too, but he wouldn't be specific. My guy said he wouldn't want to meet him in a dark alley—or anyplace else, for that matter. He made the man sound thoroughly unpleasant. He also mentioned that there would be no criminal record—or, if there had been one, it would have been quietly expunged from all the relevant computers. The guy sounds like a rollover."

"What's a rollover?" Holly asked.

"A rollover is somebody who gets caught doing something naughty, and the people who catch him realize he might be more valuable doing naughty things for them, rather than being put in a prison cell. So they roll him over—give his background a shampoo and a haircut, and he belongs to them."

"Until he retires," Ham said.

"There's no pension plan for people like this," Harry said. "In fact, my guy said that if I ran across Charlesworth in person, he'd like to hear about it. He was real casual about it, but what this says to me is that Charlesworth bailed out of whatever program they had him in, and that they would either like to have him back or give him a new haircut, starting at about the Adam's apple."

"Well," Holly said. "This is wonderfully murky. We never ran into stuff like this in the MPs."

Everybody laughed.

"I don't get it," Ham said. "What would a guy like this be doing involved with some half-baked gun nuts like these folks out at the lake? You think they're robbing so many banks that they need somebody to launder the proceeds?"

"I wouldn't think so," Harry said. "We tend to notice when somebody starts robbing a lot of banks, even if they're spread out all over the country. Bank robbers always have a modus operandi, and they stick to what works for them. So far, we've got a pattern of only two, separated by a number of years. If the same group did both jobs, then they've more than likely got the proceeds salted away and are spending it on groceries and plumbers and orthodontists and car repairs."

"And weapons," Ham said.

"There is that," Harry said. "And if, as you say, this guy John has been away for a while, then where has he been?"

"Laundering money?" Holly ventured.

"I really don't think they've got that much money," Harry said. "What occurs to me is that maybe John is a traveling man, going from place to place and, maybe, from group to group."

"That would fit in with my impression of him," Ham agreed.

"Be interesting to see how much you see of old John in your visits to the group," Harry said. "He wasn't there for the first few visits, but he's here now, or was. I want to know if he's there on your next visit."

"Okay," Ham said.

"And Ham," Harry said, "I don't think you can keep going back out there without asking at least *some* questions. It wouldn't seem natural to have no curiosity at all about what you're seeing there."

"What do you want me to ask them?"

"Don't get too pointed, just be easy about it. I think, at some point, you have to let them know that you're not going to get too involved until you know what's going on. It's a matter of when you believe they're starting to trust you."

"I see," Ham said.

"Of course, you don't want to get *too* curious," Harry said. "If they think you're too curious, they might choose to do something about you, and we wouldn't want that, would we?"

"No," Holly said, giving Ham a worried look, "we wouldn't."

Ham walked down the line of shooters, who were in the prone firing position, kicking their feet farther apart, telling them to get their arms vertically under the stock and to relax. They were dry-firing at paper targets no more than twenty-five feet away.

"When do we get to fire?" one of them asked.

"When you can hold the weapon steady enough and pull the trigger slowly enough to keep a bead on the center of that target without any movement whatsoever."

Ham glanced at John, who was standing a few feet away, watching the procedure.

John gave Ham a big smile. "That's telling 'em," he said.

Ham walked over and stood beside him. "They all think they're hotshots," he said. "They don't like being made to dry fire, but dry firing can make the difference between firing expert and constantly looking at Maggie's drawers." He was referring to the red flag that was waved by the checker when a shooter had missed the target entirely.

"How long will you keep them at it?"

Ham called out to the group. "Who's getting it right every time?"

A skinny kid in camouflage fatigues that were too large for him raised his hand.

"Okay, son," Ham said, "you go on over to the range and have them put up a target for you. I'll come take a look at it after a while."

The boy got up and left.

"Depends on the shooter," Ham said. "That boy might turn out to be good. We'll know in a little while."

"I'm surprised they're not all raising their hands," John said.

"They won't do that, because I've already told them that if they pass themselves too quickly, then screw up on the range, I'll send them back to dry firing, and that would be humiliating."

"You sound like you've done some time as a drill sergeant, Ham," John said.

"I've done some time at just about everything an NCO can do in the army," Ham replied.

"You know," John said, placing a friendly hand on Ham's shoulder, "I think you're going to fit in just perfectly around here."

"Nice of you to say so," Ham replied. "Now maybe you'll answer a question for me."

"Sure. What do you want to know?"

"Who the hell are you, and what's going on around here?"

John burst out laughing. "You get right to the point, don't you, Ham?"

"Why waste your time and mine?"

"Let's go over there and sit down," John said, nodding toward a picnic table under an oak tree. They went and sat down. John put a cooler on the table. "You want a beer?"

"Sure," Ham said. "It's hot out here."

John handed him a Budweiser, and they both popped the tops. He took a long swig and set the beer on the table. "Ham," he said, "let me tell you about you."

"Okay," Ham replied.

"You're like a lot of our folks; you don't like the direction the country has taken since—"

"Since the Vietnam war," Ham said.

"Right. That was the breaking point for a lot of us. The politicians got us into a shooting war and wouldn't let us win it. The result of that, among other things, is that blacks and Jews started to get more political power, to the point that you can't really get anything done in this country unless you kiss their asses."

"That's God's truth," Ham said.

"Now you're out of the army that gave you a reason to live for thirty years," John said, "and you're bored rigid."

"Right again."

"What would you say if I told you I could offer you work that would, one, end your boredom, and two, help bring about a new American revolution, one that would put real people like you and me in power?"

Ham looked him in the eye. "I'd say that's a mighty big statement."

"I can back it up," John said.

"I'm listening."

"All right. I have two things that will help me make it happen: one, I've got the makings of an army of absolute loyalists who are being trained to make that revolution happen, and two, I've got the financial means to support the effort—or I will have, and sooner rather than later."

"I'm still listening," Ham said.

"Ham, you've been a noncom for most of your adult life. How would you like to be a general?"

Ham allowed himself a small smile.

"You'd be good at generaling, wouldn't you?"

"You're damn right I would, but if you try to take over the country, you're going to have to deal with the military, and that's a very big job."

"Think back on your military experience, Ham. How many officers you knew would fit into the kind of revolution I'm talking about?"

"Damn few."

"But the enlisted men and noncoms were a different story, weren't they."

"They were. A lot of them were smarter than the officers who commanded them." Ham was getting good at lying.

"So, you see, we don't have to fight the military. We take it over, and we do so by elevating the noncoms to command status."

"And you do that by eliminating the officers?"

"Not all of them," John said. "There are some who can be trusted. We're already in touch with a lot of them."

"So you're talking about getting rid of most of the officers, establishing martial law with a new military, then dumping the Constitution?"

"No, no, no," John said. "The Constitution of the United States is a magnificent document, a blueprint for the perfect society. The problem is the people who are interpreting it and enforcing it. What we need is about five years of military dominance to cleanse this country of its worst elements and to establish a new judiciary. Then we can hold elections with confidence. Free elections are a wonderful thing, when you're dealing with an electorate purged of anti-Christian elements and reeducated to think about their country in a new way."

"Well, that's all very exciting," Ham said, "but do you really think you can pull this off?"

"I don't believe in fantasy, Ham; I deal in reality. The right man, with the support of like-minded people like you, can make his own reality."

"Nothing like this has ever been done before," Ham said, shaking his head.

"Sure it has," John replied. "Go back and look at Germany in the twenties and thirties. Adolf Hitler did something very like what I'm talking about. He didn't lead the sort of revolution they had in Russia; instead, he infiltrated his country's institutions, built public support, co-opted industry and the army, and, in a very few years, got himself elected dictator with over ninety percent of the vote. It can be done here, too."

"Well," Ham said, gazing at the lake, "this is all pretty breath-taking."

"I understand how you feel, Ham, and you're right to be skeptical. You stick with me, and by the time a few weeks have passed, you'll see a bigger picture, and you'll come to know in your very bones that what I've been telling you can and will happen."

"I'm looking forward to learning," Ham said.

John clapped him on the shoulder. "Great! Now you get back out there and make marksmen of those boys. We're going to need them!"

Ham walked back toward his students in a daze.

36

Ham drove quickly back to Orchid Beach, watching his rearview mirror to be sure he wasn't followed. He drove down A1A to the South Beach area, turned in to a driveway and waited for a car to pass. Nothing did for one minute. He backed out, drove to Holly's house and parked the car. She wasn't home, so he hiked along the beach to the house next door and found her having dinner with Harry, Doug and Eddie.

Harry saw him at the sliding door and waved him in. "Ham, it's dangerous for you to come here a lot."

"Nobody followed me," Ham said. "I checked thoroughly, then I parked at Holly's."

"Get yourself a beer," Harry said. "You want some pizza?" He waved at the three open boxes on the table.

Ham got himself a beer, grabbed a slice of pizza and took some deep breaths.

"What is it, Ham?" Holly said. "You look funny."

"I feel funny," Ham said.

"What?" Harry demanded.

"Listen, Harry," Ham said, "when I got into this, I thought I was looking for bank robbers, you know?"

"Right."

"And then I thought maybe it was a little more complicated than that, but . . ." He stopped.

"Ham, what is it?" Harry asked.

"This is a lot bigger than any of us thought." Ham repeated his conversation with John, word for word.

When he had finished, Harry and Holly sat and stared at him, saying nothing.

"Well?"

"Well, shit," Harry said, putting down his slice of pizza and taking a big swig from his beer bottle.

"What do you want me to do, Harry?"

"Do you think this guy was just blowing smoke up your ass? You think he's fantasizing all this?"

"Not for a minute," Harry said. "If you'd been there, you wouldn't think so, either. This guy is perfectly serious."

"You think maybe he was exaggerating a little?"

"No, I think he was holding a lot back."

"Of course, they have checked you out thoroughly," Harry said. "They've got to believe you're who you say you are and not a Fed."

"I'm sure they do. Jesus, I wish I had been wearing a wire."

"Did they search you for one? Have they ever?"

"No, never."

"That's kind of weird, in a way," Harry said. "You'd think they'd be more careful."

Eddie the Hacker spoke up. "They don't necessarily have to frisk him, you know. They could have something that could pick up transmissions."

"Yeah, but that sort of thing couldn't pick up a recorder."

"You've got to start wiring me," Ham said.

"I know," Harry replied, "but I'm reluctant. If they should ever really search you . . ."

Eddie spoke up again. "We don't have to send him in there with a conventional wire. We can do a lot better than that, if you'll make a call to Washington for me."

"I'll make the call," Harry said.

"He's talking about subverting the army, Harry," Ham said. "I don't really see how he can do that. I mean, this is not Germany in nineteen thirty."

"We know there are right-wing, racist groups in a lot of army outfits," Harry said. "We keep a very close watch on that sort of thing. I don't think they could actually do what John says they're going to do. I'm more interested in how he's going to finance all this. He can't rob that many banks."

"He said he'd have the financing soon," Ham said. "I didn't press him on that."

"He must have a benefactor," Harry said. "Somebody with big bucks, who's willing to invest in a future he thinks he can control. I'd sure like to know who that might be."

"I don't think that's the kind of thing he'd tell me," Ham said.

"I agree. You're too new."

Ham turned to Eddie. "Have you got some equipment I can plant out there? They seem to hold a lot of meetings in Peck's office; that would be a good place to bug."

"Depends on how paranoid they are," Eddie said. "If they sweep the place and find something, then we're screwed."

"You mean Ham's screwed," Holly said.

"Come on, Eddie, you must have something that would work."

"I've heard rumors about stuff," Eddie said, "but I don't think the Bureau is in charge of it."

"You're talking about the National Security Agency, aren't you?" Ham asked.

"Yeah. I've heard rumors about their capabilities, and they're scary. They could be listening to us right now."

Holly looked at Harry. "Why do I think you wouldn't want to bring another government agency into this?"

"Don't needle me, Holly."

"Something's building out there," Ham said. "I don't know what it is, but if all you've got is me, then I think you need a lot more help, Harry."

"I guess at some point I'm going to," Harry admitted. "But not yet. In order to get the NSA in on this I'd have to go right up the Bureau's chain of command to the director, who'd then chat with the attorney general about it, and if he thought it couldn't damage him politically, then he might talk to the director of Central Intelligence, and if he felt like it, he might authorize the director to talk to somebody at NSA. But there's no way to be sure of that, and before I go that route, I want some hard information."

"I believe this is a catch twenty-two," Holly said. "We can't get the information without outside help, and you don't want to ask for outside help until you have the information."

"That's about it," Harry said. "What I can do, though, is get Washington to equip Eddie with something cuter than a regular tape recorder. You'd like that, wouldn't you, Eddie?"

Eddie nodded enthusiastically.

"I'll make the call in the morning, after they've had their coffee," Harry said. "We'll get hold of something."

Holly chimed in. "Get hold of something that won't get Ham's ass fried, will you, Harry?"

37

Ham was spending every day at Lake Winachobee now, and his students were becoming expert shots, one after another. Only occasionally did he find someone who could not learn to shoot reasonably well. They were usually people with shaky hands.

One morning, after sending a shooting class to the range, Peck whistled at him from his house and waved him over.

"What's up?" Ham asked.

"I want you to hear a little presentation John's giving to some of our newer folks," Peck said, ushering him into his study. A dozen people sat around the room, and John sat in a comfortable armchair, chatting easily with a couple of them. He looked up and saw Ham and Peck enter.

"All right, listen up," John said to the group. "We know from our previous discussions that the founding fathers of our country intended that it should be run under principles set down in the Bible:

whites are the chosen people of God; homosexuals are an abomination and should be exterminated. Also, the paper money issued by the government is unconstitutional, and so are the income tax laws, but of course, we have no chance of getting the Supreme Court to rule that, not without a new Supreme Court. Now, we're going to see what can be done about avoiding taxes and keeping our financial dealings secret."

John stood up and went to an easel. He took a felt marking pen and began drawing a chart. "What we've done is set up something called a warehouse bank," he said, pointing to the first block. "We take deposits into numbered accounts, and that's very important. Once we establish an account and give you a number, we destroy any record that would show who owns the account. This drives the IRS crazy. I saw a quote from one official who said that investigating a warehouse bank is like looking for a needle in a stack of needles." This got a good laugh.

"Now, let's say you open your account with ten thousand dollars. We then transfer these funds to certain western banks. When you want to pay a bill, you send an e-mail to the warehouse with your instructions and your account number; that is transmitted to the partner bank, which sends a banker's draft to your creditor. So the bill is paid without your name being mentioned, only your account number with the creditor. If you want some cash, you request that by e-mail, too, and the money is sent by certified mail or an overnight delivery service.

"At no point in this process are you identified by anything other than an account number, so the IRS can't examine your bank records to find out how much money you're depositing or how much you're spending. This effectively puts a stop to the enforcement of the income tax laws."

A man raised his hand. "How much can we save in taxes this way?"

"Depends on how much you earn," John said. "Recently, one of our warehouse bank customers became the first of us to save one million dollars in taxes. I can tell you that we've saved our members, collectively, a quarter of a billion dollars in income taxes."

There was a murmur of approval from around the room.

"Also," John continued, "we print our own currency, which we use only among our member groups." He passed around a banknote for everyone to look at.

Ham inspected the paper, which bore an engraving of Jefferson Davis. It had the look and feel of money.

"By drawing our own currency from the warehouse bank instead of U.S. currency, we can trade among ourselves without fear. We also encourage the use of false social security numbers, which confuses the IRS, and we've learned to set up trusts that help us do business without attracting their attention."

"What are the chances of our getting caught doing this?" someone asked.

"We've been doing it for more than ten years, and none of us has even been arrested," John said. "You may have seen accounts in the Jew press of arrests, but they weren't our people. From time to time, we shut down the warehouse bank and create a new one. We're a constantly moving target, and the antitax forces in this country have influenced the U.S. Congress to cut funds for IRS audits and investigations, which makes it harder than ever for them to track us down."

"How can I open an account?" a man asked.

"Peck is going to distribute account application forms now," John replied. "You'll notice that nowhere on the form do we ask for your name. You make deposits in cash, and we give receipts to numbers. Not even I know who has which account number."

Ham received one of the forms and put it in his pocket as the meeting broke up.

Peck walked over. "You going to open an account with us, Ham?"

"I'm going to have to take a close look at this, Peck," Ham replied. "My income comes mostly from my army pension, although I have some investments. I think I might be too much on record to start hiding stuff. I might raise a red flag that could cause trouble for you."

"I see your point," Peck said, "and I appreciate your concern. You let me know what you want to do. I'm sure it will be all right with John."

"Can I buy some of your currency?" Ham asked. "That makes a lot of sense."

"Sure, how much you want?"

"I've got a couple hundred in my pocket, I guess," Ham said, digging out some money. He handed Peck four fifties.

Peck went to a safe in the corner, opened it and returned with twenty ten-dollar bills. "Use it to shop at the gun show this weekend."

"Right," Ham said. He walked out to the range, his head spinning.

38

Ham let himself into the beach cottage through the sliding doors. They were all at dinner again. "My God," he said, "don't you people ever eat anything but Chinese food and pizza?"

"You got a Mexican restaurant in this town?" Harry asked. "We'd go for that."

Ham rolled his eyes and pulled up a chair.

"What have you got?" Harry asked.

"Fellas, it's a whole new ball game every day." He pulled a sheet of paper from his pocket, unfolded it and handed it to Harry.

"What's this?"

"It's an application to open an account at a warehouse bank."

"Uh-oh," Harry said.

"What's a warehouse bank?" Holly asked.

"The biggest tax dodge you ever heard of," Ham said. He explained it to the group as it had been explained to him.

Holly and the three FBI agents sat, rapt, listening to him.

"Holy cow," Holly said, when he was finished. "Harry, you're going to have to get the IRS into this."

"It can't be that big a deal," Harry said.

"Would you believe a quarter of a billion dollars?" Ham asked.

"That's *billion* with a *B*?"

"Correct. That's how much they claim to have cost the IRS over the past ten years."

Harry stared at him blankly. "How many people are we talking about here?"

"I have no idea," Ham replied. "John did say that, recently, someone had become their first member to avoid a million dollars in taxes." He pulled the group's paper money from his pocket and placed it on the table. "They also print this for themselves."

Harry picked up a note. "Jefferson Davis? I don't believe it."

Eddie was holding a bill up to a bare lightbulb. "This is first-class work," he said, "and with Jeff Davis on it, it could never be considered counterfeit currency, legally, unless it was counterfeit Confederate currency."

"How do they use this?" Harry asked.

"They buy and sell among themselves at these gun shows."

"Shit," Harry said, tossing the note onto the table. "We're going to end up with every law enforcement agency in the federal government in on this. There'll be nothing left for us."

"You're forgetting the bank robbery," Holly said. "And there's the murder for me."

"Oh, right."

"Harry, I think you've got to start making some calls to other agencies."

"Yeah, I guess so," Harry replied disconsolately. "And once I call one, I'll have to call them all. I still want some hard information, though. Eddie?"

Everybody turned and looked at Eddie, who was grinning.

"You look like the cat who got into the goldfish bowl," Holly said.

"You could say that," Eddie replied. "Ham, describe the room, Peck's study, where all these meetings take place."

"It's big, maybe twenty by thirty, fairly high ceiling, windows on two sides. The venetian blinds are almost always drawn."

Eddie set a cardboard box on the table. "This stuff was couriered in today." He held up what appeared to be a smoke detector. "This is really neat: all you do is stick this to the ceiling somewhere in the room, and it sits there, listening. It'll pick up anything said anywhere in the room, then it transmits what it's hearing to an NSA satellite. They can listen to real-time conversation and transmit it to us over phone lines. We'll know everything that's going on."

"What happens if they sweep the room?" Ham asked.

"They'll probably be using readily available commercial stuff, which is pretty good, but very short-range. They'll walk around the baseboards, then the lamps and phones with a detector; they'll look behind pictures and under the rug. Meanwhile, ten or twelve feet above their head, this thing is sending a highly directional signal straight up. Have you noticed that nobody ever looks up in a room? Well, they won't sweep up, either."

"Suppose they do?" Holly asked. "Suppose Peck looks up and says, 'Hey, I didn't install a smoke detector in here.'"

"If Peck takes it down and looks at it, he's going to see a smoke detector. It will even work like a smoke detector. If you blow cigarette smoke at it, it'll squawk. What he won't see is a layer of electronics that's sealed into seamless plastic."

"How is it powered?" Ham asked.

"The only difference between this and a regular smoke detector is it has two nine-volt batteries, instead of one. Except they're not really nine-volt batteries, they're made of a new, extremely high-powered battery material developed by the NSA. They're disguised to look like regular nine-volt batteries. The two of them would give you a month's talk time on your cell phone, and this unit uses a little less power than a cell phone."

"Neat," Ham said.

"What's *not* neat," Holly pointed out, "is that Ham has got to go into that room and install the thing."

"All he does is peel off a strip of plastic, exposing a sticky tape and glue it to the ceiling."

"You're missing my point," Holly said. "Ham has to do it; he has to go into that room, unseen by anybody, get on a ladder, or something, and stick it to the ceiling without getting himself shot."

"Well, there is that," Eddie admitted.

"Ham, have you ever been alone in that room?" Harry asked.

"No, there have always been at least half a dozen people there."

"How long do you think it might take you to get in there by yourself?"

"I don't know," Ham said, "I can only try."

"There's more," Eddie said. "Ham, you wear your old army fatigues a lot, don't you?"

"I do when I go out there," Ham said.

Eddie held up a button. "They have buttons like these, don't they?"

"Yes."

"You sew this onto your fatigues, top front button, or on a pocket. There's a tiny microphone inside that transmits a very short-range signal."

"What good is a very short-range signal going to do us?" Ham asked.

Eddie took a pair of well-worn combat boots from his box. "It has to broadcast only as far as your feet. These will fit you," he said. "We got your shoe size from your military record." He took a tiny screwdriver from his pocket. "This is the kind of tool you use to replace a screw in your eyeglasses. You also use it to switch on a tape recorder in the right heel of the boots." He demonstrated. "Insert it a quarter of an inch, make sure it mates with the screw head inside and give it a short turn clockwise. You're up and running, and you have an hour and forty minutes recording time on two memory sticks imbedded in the heel."

"What if he's swept while it's running?" Harry asked.

"Then they'll pick it up and zero in on the button." He turned to Ham. "Don't let that happen," he said.

"Gee, I'll try not to," Ham replied.

39

Holly, Daisy, and Ham walked back up the beach toward her house. "I'm worried about this," she said.

"What, you don't think your old man can handle it?"

"That's not what I'm worried about. Harry is acting funny."

"What do you mean?"

"I mean that, based on the information you've given him, he ought to be ordering a full-scale investigation and on the horn to Washington, networking with the other agencies involved, which—so far—includes the Secret Service, the IRS, Alcohol, Tobacco and Firearms and God knows what else."

"You don't trust Harry?"

"Of course, I trust him, on a personal level, but he's playing some sort of political game, and I think that's dangerous."

"Well, I'm going to have to leave the politics to you and Harry," Ham said. "What I'm going to do is go home and sew this button on my fatigue shirt, then, tomorrow, I'm going to go back out there and try to plant this smoke detector thing."

"I know you are, Ham. You wouldn't do it any other way."

"Straight ahead is the only way I know."

They stopped outside her house. "You want to come in for coffee?" she asked.

"Nah, I'd better get home, I guess."

She kissed him on the cheek. "You watch your ass, you hear?"

"Don't I always?" he replied. Then, with a wave, he walked toward his car.

When Holly entered the house, the phone was ringing and she picked it up. "Hello?"

"Holly? It's Stone Barrington, how are you?"

"Oh, Stone, I don't know."

"You sound tired."

"I'm depressed and exhausted."

"Trouble with your case?"

"Oh, we're making progress by leaps and bounds on that," she said. "I'm just worried about it."

"What's the problem? I'll help if I can."

"When you were a cop, did you ever have any dealings with the FBI?"

"From time to time."

"What did you think about them?"

"New York City cops don't trust the FBI; maybe cops everywhere don't. I was naive the first time I had to deal with them, but I learned."

"Learned what?"

"That Mr. Hoover's boys want all the meat for themselves and their agency, and if you deal with them, you end up with the bones and gristle."

"I was afraid you were going to say something like that," she replied.

"You think the Feds are trying to screw you?"

"I don't think my friend Harry would do that, but I think he's trying to screw every other government agency."

"They'll do that, too."

"What should I do about it?"

"Do you have anything solid that would justify bringing other agencies into it?"

"Sort of, but nothing hard."

"Then you're going to have to ride the pony you rode in on," Stone said. "If you try to bring other agencies into it, your sweet Harry is going to cut you off at the knees, believe me."

"I don't think he'd hurt me," she said.

"Oh, he won't hurt you, he'll just box you in, well away from your case, until he's milked all the credit he can out of it. It's not just Harry, believe me; it's the way the Bureau works. They'll put themselves up front every time."

"I worked with them once before, and it came out all right," she said.

"Yeah, I read all about that. You brought them into it, didn't you?"

"Yes, and we worked on it side by side."

"But no other federal law enforcement?"

"No."

"Then they didn't have anything to worry about. If you'd gotten in their way, they'd have patted you on the head and sent you home, while the big boys in the Bureau did the heavy lifting."

"You're a cynic, you know that?"

"Me? I'm Sunny Jim; I've just had experience with them. I've had them walk into a case, steal my collar and confiscate the evidence my partner and I collected. I got to read about it in the papers later, and my name didn't get mentioned."

"Stone, don't get me wrong, I'm not worried about getting credit. My father is up to his neck in this, and I'm afraid that they're not putting enough resources into this case to protect him if he gets into trouble. I don't want to go into detail, because it's all confidential."

"I understand. Well, it sounds like you're going to have to give them some more rope, and hope they don't hang themselves and your father. If it's an important case to more than one agency, then a time will come when your Harry will have to call them in, whether he likes it or not. I think what he's doing is maneuvering to be in a position to keep the case from being taken away from him by some other bunch of Feds."

"I think you're right," she said.

"Is he a smart guy, this Harry?"

"Yes, very."

"Then you're going to have to trust him for a while longer. If he screws up, then you can always threaten to go elsewhere, or over his head."

"I guess you're right," she said.

"Are you all right otherwise?"

"Oh, I haven't had time to worry about myself; I've been too busy worrying about Ham."

"Who?"

"My father."

"Have you thought about taking some time off the job? Might do you good."

"No, it wouldn't. I'd just worry, and I'm better off occupying myself to the hilt right now."

"You're the best judge of that," he said. "Take care of yourself, and call me if I can do anything to help, or if you just need to talk."

"Thanks, Stone, you take care, too." She hung up and went upstairs, pulling clothes off along the way. She missed Jackson terribly at this moment. She wanted to crawl into bed and rest her head on his shoulder, while he stroked her hair.

Instead, she crawled into bed and waited for Daisy to settle in next to her. Daisy wasn't Jackson, but she was the best friend Holly had.

40

Ham arrived at Lake Winachobee the following morning, and before he could join his shooting students, he was intercepted by Peck Rawlings.

"Good morning, Ham," Peck said.

"Morning, Peck."

"John wants you to attend some classes for the next few days," Peck said.

"Classes?"

"It's time you got to know more about the foundations of what we believe in. I know that most of this stuff is going to be old hat for you, but John thinks it's important, just so you'll know how he and the leadership think."

"Well, sure, if that's what John wants. But leadership? I thought John was the leadership."

"He's one of a group, and he communicates the leadership's messages to all of us."

"You mean all of us at Winachobee?"

"No, all over the country. John does a lot of traveling."

"Oh. Just how big an organization are we?"

"You'll be told all about that in due course," Peck said. "You better hurry; the class is getting started. It's in my study."

"Sure, just let me get a notebook out of my truck."

"Hurry."

Ham trotted back to the truck, removed the smoke detector from its box and stuck it in the pocket of his fatigues. Then he retrieved the tiny screwdriver, inserted it into the heel of his boot and gave it a quarter turn. He started back toward the house. "Okay, I'm recording," he said. "Peck has sent me to class." He stated the date and time.

Ham entered the house and walked to the study. The other students, half a dozen of them, were scattered around the room, and John was standing before them. "Morning, Ham," he said. "Take a pew."

Ham found a chair and got set to listen.

"Now," John said, "we're going to talk about the group and the things we believe in. I know you're all new to the group, but we've taken a close look at each of you, and you wouldn't be in this room if we didn't think you believe what we believe."

Ham listened as John launched into a quiet diatribe that seemed to include every crazy thing he'd ever heard about fringe militia groups. John covered all the bases—hatred of blacks, Jews and homosexuals, hatred of the government, hatred of anybody who didn't share the group's views. Ham was bored stiff, and he took the opportunity to look around the room, especially the ceiling. He wanted to get the smoke detector up and running as soon as possible. Then he suddenly snapped back to attention. John was talking about surveillance.

"We're very careful about being listened in on," John was saying. "The government gets better and better at watching over people's lives, especially people who despise them, as we do. You shouldn't have realized it, but each of you has been swept for bugs every day you've been here, and every room in this compound is swept every day. That's so that we and you can know that we can speak freely to each other without having to worry about some spook listening in on us. Believe me, our antisurveillance techniques are just as good as their ability to bug us. In fact, Peck is standing at the back of the room there. Sweeping each of us right this minute."

Ham looked over his shoulder and saw Peck standing by the door, holding a small black box with an extended antenna. He felt sweat break out in his armpits. Surreptitiously, he took out the little screwdriver, crossed his ankle over the other knee and rested his hand on his boot, trying to look as relaxed as possible. Staring hard at John, he got the screwdriver into the heel of his boot and switched off his recorder, then he crossed his legs in the opposite direction and pocketed the screwdriver.

Peck was walking slowly around the room now, waving the antenna.

"You got something, Peck?" John asked.

"I did for a minute," Peck said. "Then it went away. Just a small surge, but definite."

"All right everybody," John said, "we're now going to show you just how careful we are. Stand up and line up against the wall over there."

Everybody did as instructed.

Peck went down the line and, one by one, had each man extend his arms away from his body, then swept the antenna over his clothing. Ham was third in line, and he watched out of the corner of his eye while Peck did his work. Finally, Peck was in front of him, and he gave Ham a wink that said, "Don't worry pal, this is just for show."

Ham hoped to God that turning off the recorder in his heel also turned off the microphone in his button, because if it didn't, he was about to be nailed. He began thinking about how fast he could get out of there and to his truck, and the answer he came up with was, Not fast enough.

Peck went up and down the top and bottom of each of Ham's arms, then his legs and crotch. "I'm not feeling you up, Ham," he said, "it's just that undercover cops just love to hide bugs in their crotches."

"Don't worry, Peck, you're not my type anyway."

Everybody laughed.

Peck then moved the antenna to the top of his head and worked his way down both sides of his torso. Ham turned to allow him to sweep his back. Peck moved on to the waist, paying particular attention to Ham's belt buckle, then, as he started up the torso, the black box beeped. "What you got in that pocket, Ham?" Peck asked, pointing.

Ham reached into his pocket and produced the smoke detector.

John walked over and took it from him. "What's this?"

"A smoke detector," Ham said. "I was putting some up last night, and I guess I forgot about that one."

John unscrewed the two halves of the detector and looked inside. "Two batteries," he said. "That's unusual."

"Is it?" Ham replied. "First ones I ever had anything to do with."

John motioned with his head for Peck to sweep the smoke detector, and Peck complied. A tiny beep came from the black box.

"Interesting," Peck said.

"Not really," John replied. "You've got some electronics in there, and the batteries. You sometimes get a reaction from small devices, even when they're not transmitting." He handed the smoke detector back to Ham. "Let's get this finished up, Peck, and get back to our class. I've got a lot of ground to cover."

Ham stuck the smoke detector back into his pocket and tried not to look relieved.

41

Ham entered the beach house, and for once, no one was eating.

"Ham, I don't know if you should be here every night," Harry said.

"I had a close call today, and I want to talk about it."

"What happened, Ham?" Holly asked.

"I found out that they have been sweeping the place, and not just the place, but people, too. Can they do that without anyone knowing?"

Eddie shrugged. "It could be done, but they'd need some pretty sophisticated equipment. Somebody could carry around a small sweeper in his pocket that would signal if he got close to somebody wearing a transmission device."

"I'm glad I haven't been wearing anything up to now."

"Ham, tell us what happened," Holly insisted.

Ham told them about the lecture and Peck's sweeping of the participants. "I managed to turn off the thing in my heel," he said, getting his foot out of the boot and handing the shoe to Eddie. "When it's off, does the button emit any signals?"

"No," Eddie said, working to remove the heel from the boot. "When you turn it on, it activates the button microphone."

"Their sweeper beeped when Peck got to me," Ham said. "They found the smoke detector."

Everybody stared at Ham aghast.

"Then how did you get out?" Harry asked.

"I walked out, like always. John examined the thing and said it was a smoke detector. He noticed the two batteries, though."

"Did he question that?"

"No, but now you're going to have to do two things," Ham said.

"What?"

"Eddie, first you're going to have to take one of the batteries out."

"But that will halve the transmission time," Eddie protested.

"I don't care. I'm not going to put this thing up while it's got two batteries in it. John has seen the insides of it, and if, for any reason, they should pull it down and it has two batteries, then I'm gone."

"Do it, Eddie," Harry said. "And right now. What's the second thing, Ham?"

Ham handed the smoke detector to Eddie, who went to work on it. "You've got to give me some smoke detectors with two batteries that I can install at my house."

"Oh, no," Eddie groaned.

"I told him I had been installing them, so whatever's there has to have two batteries."

"I'll ask for them tomorrow," Harry said.

"Okay," Ham replied.

"Also, Eddie," Harry said, "we've got to set up another way to communicate with Ham. He can't keep coming here nearly every night."

"You can ask Washington for a couple of scrambled cell phones," Eddie said.

"Yes, I can," Harry agreed, "and I'll do it first thing in the morning."

Ham spoke up. "If I use a scrambled cell phone and somebody is listening on a scanner, what will they hear?"

"Nothing," Eddie said. "It will operate on a government frequency that commercial scanners can't detect. And even if they could, all they'd hear would be static."

"Okay, that sounds great."

"Ham," Harry said, "do you think that once Eddie gets the smoke detector operating on one battery, you'll be able to place it?"

"I don't know," Ham said. "That room is used a lot, so it could be tough. The good news is, there's a smoke detector there already, so if I can replace it with ours, that should lessen the chances of someone messing with it."

Eddie spoke up. "Before you remove the old one, be sure it's a stand-alone, battery-operated unit, and that it isn't hardwired into a fire and burglar alarm. If it has a wire attached that goes into the ceiling, leave it alone."

"What about this sweeping equipment of theirs? Will it detect our unit?"

"Very unlikely," Eddie said. "It will still be a short-range thing, and you said the room has a fairly high ceiling. And its signal is highly directional, straight up."

"Good."

"Harry, you want to listen to Ham's boot?"

"Yes," Harry said.

Eddie connected a box to the electronics in the heel and pushed a button. John's voice, tinny but clear, came out of it. Everyone listened raptly.

"Is it all as mind-numbing as this?" Harry asked after a few minutes had passed.

"I'm afraid so. It's straight indoctrination, although I think he's preaching to the converted."

The recording finished, and Eddie replaced the two memory sticks with fresh ones, then replaced the heel. "There you go."

"You got anything else for me?" Ham asked.

"Be careful using that recorder. Save it for when you're alone with John."

"Okay," Ham said. He took the altered smoke detector back from Eddie and left.

When Ham had left, Harry said, "Holly, your old man is one standup guy."

"Yeah, I know," Holly said. "That's what I'm most afraid of."

42

Today's lesson was about loyalty, and Ham struggled to look interested. He was astonished that John had the wind to keep at this stuff, and he prayed for it to be over soon. His prayers were not answered until lunchtime.

"That's it, gentlemen," John said. "I think you understand what you're a part of now. Any questions?"

A man raised his hand. "Just one thing I don't understand," he said.

"What's that?"

"Do we have a name?"

Ham could have kissed him.

"Before I can tell you that," John said, "there's an oath to take. Are you ready to take it?"

There was a murmur of assent.

John turned a page of his drawing pad, and in neat block capitals was written: "I pledge that I accept the principles of The Elect whole-heartedly and without mental reservation. I pledge to advance the cause of white Christians with all the energy I possess. I vow to accept the orders of my superiors without question and to carry them out at the cost, if necessary, of my blood or my very life. If I should break these vows I understand that I am subject to swift punishment by death at the hands of my superiors. I swear all this by my sacred honor and by Almighty God."

"Read that and think about what it means for a few minutes," John said. He left the room and closed the door behind him.

There was perfect silence in the room. The group stared at the oath, and when Ham chanced a glance at his companions he saw tears on the cheeks of some of them.

Five minutes passed before John returned to the room. "Are you ready to take the oath?" he asked.

A chorus of affirmation rang out.

"Then repeat after me," he said, then began reading.

The group followed him, speaking every word.

When they had finished, John took his felt marker and underlined "The Elect." "That is our name," he said. "We never speak it but to a man we know to be one of our number." He ripped the pages from the drawing pad, flicked a lighter and set fire to them, dropping the flaming paper into a metal wastebasket. "I welcome you all," John said, and began shaking their hands.

Suddenly, from over their heads, a loud beeping began. Everyone looked up. The smoke detector on the ceiling had gone off.

John led the laughing. "Ham, you know about these things. Can you turn it off?"

"Sure," Ham replied. He dragged a chair over and tugged at the alarm. It came away in his hand, stuck to the ceiling only by tape. "Give me a minute, and I'll get it reset," he said.

"Come on, men," John said. "I'll buy you all a beer. Ham, join us when you tame that thing."

"Be right with you," Ham said. He took a pen from his pocket and pretended to do something to the alarm. As soon as they left the room, he pressed the reset button and the beeping stopped. He took Eddie's unit from his pocket, ripped off the plastic covering the tape and stuck it to the ceiling. Then he pocketed the old alarm and went to find the others. On the way, he stopped at his truck and tossed the original alarm inside.

"Thank you, Jesus," he said aloud, as he made his way toward the picnic area.

Half an hour later, Harry was on the phone in the den of the beach house when someone turned on the radio in the living room. He covered the receiver and yelled, "Will somebody turn that goddamned thing down?"

Eddie stuck his head in the door. "Are you sure, Harry? Ham's smoke detector just went on the air."

"Holy shit!" He uncovered the phone. "Sorry, sir, I've got to run. Will you overnight that equipment to me?" He hung up without waiting for an answer and ran into the living room.

Doug and Eddie were staring at the speaker as if were a television. The voices were clear, except when someone mumbled.

"Everybody take the oath?" someone asked.

"Every man jack of them," another replied.

"Ham, too?"

"You bet."

"That man's a real find, isn't he?"

"Peck, you spotted him. You get all the credit for bringing him in."

"That's Rawlings," Doug said.

"Is the other one John?" Harry asked.

Eddie held up a hand for quiet, then he fumbled with a tape recorder and started it.

"I think it's time we got Ham started, don't you?" the other man asked.

"I believe it is," Peck replied.

"Let's get him moved in here, then," the other man said.

"John, I don't know about that. He's got a real sweet place out on the river, and he's not going to want to leave it to move into a bunkhouse."

"All right, feel him out about it. I don't want to piss him off at this stage, so go gently, but he's going to have to be in residence here before the day."

"On the day," Peck said.

"On the day," John echoed.

43

Ham finished his marksmanship class for the day and glanced at his watch. Nearly six. He would go straight to the beach house and see if his newly planted bug was working. He was walking toward the truck when Peck Rawlings approached.

"Well, Ham, this was quite a day."

"It sure was, Peck, and I want to tell you I'm proud to be a part of all this. Anything you want done, you just ask."

"How would you feel about moving out here?" Peck asked.

"Moving?" Ham was alarmed, but he took care not to sound it. "Where?"

"We've got a bunkhouse down in the woods there." Peck pointed off to the south of the range. "Right along the lakeshore. It's real comfortable."

"Well, Peck, I'm pretty comfortable where I am," Ham replied. "I don't mind a little commute."

"Sure, I understand," Peck said. "You just stay where you are for the time being. Of course, when we start an operation, you'll have to move out here a few days ahead of time. We don't want anybody loose in the world who knows what we're going to do and when."

"Oh, sure, I understand."

"Tell you what, you pack a duffel bag with a week's clothes and leave it out here tomorrow. That way, if something comes up, you'll be ready instantly."

"I'll do that, Peck." He glanced at his watch. "Well, I'd better get going. I've got my once-in-a-blue-moon dinner with my daughter."

Peck took his arm. "Ham, you've got to be careful about seeing her. John is aware that she's . . . well, aware of who she is, and—"

Ham held up a hand. "Don't worry, Peck. I've never said a thing to her about the group, and I never will. In fact, it occurs to me that when we do get into a project, it might be an advantage having her as a kind of personal reference. She'd say, 'What, my daddy involved in that? That's completely crazy,' and they'd believe her."

"I see your point," Peck said. "Just be careful around her."

"You bet I will." Ham turned to go.

"Oh, by the way," Peck said, stopping him with a hand on his arm. "You've taught your last shooting class for a while."

"Oh? You got something else for me?"

"You better believe it," Peck said.

"What is it?"

"Now, don't get too curious. You'll find that, in The Elect, you get information slowly, when your superiors think it's necessary. I will tell you this, though. John wants you to start working on the Barrett's rifle first thing tomorrow morning. He wants you up to speed on that weapon in a hurry, able to hit anything from any distance."

"I think I'll enjoy that," Ham said.

"See you tomorrow, then. Enjoy your dinner with your daughter."

Ham sighed. "I'll try," he said.

· · ·

Ham parked at Holly's and ran all the way to the beach house next door. As he walked into the living room, Harry jumped up and hugged him.

"You did it!" he yelled gleefully. "Those sons of bitches are on the fucking air!"

Doug and Eddie were pounding on his back, congratulating him.

Holly came and put an arm around him. "My old man!" she exclaimed. "How did you ever do it?"

"You're not going to believe it," Ham said. "Our lessons ended this morning, and after we took the damnedest oath you ever heard, John ripped up his class notes and burned them in the trash can, and the smoke detector in the room went off. John remembered I said I'd been installing them, and he asked me to fix it."

"And you switched detectors?"

"You bet your sweet ass I did. Have they been talking?"

"Yes," Harry said, "and they were talking about moving you out to the lake."

"Yeah, Peck brought that up, but he didn't push it. He wants me to keep a week's clothes out there, just in case."

"In case of what?"

"Something's in the wind, some sort of operation."

"Any clues?"

"Not really, but John wants me to start training on the Barrett's rifle tomorrow morning."

"Damn," Harry said. "What the hell are they going to do with that thing?"

"When I find out, I'll let you know," Ham said.

"I think this is a scary development," Holly interjected. "The idea that they might actually shoot that gun at something or somebody is terrifying."

"Tell me about this oath," Harry said.

"Well, it pretty much called for me to hand them my ass on a platter, and if I do something they don't like, they have my permission to shoot me."

"Swell," Holly said.

"Harry, did you get the scrambled cell phone?"

"It'll be here tomorrow morning, and you can pick it up tomorrow evening."

"I'm getting to the point where I really want a way to communicate," Ham said.

"Well," Eddie put in, "you can always go into Peck's study and talk to the ceiling. We'll be listening."

"Are you getting real-time transmissions?"

"As far as we know," Eddie said. "Who knows what those spooks at NSA are doing with this stuff. There may be some sort of delay piping down here to us."

"Can we find out? That's something I'd really like to know."

"I'll try," Harry said, "but those boys and girls don't talk much."

"Who else is hearing it besides us?" Doug asked.

"Hell, I don't know," Harry replied. "They could be playing it in the NSA cafeteria, for all I know. My guess would be that the attorney general is getting at least a digest of what's being said, and certainly, the director, but I asked for it to be as closely held as possible."

"Oh, by the way, the group has a name."

"What is it?"

"The Elect, and by telling you, I've just made myself eligible for a bullet in the brain."

"We came up with that name in the militia database. Now, who wants pizza and who wants Chinese?"

44

The following morning Ham packed a large duffel with clothing, including several fatigue shirts. He was going to have to sew that microphone button on a different shirt every day, he reflected. He had grown to hate and fear the recorder in his boot. It was too damn hard to turn on and off, and it had already nearly gotten him caught. He wished he had complained about it to Harry and made them get him something simpler to use. He resolved not to use it again, unless he absolutely had to.

He packed his cell phone and charger into the duffel, and as an afterthought, included a bottle of Wild Turkey. He had a feeling he was going to need a drink every now and then, if he had to start living with those people.

He drove out to the lake and found Peck.

"I expect you want to draw the Barrett's rifle and some ammo," Peck said.

"Right."

"Follow me." Peck led the way into the house, to an innocuous-looking door that turned out to lead to a cellar. Cellars weren't big in Florida, and Ham thought they must have gone to a lot of trouble to waterproof it.

The cellar turned out to be quite something, bigger than the house it served. There was a pistol-shooting range, several storerooms and what could only be described as an arsenal. "Wow," he said, when Peck opened the door.

"Yep, we're pretty well equipped, aren't we?"

Ham spotted assault weapons, grenades, shoulder-mounted anti-aircraft missiles, antitank weapons and cases of handguns. Peck selected the Barrett's rifle case from a group of four. "Grab that ammunition box," he said to Ham.

Ham shouldered the 500-round box and followed Peck up the stairs, out of the house and into the sunshine. Peck put the rifle in the back of Ham's truck and got in. "We'll drive," he said.

Ham put the ammunition into the truckbed and got behind the wheel. "To the range?" he asked, starting the engine.

"Past the range," Peck replied. "I'll direct you."

Ham drove off down the dirt track that ran past the shooting range and into the woods behind.

"You know, Ham," Peck said, "you're moving very fast in this organization."

"I am?"

"You certainly are. We have a process for recruiting new members that normally takes a year or more, depending on the man. But you came to us whole, ready to go; it was like a miracle. Your army service and experience made you perfect for us, and your personal beliefs already matched ours. I want to tell you that John is absolutely delighted with you. I've never seen him so happy with a new man."

"Well, that makes me feel good," Ham said.

"I don't mind telling you that it took me a good three years to be trusted by my superiors the way John trusts you."

"I don't know anything about the structure of the organization," Ham said. "Is John the top man?"

"As much as anyone is," Peck replied. "We have a leadership made up of a council, and I guess you could say that John is the de facto head of the council."

"He's a very impressive man," Ham said.

"That's why the council trusts him. John is a brilliant planner, but a cautious one. He knows how quickly a bungled operation can bring this whole thing down on our heads, and he's intolerant of error. I can tell you that he's been planning our next operation for the better part of a year."

"What sorts of operations have you been doing in the past?" Ham asked.

"You don't want to know that just yet," Peck replied. "Too much information is not a good thing when you're new to the group. I can tell you that the operations are roughly divided into three categories: training, infiltration and what you might call fund-raising. All these are aimed at supporting operational work; you can't bring off a successful operation without all those things lined up and working."

"How do you raise funds, from the members?"

Peck smiled. "Let's just say we go to outside sources. Take a left here."

Ham turned left at a fork in the road and shortly they came to a long, narrow strip of grass. "You could fly an airplane into here," he said.

"And we do," Peck replied, nodding toward a large metal building beside the strip that had been painted in camouflage colors. "John's airplane is in there, and we get occasional other visitors, too. But the really nice thing about the strip for you is that it gives you four thousand feet clear for shooting. Stop right here." Peck got out of the truck, went into the hangar through a small door and came back with a roll of paper under his arm. "Drive down to the other end of the strip," he said.

Ham did as he was told, then he helped Peck tack targets to the trees. They were of different sizes and shapes, some were silhouettes of men.

Ham drove back to the other end of the landing strip and parked the truck. Peck took the big leather case from the truckbed and opened it. Inside were the Barrett's rifle, an aluminum tripod, some cleaning equipment and half a dozen ammunition clips.

"Let's do some loading," Peck said. He opened the ammunition box, grabbed a handful of cartridges, set them on the truck's tailgate and began loading clips.

Ham helped him. "Six-cartridge clips," he said.

"If you haven't hit what you're shooting at by the time you've fired half a dozen times, you'll have attracted enough attention to yourself that it's time to run, anyway," Peck explained. "I suggest one clip in the weapon and one in your pocket, when you're working."

They finished loading the clips. Peck set up the tripod, and screwed it into a receptacle on the rifle. "It's not exactly a handheld weapon," he said. "Not for the kind of accuracy we're looking for. When you don't have a tripod, you have to find some way to brace the thing." He handed Ham a pair of foam earplugs, put some in his own ears, then stepped back and indicated that Ham was to proceed.

Ham worked the action a couple of times to be sure it was smooth, then he shoved a clip into the rifle and worked a cartridge into the chamber. He stepped up to the weapon, sighted down the barrel, then stepped back and raised the tripod a couple of inches.

"That's right, you're tall," Peck said.

"Just getting comfortable." Ham sighted again, then flipped off the safety. He took aim at a full-length target of a man, sighted on the middle of the chest and fired, making a big noise. A moment later, the .50 caliber bullet struck the target dead in the crotch, exploding a big chunk out of the tree it was attached to.

"Right on line, but low," Peck said, looking through a small pair of binoculars he had produced from a pocket.

Ham made a small adjustment in the sight. "Nice that there's no wind on the strip, since we've got trees on both sides," he said.

"You can't hit anything with this weapon if there's wind," Peck said. "We wouldn't ask you to shoot under those circumstances."

Ham gripped the big rifle again. He fired, and the middle of the target's chest disappeared.

"Right on," Peck said, checking through his binoculars. "Try for a head shot."

Ham fired again and took off the target's left ear. "My fault," he said. "I pulled too quick." He tried again and blew off the target's head.

"That's terrific shooting," Peck said.

"I'm ready to go to work," Ham replied. "I'll do whatever I can to help. When do I start?"

Peck smiled. "How about next week?"

45

Ham fired through the morning at targets of varying sizes, hitting everything with monotonous regularity.

"Tell me, Ham," Peck said, "how do you sight this thing in if you're in a place that's new to you?"

"Will we know the distance ahead of time?"

"Approximately."

"If somebody can pace it off, then I can preset the elevation; windage is another thing. I'll just have to guess, and I can't guarantee you a kill on the first shot."

Peck nodded gravely. "That's about what I thought."

"Would this be in a public place?"

Peck nodded again.

"You planning to use explosive shells?"

"Probably."

"Then I'd suggest firing a nonexplosive round the first time, followed by an explosive one. Won't take more than a couple of seconds to adjust the sights."

Peck nodded thoughtfully, then he looked at his watch. "Let's get some lunch," he said.

They got back into the truck, and Ham headed back toward Peck's house, but halfway there, he was directed to make a right turn, toward the lake.

"Let's drop your gear off at the bunkhouse," Peck said.

"Okay."

They arrived at a low, clapboard building, and Ham got his duffel from the back of the truck. It was much like a military barracks, one big room with a small office and heads at one end. There were two dozen bunks, and a dozen of them had gear piled on them.

"Pick a bunk," Peck said.

Ham chose the bunk nearest the heads. "Looks like you've got some new arrivals," he said, nodding toward the luggage on the other bunks.

Peck nodded. "By the way, have you got a cell phone?"

"Yep. In my duffel."

"Let me have it."

Ham retrieved the phone and handed it to Peck, who slipped it into a pocket. They got back into the truck, and Ham resisted the urge to ask why Peck wanted his cell phone. Peck answered his question anyway.

"We've been locked down since nine o'clock this morning," Peck said. "Nobody leaves for any reason, not even to buy groceries, without John's permission. Nobody makes a phone call; nobody sends smoke signals; nobody uses a reflecting mirror. Nobody travels or communicates, unless he wants to catch a bullet."

"Okay," Ham said, because he couldn't say anything else. "When do we jump off?"

"Next week. You'll be told when you need to know."

Today was Wednesday, Ham reflected, and these people were planning something very public the following week, and he had no way to communicate with Holly or Harry.

They drove back to the main house, got into line for food and sat at a picnic table with John.

"Peck told you we're locked down?" John asked.

"Yes."

"That okay with you? You got any loose ends that need tidying?"

Ham shook his head. "I'm ready to go when you are."

"I know you are, Ham. I think I'm beginning to know you better than you know yourself. I'm not ready to tell you what we're doing, but I can tell you this: you're going to be doing something good for your country and for the group. And you're going to enjoy it."

"Sounds good to me," Ham replied. "Excuse me, I've got to take a leak." He took his tray back, then walked toward the house, thinking furiously, trying to work out a plan. He entered the house, and on the way to the john, looked into Peck's office. A group of men was in the middle of some sort of discussion. He used the toilet, then slowly washed his hands, taking as much time as he reasonably could.

He left the john and walked back down the hall. Just ahead of him, the group from Peck's study were filing out of the room, no doubt headed for lunch. He made a show of looking at some flyers on a bulletin board, advertising right-wing literature for sale by mail order, then, when the last of the group was out of the house, he ducked into Peck's study.

He stopped directly under the smoke detector. "This is Ham," he said. "Listen up. They're planning something for next week, I don't know what or when, and the place is locked down, so I can't leave. You're going to have to get a phone to me, and it's going to have to be by water. I'm staying at a bunkhouse down by the lake, looks like a military barracks. I'll try to leave a light on to guide you. Put the phone in a plastic bag and leave it under a rock on the shore as close to the bunkhouse as you can. Do it tonight. I'll find it. That's all."

He hurried back to the picnic table and joined John and Peck.

"You were a long time," John said.

Ham patted his stomach. "I was a little late this morning; usually my bowels go like clockwork."

John nodded. "Peck tells me you're ready with the Barrett's rifle," he said. "I didn't expect it to happen so quickly."

"Given the circumstances, what I've got to do is practice sighting in the rifle with one shot," Ham said.

"I want to work on a moving target, too," Peck added. "Just in case."

"Good idea," John said. "You never know what might happen, the target could be rolling."

"Can you slow it down?" Ham asked.

"Probably."

"Then it shouldn't be too much of a problem."

"You see?" John said to Peck. "I told you he was a can-do guy."

46

Holly left her house with Daisy at sunset, ran through the dunes with her for a while, then went next door to Harry's rental. To her surprise, she smelled cooking.

"You guys get tired of Chinese and pizza?" she asked, letting herself in through the beach door.

"I got a steak here for you," Harry replied. "How do you like it?"

"Medium rare. Did you get any wine?"

"I bought a mixed case," Harry said, nodding toward the carton. "I figured we'd be here long enough, and I was getting tired of beer." Harry flipped a steak over.

"Eddie, what did you get from the compound today?"

"Zip," Eddie said. "I don't even know whether it's working."

"Don't you think you'd better find out?"

"Harry, you'd better call somebody," Eddie said.

"I'll call my contact at home after we eat," Harry replied. "I'm not too exercised about this. It's early days in this surveillance."

"I don't want to miss a thing," Holly said. "You know, I thought Ham would be here by now."

"Maybe he went home to change or something," Doug said.

"Maybe, but he's been here by sunset just about every night."

They dug into their steaks and baked potatoes. "The wine's nice," Holly said.

"Australian," Harry replied. "Black Opal."

"I'll try to remember that." She suddenly remembered that she hadn't opened a bottle of wine since Jackson's death.

"The scrambler phones came," Harry said. "I got one for you, too, so we can talk between the houses without having to worry about ears."

"Good," Holly said. She looked at her watch again. "I'd like to call Ham. He shouldn't be this late."

"No good, Holly. The bug is still on his phone."

"Oh, yeah," she said, and resumed eating.

They were scraping the plates when Holly stood up. "I'm going out to Ham's," she said. "Something's wrong."

"Doug, go with her," Harry said. "Meantime I'll make that call."

Holly and Doug walked next door with Daisy to pick up Holly's car, and shortly, they were driving north on A1A.

"I've never seen Ham's place," Doug said. "I hear it's nice."

"It sure is. My former boss left it to him." She took a left and drove over the North Bridge, then turned left onto the little dirt road that led to Ham's island.

"Don't park too close to the house," Doug said. "That bug's still in place, and I don't want them to hear car doors slamming."

Holly parked well away, then led Doug to the house, opening the door with her key. She used a flashlight instead of turning on the lights, walking softly around the place. Everything seemed to be in order, except that Ham was not there. She motioned Doug outside.

"You think he hasn't been back here tonight?" Doug asked.

"That's what I think."

"Maybe they asked him to stay for dinner, and he couldn't say no."

"I hope that's what happened," Holly said. "Come on, let's get back to your place. Maybe he's turned up."

They arrived back at the house to find Harry and Eddie sitting beside the radio.

"NSA has just downloaded today's transmissions," Harry said.

"What are they saying?"

"Pretty dull stuff—a Bible class, kind of twisted, and a discussion group about race."

The men on the recording were making wrapping-up sounds, moving away from the bug. There was a moment's silence, then, suddenly, Ham's voice came through.

They sat, transfixed, listening to his short report.

"Holy shit," Harry said. "We could have missed it. I'm going to get word to NSA that we want everything in real time from now on."

"I'm going to take him the phone," Holly said.

"No, Doug will do it," Harry replied. "I don't want you at risk."

"Fuck the risk," Holly said. "Ham needs a way to communicate, and I'm taking him the phone. Now, do you have a large-scale map of the place?"

"Yes," Harry said, spreading it out on the table.

"What about aerial photographs."

"Eddie, get the sat shots."

Eddie came back with some surprisingly detailed photographs.

"Why haven't I seen these before?" Holly asked.

"They arrived today, with the phones."

"Okay, there's a dock on the lakeshore here, about what, two or three miles from the compound."

"Looks like that. Where are we going to get a boat this time of night?"

"Ham's got an aluminum dinghy," Holly said, "and one of those little trolling motors that runs on a car battery."

"Where is it?"

Doug spoke up. "It's lying next to Ham's house," he said. "I saw it when we were out there."

"You've got a pickup, Doug," Harry said. "Go get it and bring it back here, and don't forget the motor and some oars."

"Be back shortly," Doug said, then left.

"Ham's battery will be on a trickle charger, but I want a spare, just in case," Holly said. "We'll cannibalize one of your cars."

"Okay with me," Harry replied.

Holly looked at the sat shots again. "This must be the barracks," she said. "It's the only thing that fits the description. Eddie, show me the phone."

Eddie left and came back with half a dozen tiny phones in a cardboard box. "They're Motorola V-phones," he said, "that have been modified to scramble." He showed her how the phone worked, while Holly began composing a note to Ham.

"He's going to need some extra batteries," she said.

"I've got some in the charger. They're small, but they're good for eighty minutes of talk time each, and about twenty-four hours of standby."

"Can he take a call without the phone ringing?"

"It has a vibrate mode. You can't hear it, but you can feel it if it's clipped to your belt or in your pocket."

"Show me." She wrote down the instructions for Ham.

"Do we know whether there's even cell phone service out there?" Holly asked.

"I don't know," Harry said. "We'll try it when we get out there, and if there's no service, I can have a portable cell transmitter and antenna in here by tomorrow morning that has a range of about five miles. It'll be on a van, and we can park it as close as possible."

"Good," Holly said. She looked at the sat shot. "This looks like a grass landing strip," she said.

"I agree," Harry replied. "Might come in useful before this is over."

Doug came back with the boat, and they loaded it into the pickup.

"Eddie," Harry said, "you stay here and monitor the bug in the compound. Call us on the scrambled phone if anything important happens."

"Will do," Eddie replied.

"Let's get out of here," Holly said, and got into the truck.

47

Ham had dinner at the table with John and Peck. A pecking order seemed to have been established in the compound, and he figured, from the seating arrangements, that he was pretty near the top of it.

"Peck," John said, "you think you can find a bed for Ham in one of the houses?"

"Sure," Peck replied.

Ham raised a hand. "Listen, guys, I appreciate the thought, but I'm real comfortable in the bunkhouse. I've spent a big chunk of my life in barracks, and I like it." This was an outright lie. He'd spent as few nights in barracks as possible, and he didn't care if he ever spent another one there, but he had to be on the lakeshore when his people showed up with the phone, as he had no doubt they would do.

"Whatever you say, Ham," John replied. "As long as you're comfortable. If you change your mind, let me know."

"Okay," Ham said.

. . .

Harry, Holly and Doug, in the pickup truck, worked hard with the large-scale map and a flashlight to find a way to the eastern shore of Lake Winachobee. The dock didn't seem to have a real road leading to it, and they had been picking their way along overgrown lanes for more than two hours.

"The hell with the dock," Holly said. "It's after midnight, and we can launch the dinghy from the shore. I don't mind getting your feet wet."

"Thanks," Harry said.

"Just drive west until we end up in the lake," she said.

"I'm doing the best I can, Holly."

"There," she said, pointing to an opening that appeared in the headlight beams. "That track looks like a car might have once driven down it, and it's headed in the right direction."

Harry turned down it, and a deer ran across the road, nearly striking the truck. "That's all I need," he said.

Then the track opened into a clearing, and the starlight glinted on water.

"There!" Holly nearly shouted. "Douse the headlights."

Harry switched them off and stopped the truck. They sat and waited for their eyes to become accustomed to the darkness.

"Thank God there's no moon tonight," Harry said.

"Not yet, anyway," Doug replied. "We should have checked an almanac."

"Come on," Holly said, "let's get the boat into the water."

They got out and heaved the lightweight dinghy off the truck and to the lakeshore. Holly took off her shoes and rolled up her jeans. "Hand me the motor." She accepted it from Doug and clamped it to the stern of the dinghy. "You can handle the batteries," she said. "Put them side by side." She climbed into the dinghy.

Doug placed the batteries in the bottom of the boat and fixed the alligator clips to the terminals of one. "There you go," he said. "Are you sure you don't want company?"

"I can handle it alone."

"Look across there," Harry said, pointing. "The house with all the lights must be Peck's place. The barracks has to be farther along the shore to your left. I'd stay away from it, just use it as a landmark."

Harry suddenly grabbed at his belt. "My phone's ringing." He opened it. "Yeah?" He listened for a moment, then hung up. "Eddie says they've just broken up for the evening. The main house seems to be emptying out."

"How far do you reckon it is?" Holly asked.

"Three, maybe four miles, I'd guess. I think we're south of the putative dock."

Ham left Peck's house with four other men who were also quartered in the bunkhouse. None of them was over thirty, and they were talking excitedly about the group and their part in it. They reached the bunkhouse and began to unpack their things, placing their clothes in lockers. Ham took his time; he wanted them all asleep before him. With that in mind, he wrapped a towel around himself, went into the heads and took a long, hot shower.

When he came out, two of the boys were still talking quietly, but soon they drifted off, and the barracks was quiet. Ham checked his watch and waited for another hour before he made a move. He got silently out of bed, took a blanket and a pillow from the empty bunk next to his and walked quietly out the lakeside door. Once outside, he stopped and listened for a full two minutes to see if anyone was stirring inside the bunkhouse or outside. Hearing nothing, he made his way across a neatly trimmed lawn toward the lake. Once there, he stopped and listened again. His watch showed nearly half-past two in the morning.

Holly sat in the bottom of the dinghy, the motor humming quietly behind her, only her head and shoulders above the boat's gunwales. Peck's house had only one light now, and it appeared to be an outdoor lamp that stayed on all night. This was good, since it gave her a landmark. Then, as she made her way slowly across the lake, the moon began to rise, and this was not good. It was nearly three-quarters full, and it gave a lot more light than Holly needed or wanted. She reckoned she was a mile from shore now, and remembering that even small sounds carried across water, she switched off the little motor and let the boat drift. Then she made her way forward to the stem, knelt down and began paddling with an oar, using a J-stroke, the way she had been taught at Girl Scout camp, so that she wouldn't have to lift it from the water.

Ham hadn't noticed the motor until it was turned off, but when it went quiet, he knew what the sound had been. The moon was rising, and he didn't like that at all. He walked back to the bunkhouse and stuck his head inside the door. Four lumps lay inert in the bunks, one of them snoring softly. He went back to the lakeshore and, bothered by the moon, lay down on the blanket. He didn't want to be spotted in the moonlight.

Holly could see the dark outline of the bunkhouse, and she made for it, resisting the urge to paddle faster. Then, as she approached the shore from fifty yards out, two things happened. Ham, who had apparently been lying down, stood up.

Then a light went on in the bunkhouse.

48

48

Ham hunkered down under his blanket and pretended to be asleep. The light had alarmed him; he didn't know who might be behind him. Then he heard a screen door shut and someone walking across the lawn toward him.

"Ham?"

"Huh?" he grunted. He turned over and found one of his four bunkhouse mates, a kid named Jimmy, standing over him. "What's up?" he asked sleepily.

"There's a boat out there, about fifty yards away," Jimmy said.

Ham sat up on an elbow and looked toward the dinghy, which appeared to be empty. "Just somebody's dinghy came untied," he said grumpily. "Why the hell did you wake me up? I came out here to get away from the snoring, and now I've got you making noise. And why is that light on in the bunkhouse?"

"Sorry, Ham, I didn't know you were sleeping." He started toward the edge of the water. "I'm going to swim out there and check out that boat."

"Hold it right there," Ham said, and he brought authority into his voice.

Jimmy stopped, turned and looked at him.

"You have any idea what the cottonmouth moccasin count is in that lake? There must be thousands, and don't even think about the alligators. They feed at night, you know."

"I didn't think of that," Jimmy said uncertainly.

"You get your ass back into that bunkhouse and into bed, and don't you fucking wake me up again."

"I'm sorry, Ham, I—"

"Just get back in there. If the boat is still there in the morning, I'll check it out."

"Okay, if you say so. Good night."

"It better be."

Jimmy walked back to the bunkhouse, switched off the light and, apparently, went back to bed.

Ham lay on his side, staring at the boat. He lay that way for better than half an hour, then he saw a movement in the boat, and a figure sat up. There, in the moonlight, was Holly.

"Oh, shit," Ham said aloud.

Holly was on one of the boat's seats now.

Ham stood up and waved her off. "Get out of here," he whispered loudly. "Go on, get out." He hoped his voice would carry over the water. Then he saw her arm go back, and she threw something. It arced high, then fell into the water, about ten yards out. Ham immediately marked the spot, taking a reference line from the corner of the bunkhouse through the spot where he stood. He bent down, found a good-sized rock and marked his position with it.

"Get out of here," he whispered hoarsely, waving her off.

She moved forward in the dinghy again, keeping low, and slowly, the dinghy turned and started moving toward the eastern shore of the lake.

Ham lay down again and pulled the blanket over himself.

When he woke up, the sun was rising and he was sore all over. It had been a long time since he had slept on the ground, and it didn't agree with his aging bones. He stood up and looked out at the lake. The dinghy was gone, to his relief, and a northerly breeze had sprung up. He heard a door behind him slam.

"You awake?" Jimmy called out.

"Yeah."

Jimmy came down to the water's edge and stood beside Ham. "What happened to the dinghy?"

"A breeze came up during the night," Ham replied. "I guess it blew away."

"Was there anything fishy about it?"

"Nah, it was just an empty dinghy. Somebody didn't tie it up good, I guess."

"I guess. You want some breakfast?"

"In a minute; I'm just enjoying the sunrise." Jimmy left him there, and Ham kept looking out at the lake. He saw Holly paddle away.

Holly and Harry stopped at a roadside restaurant west of Orchid Beach and were having breakfast.

"How the hell is Ham going to get the phone, if you threw it in the lake?" Harry asked.

"I didn't throw it in the lake on purpose, Harry," Holly replied. "I was in an awkward position in the dinghy, and it didn't go as far as it was supposed to. Don't worry, Ham will get it. I saw him mark the position, and it won't be hard to find. The water's probably only three or four feet deep there."

"You almost got your ass caught, didn't you?"

"No, I didn't. Somebody in the barracks woke up and came outside. Ham dealt with it. I waited until he was back inside for half an hour before I got out of there. And the wind helped me get back."

"You know how much that telephone cost?" Harry demanded.

"No, and neither do you, Harry. Now get off my back and eat your breakfast."

Harry took out his new, scrambled cell phone and called the house. "What's up?" he asked, when Eddie answered.

"Nothing all night. I guess they slept soundly. There are people in the house now, so I guess they're having breakfast."

"We'll be back in an hour or so." Harry punched off and turned to Holly. "You're sure the phone won't get wet?"

"Harry, it was in a sealed plastic bag. Now shut up about it and eat your breakfast."

"I don't suppose you thought to check the signal strength on the phone."

"I did, and it was dodgy—only two bars on the display."

Harry opened his cell phone again, called his office in Miami and ordered that a portable cell be set up as near as possible to the north shore of Lake Winachobee.

Holly felt awful about throwing the phone short, but she wasn't about to let Harry know it. She hoped to hell Ham could recover it.

49

Ham stood at one end of the airstrip and watched through the sights of the Barrett's rifle as a jeep towed a nearly wrecked car across the opposite end, four thousand feet away. The car was moving at about twenty miles an hour, he reckoned.

He led the car a yard and squeezed off the round. A large hole appeared in a rear door of the car. "Do it again," he said to Peck, who was standing beside him. "And I want to know how fast he's moving."

Peck spoke his instructions into a handheld radio, then he turned to Ham. "He says he was doing about fifteen miles an hour."

"Tell him to speed it up to twenty-five this time," Ham replied. "Nobody drives that slow on purpose."

Peck relayed the instructions, and the jeep turned around and started another pass, this time faster.

Ham fired again, and the glass in the front passenger door shattered.

"Right on!" Peck yelled.

"Yeah, but do you want me to hit the driver?"

"No, we want the rear-seat passengers."

"Of course, the explosive round will take out pretty much everybody in the car."

"Still, I'd like you to be able to hit the rear-door window every time," Peck said.

"Turn him around, and maintain that speed."

Ham fired the big rifle until they had to stop and let the barrel cool off.

At lunchtime, Ham was sitting with Peck when John came into the dining room.

"Productive morning?" Peck asked.

"Pretty good," John replied. He produced a cell phone and switched it on. "Tell me something," he said, "what kind of cell phone signal strength do you get out here?"

"Pretty poor," Peck said. "Sometimes you have to try half a dozen times to get a call through."

"Interesting," John said. He held up his cell phone for Peck to see. Ham saw it, too—there were five bars of signal strength showing in the display. "You know anything about cell phone improvements out here?"

"Haven't heard a thing," Peck said. "I tried to use mine a couple of days ago, and I couldn't get a call out."

"There's nothing much out here that would cause them to install a new cell, is there?"

"Not that I can think of. We're about it for twenty miles or so. Are you worried about this, John?"

"I'm not sure whether to be worried," he replied. "But I've never experienced a sudden improvement in cell phone service. I've experienced worse service many times, but never better service. If you were going to install a cell out here, where would you put it?"

"On top of something, I guess. A water tower, a church steeple, a microwave tower. The terrain is flat as a pancake for miles."

"Is there any installation like that around here?"

"No, that sort of thing is usually around I-95, to the east, or the Florida Turnpike, to the west."

"Let's take a drive," John said.

"Okay."

"Ham, why don't you join us? You're an observant fellow."

"Sure." Ham drank the last of his iced tea and followed them to a car outside. Peck drove, John took the shotgun seat and Ham sat in back.

"Take a right and drive to I-95, then turn around and come back," John said. He held his cell phone up, so that Ham could see it, too. They reached the highway and Peck turned right. "Strong signal all the way to the main road," John said.

Ham watched the cell phone display and wondered what the hell was going on.

They drove east for a few miles, then John spoke again. "Signal's dropping. We're down to two bars." A couple of minutes later: "Up to three bars, now four." Ham could see I-95 ahead. "Five bars. Turn the car around."

Peck made a U-turn and the same phenomenon occurred. "Drive right past our turn," John said, watching the phone. "Five bars at our turn," he said. A few miles later: "Signal's dropping—three, now two. The no-signal light is on. Turn around."

Peck made another U-turn.

"Ham," John said, "did you notice anything unusual along our route?"

"There was a power company van pulled over a few miles back, and a man up a pole, but I don't know if you'd call that unusual."

"Normally, not," John said, "but I wonder why the hell we're suddenly getting such good cell phone service out here. There's the power company van, Peck. Slow down as we go by."

The car drove slowly past the van, and everybody had a good look.

"One man up the pole," Ham said. "The van doors were closed."

"You want me to turn in to our road?"

"Yes," John said. He watched his cell phone signal all the way to Peck's house. "Peck," he said as they pulled to a stop, "anybody you know of have a cell phone out here?"

"I asked everybody," Peck said, "and I collected a dozen, including Ham's. Why?"

"Because I wonder if somebody has a phone we don't know about, and if somebody else has suddenly improved service in the area just so he can make a few calls."

"You want me to conduct a search of the whole compound?"

"No. If there's a phone here, I doubt if we'd find it. I want someone to monitor a scanner on the cell phone frequencies, though. We just might pick up something." He turned to Ham. "I understand there was a boat near the bunkhouse last night."

"Yes, there was," Ham said. "I went outside to sleep, because a snorer was keeping me awake; Jimmy woke me up in the middle of the night and pointed out the boat. It appeared to be an empty dinghy that someone hadn't tied up right."

"You really think it was empty?"

"I watched it for a good half an hour while I was trying to get back to sleep, and it never moved in the water. Later on, a breeze came up from the north, and it must have blown back where it came from."

"I see."

"I don't know how big a cell phone transmitter is, but I wouldn't think you could get one into a small dinghy."

"You're right," John said. "The dinghy must have been a coincidence. I don't think the signal strength is an accident, though. I want a twenty-four-hour watch on the scanner, Peck, and I want somebody to drive past that power company truck every hour. I want to see how long it stays there."

Ham wondered if this had something to do with the cell phone delivered to him, the one lying on the bottom of Lake Winachobee.

50

Holly left work, went home, walked Daisy, then went to Harry's place. Everybody was looking glum.

"What's going on?" she asked. "Have you heard from Ham?"

"No," Harry said, "not by phone or bug. There's been a lot of activity in Peck's study, but nothing was said that would give us any more information about what's going on out there."

"I wonder why Ham hasn't retrieved the phone yet?"

"There's something else," Harry said.

"What?"

"While my van was out there working to set up the portable cell, a car drove past twice, with three men in it. My people got a photograph through a window in the van." He shoved a color print across the table.

Holly picked it up. "That's Ham in the back seat," she said, "and John in the front passenger seat. I can't see the driver's face."

"You're right," Harry said. "But why are they cruising up and down the highway while my van is out there?"

Holly looked at the photograph more closely. "John is holding something in his hand, and Ham seems to be looking at it."

Harry looked at the photograph again. "Could be a cell phone," he said.

"Oh, shit," Eddie chipped in. "They were reading signal strength."

"Now, why the hell would they do that?" Harry asked.

Everybody was quiet for a moment.

"Maybe their weak signal strength out there suddenly got too good," Holly said. "Maybe they were suspicious of that."

"It's John," Harry said. "That son of a bitch is smart."

"Is there equipment out there where you can see it?" Holly asked.

"Just a whip antenna on a power pole. The van is parked a couple of miles away."

"But John saw the van there."

"Yeah."

"Eddie," Harry said, "if you were John and you thought it was strange that your cell phone signal strength had improved, what would you do about it?"

Eddie frowned.

"From a technical point of view, I mean."

"I guess I'd try to find out if somebody was using a cell phone in the compound. I'd run a scanner and see if it picked up anything."

"John could actually overhear calls, if a cell phone were being used out there?"

"He could if he has a scanner. You can buy them at Radio Shack and modify them to pick up cell phone frequencies."

"But it wouldn't pick up Ham's scrambled phone."

"No, and if it did, it would only get static."

"So if Ham got the phone out of the lake, he could use it without being caught."

"Without being caught electronically," Eddie corrected.

"If you're right about John catching on," Holly said, "then Ham would know about it, because he was in the car. Maybe that's why he's not using the phone."

"But he was here when I explained how the scrambled phone worked," Eddie said. "He heard me say that it would be undetectable."

"That's right," Harry said. "If Ham remembers."

"He'll remember," Holly said. "He's got a memory like a bear trap, better than mine."

"I hope it's better than mine," Harry said.

"Hey, listen up," Eddie said, pointing at the radio. "Ham's on the air."

Holly heard a jumble of voices, then a door close.

"Ham, I hear you're working wonders with the Barrett's rifle," a voice said.

"Damn right he is," another man chipped in.

"It seems to be going well," Ham said.

"Could you be ready to shoot by, say, Monday?" the first voice asked.

"John, I'm ready now," Ham replied.

Harry spoke up. "Eddie, is the tape recorder on?"

"Yes," Eddie replied.

"Monday will be soon enough," John said.

"You ready to tell me what I'll be shooting at?" Ham asked.

"Two, maybe three men in the back seat of a limo," John replied. "And that's all you need to know for now."

"I think we ought to start watching the weather," Ham said. "You get the Weather Channel out here?"

"Yes, on satellite," the third man said.

"Peck, that's not going to get you a local forecast."

"Why are you worried about the weather?" John asked.

"I'm worried about the wind," Ham said. "If there's more than a slight breeze, windage could be a real problem, depending on the distance. Is this limo likely to be moving through a crowd?"

"Maybe," John said.

"I don't think we want to shoot near a crowd, if there's any wind. You don't want to kill a lot of citizens, do you?"

"Not unless it's absolutely necessary," John replied.

"Well, if you have an option—I mean, if there's a route for this limo, and you could choose where to shoot, you might want to look for a spot with trees on either side of the road, and the taller, the better."

"That would help you with the wind?"

"It would, if the wind wasn't too strong."

"I can get an aviation forecast that would give me winds at the local airport twenty-four hours ahead of time."

"That would be a big help," Ham said. "The winds ought to be the same on the street."

"Well, let's go to dinner," John said, and the three men left the room.

"Well, whatever it is, it's Monday," Holly said.

"Eddie," Harry said, "I want you to get on the Internet and visit every Florida site you can find. Look for a list of events on Monday. Doug, I want you to call the FAA and tell them I want to know—in fact, I want tapes—of anybody who calls from Saturday onward asking for a forecast of local winds, not a whole briefing for a flight and not a winds-aloft forecast, just a forecast of local winds at any airport in the state."

"Will do," Doug said.

"Ham can't tell us where this is happening," Harry said, "because he doesn't know, but we do know he's supposed to shoot at two or three men in a limo, and on Monday. It's a start."

51

Ham excused himself right after dinner, claiming to be tired, and walked back to the bunkhouse. The place was empty when he arrived, so he walked out to the lakeshore. It was a cloudy night, so there was no moon, and the water looked very dark. He needed to be able to see, if he was going to find that phone. He would have to wait until morning and take a chance on looking for it in broad daylight.

The others arrived at the bunkhouse an hour later, and Ham was already in bed. He pretended that they woke him up, then he grabbed a blanket and a pillow. "I'm sleeping outside," Ham said. "You guys are going to be snoring away in a few minutes." He walked out of the house, this time dragging a bunk mattress, and stretched out beside the lake.

Half an hour later, it was quiet in the bunkhouse, and Ham was tempted to go after the phone, but he only wanted to do this once. He knew his warning to Jimmy about cottonmouths and gators might be more real than imaginary. He settled in for the night.

Holly went to bed early, with a movie on the TV at the end of the bed, but it bored her, and she was soon sleepy. She switched off the TV and lay in bed, thinking of Jackson and waiting for sleep to come.

Ham woke in the green-gray light of the predawn, and soon he could see that the sky had cleared during the night. The others would be waking soon, so if he was going to do it, now was the time.

First, he walked quietly back to the bunkhouse and looked in through a window. The four men were all still fast asleep. Then he walked to the corner of the barracks, looked for the stone he had left at the lakeside as a marker, and walked toward it. When he got to the stone, he stripped off his shorts and waded gingerly into the lake. The bottom was soft, and he stirred up a lot of mud.

"Shit," he said softly to himself, "that's going to make it harder." Then the bottom fell away in front of him, and he was shoulder deep in the water. He looked back at his reference line, then took a deep breath and went under, hoping that the lake didn't get much deeper.

The water was reasonably clear, and he swam along the gently sloping bottom for a few yards, sweeping his hands along the bottom, feeling for Holly's package. He began to run out of air, so he surfaced and looked back at the barracks. He was off his line a bit and farther from shore than he intended to be. He reckoned that the package was ten yards from shore, and he had swum fifteen or twenty.

He got back on his reference line and swam a little closer to shore, then he dove again, feeling his way along the bottom. There was not as much light as he had hoped, since the sun wasn't really up yet.

The water became shallow again, and he popped up, looking back at the barracks to be sure no one was watching him. He was, maybe, five yards offshore.

He checked his reference line again, adjusted his position, dove and started back toward deeper water. He had only swum three or four strokes when his hand brushed against something soft. He stopped and looked, but he had stirred up the bottom, and he could see nothing. He returned to the surface, got another breath and dove again, keeping as much as possible in the same spot.

He still couldn't see well, but this time he came into contact with a plastic bag. He came back to the surface again, and as he did, he saw Jimmy standing on shore, looking out at him.

With his free hand, he waved. "Come on in," he said. "It's a little chilly, but not bad."

"What about all those snakes and alligators you told me about?" Jimmy called back.

"I figure I can see them in daylight," Ham replied. He was clutching the plastic bag, dying to look at it, but having to keep it underwater. He turned on his back and floated a little, hoping Jimmy would go away.

"You okay out there?" Jimmy called.

"Just fine," Ham called back, not looking at him. A moment later, he heard the screen door slam.

He swam around for a while longer, then started back toward shore. He couldn't leave the water carrying the bag, so as he found the bottom, he began looking for a place to leave the plastic bag. He saw a clump of tall grass and headed for that, surreptitiously stuffing the bag into the grass as he passed it, then he got out and walked up to the barracks and stuck his head inside the door. "Somebody toss me a towel?" he called.

Somebody did, and he dried himself, then went back for his bedding. By the time he was back inside the bunkhouse, the four were already dressing.

"Better hurry, Ham," somebody said. "Breakfast will be ready in a minute."

"You guys go ahead," Ham said. "I'm going to grab a quick shower and get some of this lake mud off me." He went into the heads, shaved slowly, then took a shower. When he got out, they were gone. He dressed quickly, then went outside and made sure he wasn't being observed. Then he trotted over to the clump of grass and retrieved the plastic bag. He walked back to the bunkhouse, skimming a couple of rocks over the lake to appear innocent, then he went back inside.

He sat down on his bunk and unzipped the bag. The contents—a tiny phone in a belt clip, an earphone on a thin cord, three batteries and a note—were dry. He stuffed the plastic bag into a pocket and read the note.

Ham,
The phone works like any other cell phone, except when you want to scramble, you press the function key, then one, two, three, send. When you want to unscramble, you do the same thing again. The phone is set on scramble now. It's also set to vibrate, instead of ring, so if you want to leave it on, you can. Just keep it next to your body, so you can feel it vibrate. Call us whenever you can. Here are the numbers.

Love,
Holly

P.S. Now eat this note.

Ham laughed and quickly memorized the phone numbers Holly had jotted at the bottom, then stuffed the letter into a pocket. He heard a sound and looked up to find Jimmy standing in the door.

"You coming?" Jimmy asked.

"Just let me make my bunk," Ham replied, pulling the blanket over the phone and batteries beside him. "Why don't you go ahead and order me some ham and eggs?"

Jimmy went out and closed the door, and Ham quickly put the phone and batteries into separate pockets. There was no time to hide them.

He followed Jimmy out the door and back toward Peck's house, looking for someplace to ditch the plastic bag and the note. He was going to have to hide the phone, too. He didn't like having it on him.

52

Ham had breakfast with John and Peck, and he hoped to hear more about what they wanted him to do, but nothing was said. He felt nervous about having the phone on him, and he was made more so when John brought up cell phones again.

"I checked this morning," he said, "and there's an antenna on that power pole where the van was parked yesterday."

"The van was gone?" Peck asked.

"Yes. There was just the antenna and a box that could contain a transformer and some electronics."

"I've got a man stationed at the scanner twenty-four hours a day," Peck said. "We haven't heard a peep from a cell phone."

"You know," Ham said, "it's not inconceivable that they would install a new cell on that road, since it connects I-95 with the Florida Turnpike."

"Maybe," John said.

"I expect one of these days soon they'll have every square mile of the country covered," Peck added. He turned to Ham. "You shooting today?"

"I thought I might take the rifle down to the lakeshore and practice firing back toward the woods to the west. There's a breeze today, and I'd like to see how it shoots with windage."

"Good idea. I'm tied up this morning, but I'll send somebody with you."

"I don't need any help," Ham said. "I don't even need any targets. I'll shoot at trees."

"Okay," Peck said, digging in a pocket and coming up with some keys. "Take the jeep." He turned to John. "I've got a class to teach. I'll see you later."

"Right," John said, and he seemed preoccupied.

When Peck had left the table and Ham was alone with John, he lowered his voice. "John, about the cell phone business."

"Yes?"

"My assumption is that you're worried about somebody reporting our plans for Monday."

"That's right."

"I assume you've kept that information close, the way you do everything."

"You're right about that."

"I mean, *I* don't know the details. Does anybody besides you and Peck know what's going down?"

"No."

"I just wondered," Ham said. "Well, if you'll excuse me, I've got some shooting to do." He left John sitting alone at the table. That'll give him something to think about, Ham thought. He went to the armory in the cellar, drew the Barrett's rifle and some ammunition, got the jeep and drove down to the lakeshore. It was Friday; three days to go.

Harry bent and looked over Eddie's shoulder at the computer screen. "Have you come up with anything?"

Eddie shook his head. "Monday's a real quiet day," he said. "No sports events, nothing at all that would draw an important visitor. I mean, there's a convention of furniture dealers in Miami, and a literary festival in Key West, but it's not like the president—or anybody else important—is attending either of them. There's a citrus grower's meeting on Tuesday, and God knows, there's always something going on at Disney World, but we're looking for a prominent target, aren't we?"

"Yes."

"Can you check with the Secret Service and see if the president is planning some unannounced visit on Monday, something that isn't on his published schedule?"

"I'll take care of it," Harry said, then he jumped.

"What's the matter?"

Harry was clawing at his belt. "My phone just goosed me." He snapped it open. "Yeah?"

"It's me," Ham said. "This thing is working, huh?"

"Are you scrambled?"

"Yes. And a good thing, too, because they're monitoring cell phone use with a scanner twenty-four hours a day. Did you do something to jump up the reception out here?"

"Yes, we installed a portable cell. I take it John noticed."

"Right."

"Where are you now?"

"I'm out by the lake. Hang on a second."

Harry listened, and suddenly, the phone seemed to explode in his ear. "Ham?"

"Yeah? Sorry about that; I'm supposed to be practicing shooting."

"Is it safe for you to talk?"

"Yeah, but let's make it quick. I don't have any more information about what they're planning, just that it's on Monday, and it's two or three men in a limo."

"We got that over the smoke detector," Harry said.

"I'll call you back if I get any more information. Tell Holly I'm okay." Ham broke the connection.

Harry snapped his phone shut. "Ham got the phone. Thank God for that."

"Anything new?"

"Nothing. I'd better call the White House."

Ham sat cross-legged, the Barrett's rifle resting on a tripod attached to the gun's barrel. He unplugged the earphone, wound up the cord and stuffed it into a shirt pocket. He dropped the tiny phone in, too. It hardly made a bulge in the baggy fatigue shirt pocket.

He watched the movement of the trees, made a guess about the wind and fired again. He hit a tree, but not the one he was aiming for.

53

Ham finished firing for the morning. He stowed the rifle in the rear of the jeep and was about to get in when he saw a roll of duct tape on the floor of the rear seat, and it gave him an idea.

He lay down on his back in the footwell of the driver's seat and looked under the dash. Satisfied, he tore off a strip of the duct tape, stuck the phone and the three batteries to it, and taped them to the underside of the dash, satisfied that even hard bumps wouldn't dislodge them. Feeling better, he drove back to Peck's house for lunch.

Harry knew the head of the White House Secret Service detail, so he cut some red tape and called him directly. He got a voice mail tape and left a message. Five minutes later, his phone rang.

"Hello?"

"Harry, that you?"

"Chip, how are you, boy?"

"I can't complain, except they're working my ass off. I'm traveling just about all the time. Good thing I'm already divorced."

Harry laughed.

"I heard you got the Miami job. That right?" Chip asked.

"It's right, and I'm away from home right now, too."

"Where?"

"Little town called Orchid Beach, in a rented beach house."

"Sounds like tough duty. What's up?"

"I got a question for you. Is the president going to be in Florida next Monday?"

"Why? You want to take a shot at him?"

"Doesn't everybody?"

"Well, Harry, I can tell you that the president has no official visits outside Washington planned for Monday."

"What about unofficial visits. Anything that's not on the published schedule?"

"What's this about, Harry?"

"I just need to know. It's something I'm working on."

"It sounds like something the Secret Service should be working on," Chip replied.

"Come on, Chip, you know I'd call you if I thought there was a credible threat."

"Do I?"

"Sure you do. I'm not about to get my tit caught in *that* wringer."

"Let me put it this way, Harry: if the president had an unofficial visit to Florida planned for Monday, I couldn't tell you about it."

"I understand, Chip, but you could tell me if he *didn't* have an unofficial visit planned, couldn't you?"

"That depends."

"All right, Chip, what's this going to cost me?"

"The best dinner at the best restaurant in Miami in the company of the best-looking single female FBI agent in your office, the next time I'm down there."

"Oh, so now I'm pimping for you, huh?"

"You think of it any way you like, Harry. That's my price."

"All right, done. Now answer my question."

"I will. If you'd bothered to check the White House website or read the published schedule, or even watch the evening news, then you'd know that the president is receiving the prime minister of Israel and the head of the PLO at the White House on Monday morning, and talks are scheduled for all day."

"You miserable son of a bitch!"

"I'll let you know when I'm going to be in Miami, Harry, probably on short notice. Bye, now." Chip hung up.

Ham arrived back at Peck's house for lunch, just as the meeting in Peck's study was breaking up. Ham went to the john and washed his hands, and when he came out, John was waiting for him.

"Come with me, Ham," he said.

Ham followed him to the cellar, down a hall and into a room equipped as some sort of workshop, where a man wearing a loupe attached to his eyeglasses was working on something, bending close over a workbench.

The man looked up. "Hey, John," he said, "this our guy?"

"It is. Ham, meet Dave, the best document forger in the business. Dave also designs our private currency, which you've seen."

Ham shook the man's hand, and Dave didn't let go immediately. He peered closely at Ham's face. "Good tan," he said. "I'd have preferred to provide that, myself."

Ham had no idea what the man was talking about.

"Come on, Dave, just get it done."

"Well, as I understand it, we don't have time for surgery, so I'll just have to wing it."

"I always enjoy watching this," John said.

"Let's see, graying hair, but darker eyebrows. I think I'll go for a darker mustache, but with some gray in it, and heavier eyebrows." He went to his workbench, opened a large briefcase and began rummaging in it. "Here we go," Dave said. "Stand here, under the light, Ham."

Ham moved as he was directed to.

Dave picked up an eyebrow with a pair of tweezers, painted something on the back and glued it over Ham's own right eyebrow, then he repeated the process with the left one. "Yeah, this is going to work," he said. He went back to the briefcase and came back with a mustache that matched the eyebrows. After a moment, Ham was a different man.

Ham looked at himself in a mirror. "Damn," he said. "Good-looking guy."

"Let's try these, too," Dave said, picking up a pair of heavy, black-rimmed glasses. "You wear glasses, Ham?"

"Just for reading."

"What magnification?"

"Two."

"I can handle that," Dave said, going to a different briefcase and fishing out a pair of lenses. He removed the original lenses and snapped in the new ones. "Nice pair of bifocals," he said, putting the glasses on Ham. "Plain glass at the top, reading glasses at the bottom. How do they feel?"

"Loose," Ham said.

Dave made some adjustments, then returned the glasses to Ham.

Ham put them on and looked in the mirror. He would not have recognized himself, he thought.

"How's that, John?"

"Perfect, Dave."

"Okay, Ham, let's take a couple of pictures of you." He opened a folding screen and stood Ham in front of it. "We got a nice passport-model Polaroid camera here, makes four prints simultaneously." He took the picture, then handed Ham a shirt. "Put this on, and we'll take another."

Ham did as he was told, and his picture was taken again.

"This is all for your protection, Ham," John said. "We don't want anyone who gets a look at you to give an accurate description. We'll get you a hat, too." He began to look through a stack of hats on a table nearby.

"And a cigar is a good idea," Dave said. "Distorts the face."

"Hate 'em," Ham said.

"We won't bother with that," John said, picking out a businesslike straw hat and placing it on Ham's head. "Look, his own mother wouldn't recognize him. You own a suit, Ham?"

"Yes, back at my place."

"I'll send somebody over there to pick it up for you. Let me have a key."

Ham unhooked his house key from a ring and handed it to John.

"We'll burn it after you wear it," John said. "I'll spring for a new one, though."

"I've only got one, and I was thinking of burning it, anyway," Ham said.

Everybody laughed.

54

Holly was visiting Harry's place after dinner on Friday evening, when Eddie, who was listening to his smoke detector bug with a headset, whistled and flipped a switch. John's voice came into the room, but there was some sort of static, too, and there were gaps in the transmission.

"May I have reservations, please," he said. "Hello? My name . . . Owen. . . . I'd like to confirm a reservation I made recently. . . . nights, arriving tomorrow, departing Tuesday morning. No-smoking, that's correct, and I'm on the beach side of the hotel? . . . floor will be fine. Yes, I understand there won't be an ocean view, but I'll be working too hard to enjoy it, anyway. . . . see you tomorrow." He hung up, then he could be heard moving around the room, but he didn't speak and no one entered the room.

"Damn, Eddie, can't you do anything about that reception?"

"No, Harry, it's somewhere between here and a satellite a few hundred miles up."

Harry wrote down the name Owen. "I wonder if that's his real name," he said.

"I doubt it," Doug replied. "The guy's probably got a dozen or more aliases. I think Alton Charlesworth is as close as we're going to get without prints. Even if we ran them, we'd find a CIA hold on the record."

"You're probably right," Harry said.

Then there were two voices in the room. "Hey," Peck's voice said. "We all set on paperwork?"

"Dave's working on it now. We took the photographs, and they look great. He'll have everything ready before he goes to bed tonight. Has Ham turned in?"

"Yeah, he left a few minutes ago."

"Does he still have the jeep?"

"No, I've got it."

"Let me have the keys. I want to take a drive out to the strip and make sure the machine is ready."

"I took care of the list you gave me," Peck said.

John's voice took on a new tone. "Peck, are you carrying your cell phone?"

"Yeah, sure. I always do."

"Make any calls today?"

"No."

"Let me have it, will you?"

"Sure, here. I'd like it back tomorrow."

"I know you would, but I may need it more than you."

"Whatever you say, John." Peck sounded abashed.

"Good night."

"Good night, John."

The door could be heard to close, then a television came on.

"He's listening to the Weather Channel," Harry said. "The seven-day forecast. I wish we knew for sure which city, and especially, which hotel."

"It's near a beach," Doug replied.

"Like half the hotels in Florida."

Ham woke up the following morning to find himself alone. When he had returned to the bunkhouse the night before, his companions and their luggage had gone.

"Hello!" a voice called from outside.

"Yeah, hello!" Ham called back.

A young man Ham had never seen before came into the barracks carrying a cooler. "Breakfast," he said.

"Breakfast in bed?"

"If that's where you want it," the young man replied. "It's all there, what you usually have. John said to tell you you're to stay here this morning, until he sends for you."

"Something special about Saturday mornings?" Ham asked.

"Just the gun show. But you're confined to barracks until further notice." He smiled, waved and left.

Ham opened the cooler to find hot scrambled eggs and sausage, juice and a Thermos of coffee. He ate breakfast slowly, then showered and shaved and lay back down on his bunk in his shorts. He had nothing to read, no television to watch. He was bored. Then he noticed his blue suit hanging on a hook near the door. Someone must have put it there during the night, he thought. He decided to go back to sleep.

Harry was eating breakfast when Eddie waved at him and turned up the volume on the radio. Lake Winachobee was on the air again.

"Good morning," John's voice said. "This is November one, two, three, tango foxtrot. Would you please brief me for an IFR flight from Vero Beach to Miami, Opa-Locka, departing at seven P.M. local? I'll go low, six thousand." There was a wait as John listened to the forecast. "I'll file," he said, finally. "IFR, November one, two, three, tango foxtrot; I'm a PA forty-six stroke golf, departing Vero Beach at seven P.M. local, at six thousand. My route of flight will be Palm Beach, direct; destination is Opa-Locka; time en route, one hour. I have two and one-half hours of fuel. My name is John Wills, based Vero Beach, my phone number is (561) 555-0022. The airplane is white over gray; there will be four souls aboard. Under comments, note that I'll take off VFR and pick up my clearance in the air. Thanks, goodbye." He hung up and apparently left the room.

"You get all that?" Harry asked Doug, who was taking notes.

"Yep."

"Get somebody at the FAA out of his backyard pool and check out the ownership of that airplane, then check out the local phone number and the name John Wills. We're on the move."

"Hang on," Doug said, "the event isn't scheduled until Monday, and we don't know if Ham is going to be on that airplane."

"We'll find that out from a stakeout at Opa-Locka," Harry said. "We'll be following them wherever they go." He got on the phone to his office and his deputy. "Mark, I want you to get the loan of one of the DEA's tracking helicopters. I want the pilot to follow, but not interfere with, a light aircraft, a PA forty-six, whatever that is. I believe it's going to take off from a grass strip west of Vero Beach, heading for Opa-Locka, Miami, and the pilot will probably pick up an IFR clearance in the air. Tell him to listen in on Miami Center and get the squawk code that the Center assigns the airplane; that will make it easier to track. Set up a radio link with the chopper, so that we're in constant touch, and warn the pilot to be ready for the aircraft to suddenly change airports and go somewhere else. Above all, *he is not to lose that airplane!*"

"Got it," Mark replied.

"Next, I want you to set up a multiple-vehicle surveillance team to meet that aircraft at Opa-Locka and follow the occupants wherever they go. There should be four aboard. They're departing around seven o'clock local and should be landing in Opa-Locka an hour later, but you be ready two hours before that, and be prepared for a later landing."

"You got any idea of their destination?"

"A hotel near the beach. That's all we know."

"Anything else?"

"Yes, access the military service record of one Hamilton Barker, retired army chief master sergeant, get his photograph and try to determine if he's one of the four men aboard. I want you to photograph all four men when they land, and I'll want to see those shots the minute you take them."

"Where are you going to be?"

"I want our airplane to meet me at the Vero Beach Airport at six o'clock. I want to land ahead of the PA forty-six, and I want you to have a car there so I can run the car surveillance."

"I'll have him there."

Harry gave him the scrambled cell phone number. "Use that number when I'm on the ground. You can call me on the sat phone in the airplane. Now get going!"

"Oh, Harry, I almost forgot. You got a call from Chip Beckham from the Secret Service?"

"Yeah? Does he want me to call him back?"

"He said that wouldn't be necessary, and anyway, he'll be traveling. He said he was going to be in Miami tonight, and he's calling in your debt. He said you'd know what he meant. He gave me a cell phone number for you to get him on in Miami."

Harry jotted down the number. "Thanks, Mark." A second after he hung up, he realized what Chip's phone call meant. "Holy shit!" he yelled.

"What?" Eddie asked.

"Check the White House website and get the president's published schedule for today and tomorrow."

"Just take a sec," Eddie said, tapping some computer keys. "Here we are. Nothing for today or tomorrow."

Then what was Chip going to be doing in Miami?

The young man brought Ham lunch and dinner, too. "Be ready to leave here at six-thirty," he said. "John says wear the blue suit, shirt and tie and carry your shaving stuff and a change of clothes. Oh, and wear the disguise," he said, then left Ham alone.

Ham checked his watch. He had just enough time to eat and dress, but no opportunity to get at his cell phone, which was still taped under the dash of the jeep, unless someone had found it.

He was worried. He had expected to leave the compound on Monday morning and to have plenty of time to call Harry or Holly. He didn't like this at all.

He finished his dinner, then dressed in the suit and stuck the mustache and eyebrows on, the way Dave had taught him. He put the glasses in his pocket and tried on the hat. He looked like any salesman in the state of Florida, he thought.

He heard a vehicle stop outside, and Peck came to the door. "You ready?" he asked.

"Yep." He grabbed his bag and walked out the door. John was waiting in the jeep.

"You look great, Ham," John said.

"Thanks. I'll drive, if you like." He had to get near that cell phone.

"Nah, I'll drive," Peck replied.

Ham wanted to hit him.

55

Holly, with Daisy, arrived breath-lessly at the airport and found Harry waiting for her in the Sun Jet Aviation lounge. "I couldn't get anybody to stay with Daisy on such short notice. What's up?" she asked. "Where are we going?"

Harry took her suitcase and gave Daisy a pat. "They're on the move," he said, "and I think Ham is with them." He headed out of the building and across the ramp toward a King Air.

"But it wasn't supposed to go down until Monday."

"As far as we know, it still might. John has a hotel reservation until Tuesday morning, under the name Owen, but that's the only name we've got."

"What hotel?"

"We don't know. We just picked this up on the smoke detector bug." He stowed her luggage on the airplane, and they got in and buckled up. Doug was already aboard. Daisy settled into the seat next to Holly as if she flew every day.

"So do we have any idea of who the target is yet?"

"No, we don't. John has filed a flight plan for Opa-Locka airport. We're going to beat him there and keep him under surveillance until we know what's happening. I thought you'd like to be there."

"You're right," she replied. "Thanks. Is somebody listening in on the bug?"

"Eddie's still at the house, and the NSA is recording everything."

The pilot started the engines and, after a couple of minutes, taxied to the runway. A moment later, they were in the air, flying down the coast.

"Has Ham used the scrambled cell phone again?" Holly asked.

"No, not a word from him."

"Harry, why did you tell me to bring my sexiest dress?"

"There's someone I want you to meet. It's a surprise."

"Harry, I'm not interested in matchmaking. It's too soon."

"It's not that, Holly, it's work. I'll explain later."

Peck drove the jeep out to the landing strip, where John's airplane had already been towed out of the hangar. They began loading luggage aboard, and Ham tried to work his way into a position where he could grab the cell phone from under the dash.

"The Barrett's rifle is in the large suitcase," John said. "We've broken it down."

"Good," Ham said.

"Climb aboard. I want you in the copilot's seat, next to me."

Ham moved toward the airplane. When everyone was well away from the jeep, he stopped and felt his pockets. "I think I dropped my pen in the jeep," he said. "I'll just be a minute."

"Take your time," John replied. "I've got to do a preflight, anyway." He removed a fuel cap from the airplane and began walking around the fuselage.

Ham walked quickly toward the jeep, pretending to look for the pen. He looked back at the airplane: Peck was already on board, and

John was on the opposite side. Quickly, he leaned into the driver's-side footwell, yanked the duct tape off and, with his back to the airplane, got the phone and the three batteries into a pocket. He wadded and dropped the tape, retrieved a pen from his inside pocket and walked back to the airplane, the pen in his hand.

"Find it?" Peck asked as he got aboard.

Ham held up the pen for him to see. He made his way forward, slipped into the copilot's seat and buckled in.

John slid in beside him. "Everything's in good order," he said. "You and I will talk when we're in the air and I've gotten my clearance."

He started the engine, worked his way through a checklist, then taxied to the end of the grass strip. He did a quick runup, then put in some flaps, adjusted the trim and slowly pushed the throttle up to full power. After a brief check of the instruments, he released the brakes and the airplane began to roll.

More than halfway down the strip, John pulled back on the yoke and they were airborne, flying into the setting sun. He retracted the landing gear and the flaps, then turned to the east. The moon was rising, waning now, but still big.

Ham put on a headset that was hanging on the yoke in front of him. "Beautiful night," he said.

John held up a hand for silence. "Miami Center," he said, pressing a button on the yoke. "November one, two, three, tango foxtrot is off of Vero Beach, IFR to Miami Opa-Locka. Do you have a clearance for me?"

"This is Miami Center. You're in luck tonight. You're cleared direct Opa-Locka."

"Thank you, Center, direct Opa-Locka." He turned to Ham. "That's never happened before," he said. "Usually, my routing is more complicated."

"That will make the trip quicker, then?"

"By a few minutes." He leveled at six thousand feet and announced his altitude to Center. After a few minutes to lean the engine, he turned on the autopilot, sat back and turned to Ham, opening a zippered envelope and extracting an envelope. He handed it to Ham. "This is your identity," he said.

Ham opened the envelope and emptied the contents into his lap. He found a wallet, a passport and an airline ticket. Inside the wallet was a driver's license, some credit cards, a social security card and some photographs of a plump woman and some children.

"You're Owen Sanford," John said, "and the ticket and the stamps in the passport say you've just landed in Miami on a flight that lands about now, that originated in Cairo."

"So, if I'm arrested, it'll look like there's a Middle Eastern connection?"

"Right, but don't worry, you're not going to be arrested."

"Can I know now who my target is?"

"No, it's better that you don't for the time being."

"If you say so," Ham replied.

"Do you have anything in your pockets that might identify you?"

Ham handed over his wallet and made a show of patting his pockets.

"How about the pen you retrieved? Let's see that."

Ham showed him the pen. It was a stationery store ballpoint, undistinguished.

"You can keep that," John said. "Anything else? Even the smallest thing could identify you."

"John, if I get caught, my fingerprints will identify me," Ham said.

"You're right, of course, but we'll deal with the fingerprint problem. You having any second thoughts about your mission?"

"No," Ham replied.

"Would the identity of your target make a difference?"

"No. I trust you to make that judgment. I think of myself as a tool."

"Good," John said, with some satisfaction. "Excuse me, I have to make a phone call." He flipped a switch on the instrument panel, then dialed a number on what appeared to be a cell phone on his yoke.

Ham realized that the switch had isolated the pilot's intercom from the rest of the airplane. He couldn't hear what John was saying, and he wasn't all that good a lip-reader.

The King Air was taxiing to the terminal at Opa-Locka when the onboard telephone rang, and Harry picked it up. "Yeah? Thanks."

He hung up the phone and leaned back. "John's airplane is in the air, and they've cleared him direct. He'll be here soon."

The airplane came to a stop before the terminal and the pilot shut down the engines.

"Get this thing in a hangar and close the doors," Harry said to the pilot, then he led the way off the airplane. "They'll put the luggage in my car," he said to Holly. "Follow me."

He walked over to the base of the tower and picked up a phone. "This is Harry Crisp, FBI," he said into it, and the door buzzed open. They got into an elevator and rode to the top.

Harry shook hands with the controller supervisor.

"Anything you need?" the man asked.

"Three pairs of the best binoculars you've got," Harry said.

The man produced three large pairs of binoculars, and they sat down to wait.

56

It had started to rain. Harry, Doug, Holly and Daisy sat in the semidarkness of the tower and waited, watching airplanes land on the shiny runways, their landing lights flaring on the streaked windows of the tower.

Then suddenly: "Opa-Locka Tower, November one, two, three, tango foxtrot, with you, descending out of six thousand feet."

"One, two, three, tango foxtrot, this is Opa-Locka Tower, radar contact, enter a right base for twenty-seven right, cleared to land."

"Okay," Harry said to the supervisor, "when he contacts ground, I want you to have the lineman direct him to taxi right there," he said, pointing to a well-lit area in front of the terminal.

"Got that?" the supervisor asked the ground controller.

"Got it. I'll call him."

"Doug, is our photographer in place?"

"On the second floor, in the terminal building."

The airplane taxied onto the ramp and, directed into the light by the lineman, came to a stop. Harry, Doug and Holly had a clear view of the door.

The airplane sat, its engine idling. Holly stood, staring through the binoculars. "Why isn't he cutting the engine?" she asked.

"He's waiting for the oil in the turbochargers to cool down," Harry replied. "It'll take four or five minutes."

As they watched, a gray minivan drove onto the ramp and stopped near the airplane.

"Doug," Harry said, "let the terminal know that I want that van delayed at the gate until our people are in place."

Doug picked up a phone.

The airplane's engine finally stopped. The airstair door opened, and a man got out.

"Who's that?" Doug asked.

"It's Peck Rawlings," Holly said. "I met him at the gun show."

A second man, wearing a suit and a straw hat got out.

"How about him?"

Holly said nothing. She was staring through the binoculars. She didn't recognize the second man, but something about him was familiar.

A third man alit from the airplane.

"That's John," Harry said. "But where the hell is Ham?"

All three men had scurried into the van to get out of the rain, while the van driver loaded their luggage, which was only a few cases. He got in and drove toward the gate.

"Well, shit," Harry said.

"Are we going to run this surveillance if Ham isn't here?" Doug asked.

"I'm thinking about that," Harry said, staring out the window.

"It's Ham," Holly said suddenly.

"What?"

"The second man, the one in the suit and hat. It's Ham."

"Are you sure? It didn't look like Ham."

"It's Ham. I can tell by the way he moved."

"We're on," Harry said. "Let's get out of here." He thanked the tower supervisor and led the way down the stairs to a waiting FBI car.

The van drove up to the gate and stopped, but it didn't open.

"What's happening with the gate?" John asked the driver.

"I don't know." He rolled down the window and pushed the button on the intercom. "I'm at the gate, and it's not opening," he said into the instrument.

"We've been having problems with it," a woman's voice said. "Hang on just a minute."

"Your luggage is in the trunk," the FBI driver said, as they got in.

"Everybody in place?" Harry asked.

"Yes, sir."

"Tell 'em it's okay to open the gate."

They watched as the van moved through the opening.

Harry accepted a handheld radio from the driver. "This is number one; we're moving."

They waited until the gate closed behind the van, then drove up to it and out of the ramp area.

"Can you see them?" Harry asked the driver.

"No, sir, but I've got confirmation on my earpiece that they're in sight up ahead. We'll be working a four-vehicle pattern. They'll never know."

"I hope you're right," Harry said.

Following directions from the radio, they headed toward Miami Beach.

Ham, John and Peck all sat in the rear seat at John's direction, even though it was cramped.

"Ham," John said, "start handing our luggage from the rear up here."

Ham didn't understand, but he did as he was told.

"You hold on to the rifle. I'll take your bag."

"What's going on?" Peck asked.

"You'll see in a minute," John replied.

"Who's behind the van now?" Harry said into the radio.

"Car four."

"Can you see inside?"

"Not really. The windows have that dark vinyl stuff on them."

"How close are you?"

"Two cars between me and them."

"Drop back another car. I don't want to crowd them."

"Yes, sir."

Traffic was fairly heavy. Ham, who was sitting on the right side of the van, looked out and saw another van, a maroon one, keeping pace with them in the right lane.

"We'll do it at the traffic light," John said. "Ham, get ready to open the door."

Ham put his hand on the door handle.

The van came to a stop, and the maroon van stopped beside it, only inches away.

"Let's go," John said. "Open the door and get into the other van, Ham."

Ham slid the door open, just as the left-hand door of the maroon van opened. He tossed the rifle across, then stepped into the other van and sat down. Peck and John followed him, and the doors to both vans slid closed, clearly by remote control. "Go," John said, as the light changed. "You know the drill."

The driver made a right turn and sped away.

"Have you made the change?" Harry said into the radio. "Who's behind the van now?"

"Car two," a voice responded.

They drove along in silence for a few minutes.

"Not moving very fast, are they?" Doug said.

"I guess they don't want to risk a traffic stop," Harry replied.

"Car one, this is car two."

"I'm here," Harry said into the radio.

"Something strange. The van just pulled into a McDonald's."

"Pass it by," Harry said. "Next car, pull into the McDonald's. Everybody else pull over and wait for instructions. Who knew they would get hungry?"

The driver stopped the car. Everyone waited. Five minutes passed. Harry picked up the radio. "What's happening?"

"Car four is in the McDonald's parking lot. The driver got out and went in alone."

"Is there a big line for food?"

"No, sir. He ordered a Big Mac, and he's sitting there alone, eating it."

"Oh, shit," Harry said. "We've been had."

57

The driver of the van seemed to be working his way west, making frequent turns.

"Anybody behind us?" John asked, after twenty minutes.

"We're clean," the driver replied.

"Then go on as planned."

Peck spoke up. "Aren't we going to the hotel?" he asked.

John didn't speak, just held a finger to his lips for silence. They drove on.

Ham didn't understand any of it.

"This will do," John said, finally.

The van stopped. They were on a narrow paved road, and from what Ham could see in the headlights through the wet windshield, they seemed to be in a swampy area. He could see no house lights.

"Peck," John said, "I want to speak to you privately for a moment." He got out of the van, and Peck followed him, giving Ham a shrug and a mystified look.

The two men walked behind the van. Almost immediately, there was a pistol shot, and a moment later, another.

Ham thought, 7.65 millimeter.

A long moment passed, then John got back into the van, this time in the front seat. "Now we'll go to the hotel," he said.

The driver made a U-turn, and they went back the way they had come. Ham saw a foot protruding from a ditch as they passed where Peck's body lay.

"Peck was an informant for somebody, probably the FBI," John said quietly.

"How did you know?" Ham asked.

"A number of things: the sudden improvement in cell phone service at the compound, and Peck was the only one left with a cell phone. Even our flight clearance tonight. We would never, in the normal course of events, be cleared direct to a Miami airport. It just doesn't happen, unless someone is paving the way. There were other things, too: odd behavior. I really began to notice only after the cell-phone incident."

Ham realized that he had probably gotten Peck killed.

Holly could see that Harry was angry and depressed.

"They changed cars somehow," Harry said. "I should have been behind them myself."

"What now?" Holly asked. They were driving along the main drag in South Beach.

"I'm taking you to your hotel," Harry said.

The van pulled up in front of the Delano. It was a terribly chic South Beach hotel that Holly knew only from magazines. "I hope they like dogs," she said, clipping on Daisy's leash.

"If they give you a hard time, flash your badge and tell them Daisy is a police dog." Harry got out of the car, got Holly's luggage from the trunk and handed it to a bellman. He took Holly's arm and walked her slowly toward the door. "Now, listen," he said. "You've got the most important job in all this. You're having dinner in the hotel's restaurant at nine o'clock, with a guy named Chip Beckham."

"Harry, what is this about?" Holly demanded.

"Chip is the head of the White House Secret Service detail," Harry said. "Your job is to find out if the president is in Miami and to get his complete schedule from Chip."

"I don't understand. Why don't you just ask him?"

"Chip and I have this little competitive thing," Harry said. "He won't tell me directly."

"You mean the head of the Miami FBI office is not entitled to know if the president is on his turf?"

"Normally, yes, if I went through a lot of red tape, but there's no Miami visit on the president's official schedule, and Chip won't tell me about any unofficial visit."

"Then, if the president is in town, you think he's the target?"

"Very probably."

"And do you plan to share this information with the head of the White House Secret Service detail?"

"At the appropriate moment," Harry said, "and we're not there yet. First, I have to know if the president is in town and what he's doing."

"Harry, if this guy makes a pass at me over dinner, I'm going to stab him with a steak knife."

"If he makes a pass at you, you have my full permission to do just that."

"Does he know who I am?"

"No, only your name and that he's meeting you."

"Oh, all right," Holly said. "How do I reach you?"

"I'll reach you on your scrambled cell phone," Harry said. "Now, just go in there and register. The room's all booked, and you're the guest of the Bureau, so live it up." He left her standing in the door, which was being held open by another bellman.

Holly did not like all these games. If she were running this investigation she'd have called in everybody but the marines by now. And she doubted seriously if this was the most important job. She felt shoved aside and out of the way. Harry wasn't going to share any credit, if he could help it.

The van stopped at the entrance to the Savoy, a large hotel across the boulevard from the beach that had seen better days.

"Just go in there and register as Owen Sanford," John said. "You have a reservation; go up to your room and wait. I'll be right behind you."

Ham got out of the van, got his bag and the case containing the Barrett's rifle, and handed them to a bellman. Five minutes later, he was getting onto an elevator. Just as the doors were closing, John stopped them and got on, not looking at Ham.

"What's my room number?" Ham asked the bellman.

"Two-ten, Mr. Sanford," the bellman replied. "It's a very nice corner room, larger than most."

The elevator stopped, and Ham and the bellman got off. John got off, too, but turned in the opposite direction from Ham. The bellman opened the room door, got Ham settled, collected his tip, then left.

All Ham wanted to do was to use the phone, but as he was lifting it from the receiver, there was a knock on the door. Ham opened it and let John, who was carrying a small bag, into the room.

John looked around the room, then spent a moment looking out the window. It was an L-shaped room, with two sets of windows, set at ninety degrees from each other. "Perfect," he said. He went to the phone and dialed the operator. "This is Mr. Sanford in two-ten," he said. "Please hold all my calls until further notice." He hung up. "How about some dinner, Ham?"

"Sure, I'm hungry."

John found a room service menu, then called in their order.

Ham noticed that when he hung up the phone, he disconnected the cord from both the phone and the wall, rolled it up and slipped it into his pocket. So much for getting a call out of here, Ham thought. He discreetly patted his pocket to be sure the cell phone was still there.

Daisy lay on the bed and watched Holly get dressed. "Don't look at me like that," Holly said to her. "You're going to stay here and watch TV." She switched on the set and found CNN. Daisy liked CNN. She gave Daisy a pat and left the room. Then—scrubbed, shampooed, made up and lightly perfumed—she walked into the Delano's restaurant, wearing a straight, tight, low-cut brown wool dress that accentuated her height and figure and looked good with her tan. Men around the room turned to look at her, but one stepped up and spoke to her.

"Holly Barker?"

"Yes."

"I'm Chip Beckham," he said. He was a little taller than she, in his mid-forties, fit and good-looking in a conventional sort of way. Holly thought that, with his short haircut and erect bearing, he looked like a military man in civilian clothes.

"Hello, Chip," she said, giving him a big smile.

"Would you like a drink at the bar, or would you like to go to the table now?"

"Let's go to the table," she said.

"I've asked them to put us on the terrace. I hope that's all right."

"Of course. It's a beautiful night."

The headwaiter led them to a good table overlooking the pool. The moon and the stars were out. Holly felt distinctly odd. She had thought she would never have a dinner date with any man except Jackson.

A waiter appeared. "Would you like a drink?"

"A vodka gimlet," Holly said.

"A martini, very dry," Chip said.

"Well," Chip said, when their drinks had arrived. "You're certainly the most beautiful FBI agent I've ever met."

"Thank you, but I'm not an FBI agent. I'm the chief of police in a little town about three hours north of here called Orchid Beach."

"Oh? The terms of my deal with Harry were that he'd buy me dinner at the best restaurant in Miami, with the most beautiful, single FBI agent in his office. Not that I'm complaining."

Holly looked at him. "This was a bet?"

"No, just a trade for information."

"Well, Chip," Holly said, "this is a very weird way to meet, but cheers." She raised her glass.

58

Ham tried to sleep, but couldn't. He lay on one of the two queen-sized beds in the big room, while John slept soundly on the other. It was only ten-thirty, but John had insisted on going to bed early.

"Big day tomorrow," he had said.

He had to try to contact somebody. Ham got out of bed and in the darkened room, felt his way toward the bathroom. On the way, he got the cell phone out of his suit pocket and took it with him, closing the door behind him. He dropped his shorts, sat on the toilet and switched on the phone. He searched his memory for Holly's scrambled number. Finally, it came to him, and he dialed. It rang several times, then he heard Holly's voice.

"Hello?"

Suddenly, the door to the bathroom opened. Ham managed to close the phone and conceal it in his large hand before the light came on. John stood there, looking sleepily at him.

"What is it, John?" Ham asked, making himself sound annoyed.

"What are you doing?"

"What the fuck does it look like I'm doing? Can I have some privacy?"

"Sorry," John said, flipping off the light. "But leave the door open."

Holly was enjoying her evening. She'd had two gimlets, and Chip two martinis, and now the waiter brought a bottle of wine with their dinner. She and Chip had exchanged curricula vitae, and she had listened to his brief account of his divorce, and now she was at the point when the natural thing to do was to tell Chip about Jackson.

"What about you?" Chip asked, helping her along.

"I was engaged, but he died," she said, keeping it simple.

"I'm sorry. Long ago?"

"Not very long."

"And how did you get tied up with Harry?"

"We worked on something together last year, something on my turf in Orchid Beach."

"Wait a minute, I know about that," he said. "It was that crazy subdivision. There was a huge amount of currency involved, and it was all over the papers."

"My fifteen minutes of near-fame," she said.

"So what are you working on with Harry now? And what is it that he wants from me? He certainly didn't put us together because he's a nice guy."

"It's pretty simple," she said. "He wants to know if the president is in town."

"No," Chip said, "he isn't. Is work over now?"

"Work's over," she said, raising her wineglass. "Bon appétit."

"Bon appétit," he replied.

And then something, she didn't know what, caused her to put her hand on her small purse, which was resting on the table. She felt the vibration. How long had it been doing that?

She clawed at the handbag, got out the phone and snapped it open. "Hello?"

She heard a click at the other end, then silence.

"What is it?" Chip asked.

"Just a minute." She conjured up Harry's scrambled cell phone number and dialed it.

"Yeah?" Harry's sleepy voice answered.

"It's Holly. Did you call me?"

"No."

"Then Ham did."

Harry was suddenly wide awake. "Tell me."

"Nothing to tell. As soon as I answered, he punched off."

"He has the phone," Harry said, a note of triumph in his voice.

"He has it, but he apparently is having trouble finding a way to use it."

"They've got to be watching him like a hawk," Harry said. "What time is it?"

"Ten-thirty or so."

"You still with Chip?"

"Yes, and the president is not in town."

"Thank God for that," Harry said. "Call me if you hear from Ham again."

"Will do." She closed the phone, but she didn't put it back in the bag. Instead, she left it on the table near her hand.

"What's up?" Chip asked.

"Nothing, apparently."

"Who's Ham?"

"My father. I've been hoping he'd call."

"Was that Harry you called?"

"Yes."

"And he hopes to hear from your father, too?"

"Yes."

"This is all about some operation of Harry's, isn't it?"

"Yes."

"And you can't tell me about it?"

"No," she said.

"Not even if I beg?"

"No, not yet."

He poured more wine in her glass.

"You trying to get me drunk, Chip?"

"I'm already drunk," he replied, "so you must be, too."

"I can't tell you about it."

"Finish your wine," he said. "Think of all those winos out on the streets with nothing to drink, and there you are wasting it."

59

Holly woke early, and when she sat up, she had to lie down again. She hadn't drunk that much in a long time, or been as hung over. Finally, she managed to stand and get to the bathroom, where she was desperate to find her toothbrush.

Suddenly, she was ravenously hungry. She phoned room service for a big breakfast, then got into a shower and finished it off by standing under cold water until she was fully conscious. She toweled her hair dry, and stood looking at herself in the mirror. It made her feel better that she was in better shape than a lot of women ten years younger than she. The doorbell rang, disturbing her reverie.

She got into a robe and directed the waiter to a table by the window, overlooking the beach and the sea. She signed, leaving a very generous tip from the FBI, and, after feeding Daisy, sat down to eat. Halfway through the waffles and sausage she had so craved a few minutes before, she felt ill and had to stop eating. She was paying for her pleasures.

The evening had ended well, with Chip not getting pushy. She had given him her number at home, knowing that he would never get to Orchid Beach, and she had gotten the information Harry needed from him without trading her virtue for it. Harry could never have done that, she thought smugly.

The phone rang, and she snatched it from its cradle. "Hello?"

"It's Harry."

"What's happening?"

"We think that Ham is registered in a hotel under the name of Owen, so I've got half a dozen agents phoning every hotel near the beach and checking on that name. We ought to have something by noon."

"What am I supposed to do until noon?" she asked.

"Anything you like, just keep that scrambled cell phone handy. If you hear from Ham, find out where he is and who the target is and call me back."

"You have no idea who the target might be?"

"None. Not one of the official schedules—governor, senators, congressmen—shows anything in the city today. I almost wish the target were the president, because that would be easier to handle in a lot of ways. I'll call you if I hear from Ham first." He punched out.

Well, the hell with sitting around here all morning, Holly thought. "I'm going to the beach." She started rummaging in her bag for a swimsuit. Harry had told her to be ready to dress for anything, and she was, with a bikini. She clipped the little cell phone onto her watchband, so she'd be sure to feel it if it went off, grabbed a tote and a towel and headed for the pool, Daisy in tow.

Ham and John were having breakfast together, and John seemed a little off his feed, Ham thought. John had ordered a

Bloody Mary with his breakfast, and he looked as though he needed a refill.

"So, tell me more about The Elect," Ham said, casually, chewing on a piece of toast.

"What do you want to know?" John asked.

"The works: who are we, where are we, how many are we—anything you'd care to tell me."

"We're a tightly knit organization with a couple of dozen branches in nearly as many states—three here in Florida."

"Oh? Where?"

"Well, you know Lake Winachobee, then there's Tampa and Fort Lauderdale."

"How many members nationwide?"

"Nearly three thousand."

"Wow, it's amazing that you could get so much done with so few people."

"If you have the right three thousand, you can move the earth."

"I guess we're going to move it a little today, huh?"

"You are, Ham. You're going to do it all by yourself."

"I won't disappoint you, John. By the way, Peck told me about the bank job in Orchid Beach." This was a lie, but it was worth trying. "Wasn't that a little close to home?"

"You're damn right it was," John said, angrily. "One of Peck's people killed somebody, and for his trouble, he got a bullet in the brain."

"Why did Peck let that happen?"

"Peck wouldn't go on the job himself. That was one of the things that made me start suspecting him."

"Well, at least you raised some money."

"And another thing," John said. "We had this guy planted in the bank on an entirely separate operation, and after the robbery, he panicked and ran."

"I think I read about that in the paper. Was that the couple found in their car in the Indian River?"

"Right, and we never found the money they were stealing for us. Another job screwed up by Peck." John looked thoughtful. "You know, with Peck out of the picture, someone is going to have to run Winachobee. Would you like the job?"

"You think I'm right for it?"

"Oh, I think you're right for bigger things than Winachobee, but you've got to start somewhere."

"Sounds good to me, John."

"Starting today, you're going to be learning a lot more about the organization," John said. "And after today, you're going to be a hero in the group."

"Hold it right there," Ham said. "Who knows I'm pulling the trigger today?"

"Only the board. That's who I was referring to."

"Do they already know who I am?"

"Yes."

"Make sure nobody else knows."

"I understand your concern, Ham, and I'll do that."

"One more thing," Ham said.

"What's that?"

"Who am I killing today?"

"I don't believe it," Harry said. "Not a single Owen in any hotel in Miami Beach?"

"There was an Elizabeth Owen in one, but that didn't pan out. We've called them all," Doug said. "They all have a search engine on their computers, so it only takes them a few seconds to find out. What are we going to do?"

Harry looked at his watch; it was nearly noon. "We're going to hope to God we hear from Ham," he said.

Holly was stretched languidly on a chaise by the Delano's pool, watching the young go by, when her wrist suddenly vibrated.

She sat up and grabbed the phone. "Ham?"

"One and the same," he drawled. "Don't talk, listen: I'm in a hotel called the Savoy, room two-ten. I'm to start shooting in an hour or so, maybe sooner."

"Who's the target?" she asked.

"You're not going to—" Ham stopped talking.

"Ham?"

Silence.

"Ham, talk to me!"

Nothing.

Holly grabbed her stuff and started running. "Come on, Daisy," she yelled.

60

Holly hit the Delano lobby still running. People stared at her as she impatiently banged on the elevator button. She finally made it to her room, threw on a skirt and a T-shirt over her bikini, stuck her feet into her sneakers, grabbed her phone, purse, weapon, badge and Daisy and started running again, punching numbers into the cell phone. Harry's line was busy.

Ham set the tripod up at the bedroom window, which was perpendicular to the street, rather than parallel. John watched him in silence. Ham was still breathing hard from the fright John had given him when he came unexpectedly out of the bathroom while Ham was on the phone to Holly. He had told her what he could, but not the target's name, which he had not had time to speak.

John moved to the window. "There," he said, pointing. "The car will slow as it turns into the drive of the Berkeley Hotel, and that's your moment. The car will begin its turn, and the rear window will face you for that split second. That's when you fire. You agree?"

"I agree," Ham said. "It's perfect, like you said. And look at the palms: no wind; dead calm. We couldn't ask for more."

Ham pulled the curtains nearly shut, then fixed the Barrett's rifle to the tripod. Then he emptied all of the ammunition clips onto the bed.

"What are you doing?" John asked.

Ham got a pair of latex gloves from his bag and slipped them on. "I'm going to wipe every round, every shell casing clean of prints, then the rifle." He gave John another pair of the surgical gloves. "Put these on and start wiping down the whole room, everything from the phone to the flusher on the john, and I mean *everything*. I am *not* going to get caught doing this, now or later."

"Good man," John said, pulling on the gloves. "And I guarantee you, Ham, you won't get caught. Steps have been taken."

"I think it's time you started telling me about those steps," Ham said.

"Okay, here's how it goes: We're ready to move, so when you fire, we don't stay around to gloat. We go directly to the fire stairs, leaving the rifle here, but taking our personal stuff. You're wearing your disguise, of course. A van will be waiting for us where the fire stairs end in the rear parking lot, where the restaurant garbage is collected. The van takes us straight to Opa-Locka, and we fly out of here, back to Winachobee."

"Sounds good." He went to the window, and as he looked out, he saw a flash from a hotel room window across the street. John's binoculars were lying on the bed; he picked them up and trained them on the window. What he saw froze his blood.

Holly elbowed another woman out of the way and leapt into a cab. "Hotel Savoy," she said to the driver. "You know it?"

"Sure," said the driver laconically. "I can be there in fifteen minutes, but no dogs."

She showed him her badge. "It's a police dog. Stand on it; I want to be there in five."

"Look lady," he driver said, "I don't care if you show me a badge. I'm not losing my license for you, and I told you, no dogs."

"You want me to show you my gun?"

"Yeah, sure." He chuckled.

"Daisy, get in the front seat."

Daisy hopped lightly into the passenger seat.

"Guard."

Daisy made a low growling noise and showed her teeth.

The man froze. "You get that dog out of my car!"

Holly got out on the driver's side, opened his door, grabbed him by the belt and yanked him into the street. She got in, slammed the car into gear, went about ten feet and stopped. "Back seat, Daisy." She put the car in reverse and backed up swiftly to the stunned driver, who had gotten to his feet. She grabbed him by the front of his shirt. "Where's the Savoy?" she demanded. "And be quick about it."

Ham suddenly realized that he was about to be awarded the Lee Harvey Oswald Memorial Prize. What he saw through the binoculars was another set of hotel room curtains, across the street, drawn to leave a gap of a foot like his and, like his, with the muzzle of a Barrett's rifle just visible. And it was pointed directly at his own window.

Harry's line was still busy. Holly had reached eighty miles an hour on the boulevard, her emergency lights flashing, one hand on the horn. Hotels were flashing by her window at an alarming rate, and in the distance, she saw a building of, perhaps, fifteen stories, and high atop it was a neon sign reading Savoy. "Yes!" she said. Then a car ahead of her stupidly swung into her lane. She heard the crunch of metal on metal.

Ham, looking down the boulevard, saw a taxi, moving fast, swing into oncoming traffic, leaving a fender attached to another car, then swing two lanes to the right to get around a UPS truck, then move back into the left lane, horn blaring, lights flashing. A block behind it, a police car had turned on its flashers and was giving chase. Still farther down the boulevard, the street was empty. Something had stopped traffic. As the taxi made a wide turn into the Savoy, Ham looked a quarter of a mile up the empty street and saw a dozen sets of flashing lights, led by a platoon of motorcycles. In the midst of them was a long, black limousine, with flags flying from its front fenders.

"The time is now, Ham," John said.

Ham turned and looked at him. He was standing as far away as he could get, sweating as if air conditioning had never been invented, and he was holding a 9mm semiautomatic pistol in his hand, pointed at Ham.

"You think you need a gun to get me to do this?" Ham asked.

He turned back to the window, grabbed the Barrett's rifle, smacked a clip home and sighted through the scope, his finger resting lightly on the trigger. This was going to make a mess; he hoped no innocent bystanders would get hurt, but there wasn't a lot he could do about it.

Holly abandoned the taxi under the portico of the Savoy, and, with Daisy running by her side, sprinted through the lobby, ignoring the elevator and racing up the stairs, two at a time, her weapon in her hand.

"Halt, police!" A man screamed at her from somewhere behind. She ignored him and turned a corner. At the top of the stairs she began running, checking room numbers. She was at two-fifty when the cop yelled at her again.

"I'm on the job!" she shouted over her shoulder. "I'm a cop! Follow me!"

Ham drew a fine bead on his target. It was a perfect setup: no wind, clear air, prominent target. Steady as a rock, he took a deep breath, let out half of it and squeezed off the round. A second later, the sound of an explosion could be heard.

"Did you score?" John yelled, keeping his back hard against the wall.

Ham smiled and stepped back. "See for yourself," he said. "Don't worry, nobody's going to shoot back at us."

John reached the window, and his eyes grew large.

Across the street, a couple of hundred yards away, dead level with Ham's window, smoke and flame poured out of another hotel room, where the other Barrett's rifle had been set up. In the street, the motorcade, instead of stopping, had picked up speed and was tearing up the boulevard at a great rate of knots.

Then their attention turned to the door of the room, from which a loud noise had just erupted. John seemed frozen in place. Ham reached over and plucked the pistol from his hand, and at that moment, Holly and a uniformed Miami police officer both exploded into the room, yelling, *"Freeze!"*

John threw his hands into the air, and Ham turned and smiled at Holly. Then the police officer shot Ham in the chest.

61

Holly swung her pistol hard into the cop's face, before he could fire again. He fell to the floor, clutching his nose and yelling. Daisy was at his throat.

"Daisy, release!" She grabbed the cop's pistol from his hand and threw it across the room. "That man is with me!" she screamed at him, then she ran to Ham's aid.

John sprinted past her and was out the door. Daisy was still straddling the cop, baring her teeth.

Holly let him go and bent over Ham. "I'm so sorry," she said. "Can you talk?"

Ham nodded. "See if it went through," he gasped.

Holly rolled him on his side. There was an exit wound high on his right shoulder. "Yes," she said.

"Is there a lot of blood?"

"A fair amount."

"Then you go get John. He's on the way to Opa-Locka. He flies a Malibu, tail number one, two, three, tango foxtrot. If he gets to that airplane, he's gone. He could make Mexico."

"I'm going to stay with you," she said.

"Do what I tell you, girl. I'm going to be fine, trust me. It's not the first time I've been shot."

"All right, then." She kissed him on the forehead, then ran to where the cop sat on the floor, blood streaming from his nose. She snatched the radio microphone from where it was clipped to his shirt and pressed the button. "Officer needs assistance at the Savoy Hotel, room two-ten. Second man down with a gunshot wound to the chest, needs an ambulance, alert the nearest trauma center. Got that?"

"Got it," the operator replied. "Who are you?"

Holly handed the stunned cop the microphone and patted his pockets until she found his car keys, then retrieved them. "You explain it to your dispatcher," she said. "And you take care of that man over there. He's an FBI agent, and they'll be here soon." The cop nodded, and Holly ran.

"Let's go, Daisy!"

She got the police car started. "How do I get to Opa-Locka airport?" she yelled at the doorman. He gave her directions. She switched on all the car's lights and sirens and floored it.

With her free hand, she punched the redial button on the phone.

"Yeah?" Harry said.

"You sonofabitch," she said, "why has this number been busy?"

"Sorry, what do you want?"

"Ham is in room two-ten of the Savoy Hotel with a bullet in his chest. An ambulance is on the way."

"What happened?"

"I don't know, but I think the president *is* in town, or was.

My guess is he's headed for Air Force One right this minute. Now listen, John is headed for Opa-Locka, and I'm about a minute and a half behind him in a Miami police car. If he gets to his airplane, he could go anywhere, so you shake it, Harry! Call the tower and tell them not to clear him to take off. Better yet, close the goddamned airport!"

"I don't understand—"

"Don't even try, just move!" Holly closed the phone and concentrated on her driving. She wished to hell that she knew what kind of car John was in.

John was in the maroon van. "Just drive at a normal speed," he said to the driver. "We don't want to attract attention. How long to the airport?"

"Ten minutes," the driver said. "Where's Ham?"

"He couldn't make it." John picked up the car phone and called Opa-Locka. "Hi," he said, "my airplane, a Malibu, N123TF, is parked there. Can you tell me where the lineman put it?"

"Let me see," the woman said, consulting a list. "It's to the right, as you exit the terminal. You need fuel?"

"It was fueled last night," John said. "Please be sure that no one's blocking me, that I can taxi straight out. I'll be there in five minutes."

"Okay," she replied, and hung up.

John sat back and collected his thoughts. Then, from somewhere behind him, he heard a police siren.

Holly saw a sign for Opa-Locka, and she made a high-speed right turn in a four-wheel drift, and ricocheted off a bus, but she kept going. She was weaving in and out of traffic, which wasn't moving out of her way fast enough.

The van came to a halt outside the terminal. John opened the door. "You disappear," he said to the driver. "Get word to the board that I made it out. I'll call as soon as I can."

"Got it," the man said, then drove away.

John made himself walk at a normal pace through the terminal building. He went straight through onto the ramp, and the airplane was where it was supposed to be. Then he heard the police siren, close, and he started running.

Holly followed the signs to the ramp gate and slammed on her brakes at the intercom, switching off the siren. She pushed the button. "Police! Open the gate now!"

"What?" a woman's voice said.

"This is the police! Open the gate!"

The gate began to slide slowly open.

John got the airplane's door open, got inside and secured the door. No time for a preflight, no time for anything. He got into the pilot's seat, switched on both magnetos, both alternators and the master switch. He opened the throttle half an inch, pushed forward the mixture control to prime the engine, switched fuel tanks and repeated the procedure. The fuel gauges read full. He hit the starter button; the prop turned for three or four seconds, then the engine caught. Slowly he moved the mixture control all the way forward, then he opened the throttle more. The airplane did not move. He had forgotten to remove the chocks on the nose wheel. "Shit!" he screamed. He applied full power, and the airplane overrode the chock and lurched forward at speed. People on the ramp were running to get out of his way.

Holly spun the tires getting through the gate, then she was on the ramp. She stopped and looked around at the airplanes parked there, searching for a Malibu. She saw two, but they had the wrong registration numbers. Where the hell were Harry and his people? Then she heard the sirens. "Thank God," she breathed. Then she saw the airplane. It was taxiing out of the ramp area toward the runways, and she could plainly see the number painted, in twelve-inch numerals, on its fuselage. She switched on the siren again and floored the car.

John could hear the siren only faintly over the engine, but that was enough. He shoved the throttle forward. A training aircraft was ahead of him on the taxiway; he slammed on his left brake and turned onto the grass. As he made the turn, he could see the police car coming toward him. No more time, he thought, as he reached another taxiway. No time for a runway, either. He shoved the throttle all the way forward and, steering with his feet, tried to aim the airplane down the taxiway. Another aircraft, a large twin, was coming straight toward him, perhaps a thousand feet away.

The ground controller was yelling over the radio, "One, two, three, tango foxtrot, stop where you are; aircraft coming opposite direction on your taxiway. Stop now!"

"Yeah, well he better get out of my way," John said into the radio, maintaining his direction.

The other had obviously heard him on the ground frequency, because he was turning off the taxiway and onto the grass.

John was at twenty knots now, then forty. He needed eighty for takeoff. A corporate jet roared down the runway parallel to him, and the wake turbulence from its wingtips rocked the Malibu, but still John continued his takeoff roll.

Holly drove across taxiways and grass, dodging taxiing airplanes and tearing up turf. John's Malibu was accelerating down a taxiway ahead, at a right angle to her. She picked a point ahead of him and aimed for it. "Get down, Daisy," she said, pointing at the floor of the front seat. A collision seemed the only way. Then she realized that his wing was full of one hundred–octane aviation fuel, and she decided she didn't want to hit that.

John saw the police car coming. He put in twenty degrees of flaps, which would allow him to take off at seventy knots, instead of eighty. He was now at sixty and accelerating. A landing gear warning horn, which came on automatically at slow speeds and twenty degrees of flaps, began to bleat loudly. John's hands were slippery on the yoke.

Holly had the accelerator on the floor, and it looked as though she might hit the engine, and she wanted nothing to do with that spinning propeller, so she adjusted course. She also began groping for her seat belt, which she had completely forgotten. Daisy gazed raptly at her from the floor.

Harry's car rolled onto the ramp, leading a charge of half a dozen FBI cars. Maybe three hundred yards away, he saw a police car headed for a collision with an airplane. He picked up the microphone. "We're going to need ambulances," he said. "Send them right now."

Holly had misjudged the acceleration of the airplane. She saw his nosewheel lift off the ground, and she turned slightly to the right, nearly hitting the wing. The car collided with the tail of the airplane, and Holly, not having gotten her seat belt fastened, struck the steering wheel at the same moment she applied the brakes. The car began to spin to the left.

Harry, who was bearing down on the scene now, saw the tail assembly of the airplane break off from the fuselage, as the airplane spun left from the impact, and the loss of the tail created a weight imbalance that caused the airplane to nose over, while still at full power. The engine abruptly stopped as the propeller chewed up the ground, but the airplane had enough momentum to continue until it somersaulted and came to rest on its back. The FBI men spilled out of their cars and found themselves wading through fuel.

"Get out of it!" Harry yelled, waving them away from the airplane. He saw a fire truck racing toward them.

John hung upside down from his seat belt, but he could see all the flashing lights and hear the sirens. There was an overwhelming odor of aviation gasoline. Everything loose in the airplane now rested on its ceiling—charts, pens and, among the debris, a disposable cigarette lighter. John picked it up. "On the day," he said. Then he flicked the lighter.

The explosion of a hundred and twenty gallons of aviation fuel knocked down a dozen FBI agents and Holly, too. She had struggled from the police car and, when she saw the agents running, she ran, but the blast lifted her off her feet and dumped her onto the grass. She rolled on her side and looked back at the fireball.

"Get out of that one, John," she said, then she put her head on the grass and rested.

Daisy trotted over, careful to avoid the flames, and gave her a big kiss.

62

Holly found Ham sitting up in bed, watching the news on CNN. She couldn't believe it.

"Why aren't you in intensive care?" she demanded.

"Well, hi to you, too," Ham said, switching off the TV.

"You've just had surgery."

"Nope. The bullet missed pretty much everything important, and it removed itself through my shoulder. All they did was clean the wound and stitch it up and give me antibiotics and a tetanus shot. I wouldn't let them put me to sleep, and I'll be sore as hell when the local anesthetic wears off. They want me to spend the night in the hospital. Now that we've got that out of the way, will you tell me what the hell has happened in the past few hours?"

"As much as I know," Holly replied, perching on the edge of his bed. "I chased John out to Opa-Locka and prevented his taking off in his airplane by the simple device of driving a police car into it."

Ham laughed, then winced. "Don't, don't make me laugh."

"Sorry. Then the airplane exploded, and John is toast."

"Was it really the president in that car?"

"It was. Harry was too dumb to make an official request to find out, because he wanted the operation all for himself. He had me throw myself at a Secret Service guy to find out if the president was in town, and he told me no. He didn't lie, because the president flew in this morning to make an officially unscheduled appearance at a Republican congressional gathering in the hotel across the street from where you were waiting. It was supposed to be a surprise, since Democratic presidents don't usually show up at Republican gatherings. God only knows what the ramifications will be on relations between the FBI and the Secret Service. My guess is, everybody's ass is covered, since Harry never made an official request and the Secret Service never told him anything. They'd better hope there's never a congressional inquiry into all this. Tell me what happened in your hotel room."

"I was set up, that's what. I looked over at the hotel across the street and I saw another Barrett's rifle pointed right at me. I guess they planned to burn some bridges and I was one of them. Anyway, I blew the shit out of the other hotel room, and when the Secret Service saw the explosion, they got the president the hell out of there in a hurry. Then you arrived, and your buddy shot me."

"He wasn't *my* buddy," Holly said. "He just chased me down the boulevard and then into the hotel. I identified myself, but there wasn't time to explain the whole situation to him, and when we broke into the room, he saw you holding the gun and fired. He was young and inexperienced, but I don't think we can blame him, unless you're hell-bent on suing the Miami Police Department."

"Nah, I've already spent a couple of hours talking to them. What is Harry going to do about Lake Winachobee?"

"They're raiding it as we speak, choppering FBI men in from all over the state. We should hear from Harry soon."

"John told me there are three affiliated groups in Florida, and hundreds around the country. I hope they'll find some records there that will lead them to the others."

"I'd better call Harry about that right now," Holly said, producing the scrambled cell phone. She tapped in the number and waited.

"Crisp," Harry said. "Who's bothering me?"

"It's Holly."

"What's wrong?"

Silence.

"Where are you, Harry?"

"At the Lake Winachobee compound."

"And?"

"And there's nobody here."

"They're all gone?"

"All of them."

"Ham has just told me that John says there are two other compounds in Florida and more around the country."

"About three thousand members," Ham said.

"Three thousand members nationally. Did you find any records there?"

"No, nothing, only a few empty ammunition boxes in what was, apparently, an armory. The place has been stripped, our smoke detector bug is in tiny pieces and I can't figure out how they did it all so fast."

"They're all gone?" Ham asked.

"Yes."

He held out a hand. "Let me speak to Harry."

"Ham wants to speak to you." She handed him the phone.

"Harry?"

"Ham, are you okay? Is it bad?"

"Like a hangnail, nothing more. Listen, John told me there were groups in Tampa and Fort Lauderdale, as well as Winachobee, and others in something like twenty states. Is there nothing there that would tell you where they are?"

"Not so far," Harry said. "Of course, we've got to work this place like a crime scene, so we might come up with something. Telephone records ought to help. What I can't figure is, how did they get out so fast? We were here in no time."

"I think I know," Ham said.

"Tell me."

"After we took off from Winachobee for Opa-Locka, John made a phone call from the airplane, and he was on the phone for several minutes. I think he arranged our transfer to another van in Miami, and he must have given some orders about Winachobee, too."

"I can check that phone record, too. What kind of phone was it?"

"Looked like an ordinary cell phone, mounted on the pilot's yoke, but he kept his headset on when he was using it, and he flipped a switch that cut me out, so I couldn't hear what he said. If he gave orders about Winachobee, then they would have had, what, fifteen, eighteen hours to get out?"

"You could be right. When are they letting you out of the hospital?"

"Tomorrow. I plan to jog all the way home. And there's something else."

"What?"

"I believe John used that phone call to arrange more than the switch of vans. He used it to set up Peck Rawlings, too. Apparently, John thought Peck was working for you. You can find what's left of him in a ditch near a swamp, somewhere west of Miami, with two bullets in him."

"That's interesting," Harry said. "When you get back, I want you to come out here and walk us through Winachobee, show us what you know about it."

"Sure, glad to."

"Let me speak to Holly."

Ham handed her the phone.

"Hi."

"When you talked to Chip Beckham, did you tell him anything at all about our operation?"

"Nothing. I asked him straight out if the president was in town, and he said no. I guess he wasn't at the time."

"Yeah. Listen, a lot of shit is going to fall from the sky the next few days, and I need you to not talk to anybody about it until you and I have a chance to sit down and talk."

"Harry, it's like this," Holly said. "You may have screwed up big-time by not calling in the Secret Service on this, but I'm not looking to tell anybody that. I'll refer all questions to you."

"That's all I ask."

"But Harry, if some of your shit starts to fall on me, and I get braced for a lot of questions by some authority or other, I'm not going to stonewall them, and I'm not going to take the fifth. You'd better understand that."

"I understand, Holly, and I appreciate your help."

"Let's get this straight, Harry. I'm not helping, I'm just not hurting you if I can help it. Frankly, I don't know why the Secret Service isn't already here, talking to Ham. What I'm going to tell them when they come, and they will, is that I asked Chip if the president was in town, and he said no. I hope that will cover both your ass and Chip's, but if it doesn't, there's nothing I can do to save it. Are we perfectly clear on that?"

"Perfectly. I couldn't ask for more."

"One final thing, Harry: You and I are pretty good friends, so I'm sorry to have to say this, but I'd better get it up front. If I begin to get the feeling from the questions I'm asked by whoever that blame is starting to fall on either Ham or me, then I'm going to protect us."

"I understand, Holly, and you didn't have to say that."

"Good. We'll be home tomorrow. Call me if there's something I ought to know." She closed the telephone.

"If you hadn't told him that, I was going to," Ham said.

"You get some rest, old man."

"One more thing," Ham said.

"What?"

"John owned up to the robbery and Jackson's death. Peck planned it, and one of his people panicked and shot Jackson."

"Oh," Holly said. She suddenly had a hollow feeling in her chest. "I hope Jackson knows we got these people."

"If it helps, they offed the guy who shot him. Oh, and the two people in the submerged van? The guy, Frank, was put in the bank by John, and they put the couple in the river when they tried to run with some money."

"Well," Holly said, "that ties up a few loose ends."

"So what do we do now? Wait for the Secret Service to show and ask us questions for twelve hours?"

"I guess."

"I've got a better idea. I think my pants are in that closet over there."

"Ham, you can't do it. You've got to spend the night here."

"I told you, girl, I've been shot before. I know when it's bad, and this isn't bad."

Holly went to the closet to get Ham's clothes. His bag was there, too.

"Oh," Ham said, "how are we getting home?"

Holly went to the phone. "I'll rent a limo, and we'll charge Harry for it." She gave Daisy a pat. "Daisy's never ridden in a limo."

"That's my girl," Ham said, putting on his pants. "And don't call me old man."

I want to express my gratitude to my editor, David Highfill, and my publisher, Phyllis Grann, for their continuing care and contributions to my work.

My agents, Morton Janklow and Anne Sibbald, and all the people at Janklow & Nesbit, continue to manage my career, always with excellent results, and thcy, as ever, have my gratitude.

My wife, Chris, is my first and most critical reader, and I thank her. for her strong opinions and her love.

I am happy to hear from readers, but you should know that if you write to me in care of my publisher, three to six months will pass before I receive your letter, and when it finally arrives it will be one among many, and I will not be able to reply.

However, if you have access to the Internet, you may visit my website at www.stuartwoods.com, where there is a button for sending me e-mail. So far, I have been able to reply to all of my e-mail, and I will continue to try to do so.

If you send me an e-mail and do not receive a reply, it is because you are one among an alarming number of people who have entered their e-mail return address incorrectly in their mail software. I have many of my replies returned as undeliverable.

Remember: e-mail, reply; snail mail, no reply.

When you e-mail me, please do not send attachments, as I *never* open these. They can take twenty minutes to download, and they often contain viruses.

Please do not place me on your mailing list for funny stories, prayers, political causes, charitable fund-raising, petitions, or sentimental claptrap. I get enough of that from people I already know.

Generally speaking, when I get e-mail addressed to a large number of people, I immediately delete it without reading it.

Please do not send me your ideas for a book, as I have a policy of writing only what I myself invent. If you send me story ideas, I will immediately delete them without reading them. If you have a good idea for a book, write it yourself, but I will not be able to advise you on how to get it published. Buy a copy of *Writer's Market* at any bookstore; that will tell you how.

Anyone with a request concerning events or appearances may e-mail it to me or send it to: Publicity Department, G. P. Putnam's Sons, 375 Hudson Street, New York, NY 10014.

Those ambitious folk who wish to buy film, dramatic, or television rights to my books should contact Matthew Snyder, Creative Artists Agency, 9830 Wilshire Boulevard, Beverly Hills, CA 90212-1825.

Those who wish to conduct business of a more literary nature should contact Anne Sibbald, Janklow & Nesbit, 445 Park Avenue, New York, NY 10022.

If you want to know if I will be signing books in your city, please visit my website, www.stuartwoods.com, where the tour schedule will be published a month or so in advance. If you wish me to do a book signing in your locality, ask your favorite bookseller to contact his Putnam representative or the G. P. Putnam's Sons Publicity Department with the request.

If you find typographical or editorial errors in my book and feel an irresistible urge to tell someone, please wire to David Highfill at Putnam, address above. Do not e-mail your discoveries to me, as I will already have learned about them from others.

A list of all my published works appears in the front of this book. All the novels are still in print in paperback and can be found at or ordered from any bookstore. If you wish to obtain hardcover copies of earlier novels or of the two nonfiction books, a good used-book store or one of the on-line bookstores can help you find them. Otherwise, you will have to go to a great many garage sales.